Not as I Will, But as You Will

An Historical Novel of the Passion of Gethsemane

— Kathleen Goto —

Not as I Will, But as You Will:
An Historical Novel of the Passion of Gethsemane

Copyright ©2004 by Kathleen Goto

Publisher: Kingdomofheavennow.com

All rights reserved. No part of this publication may be reproduced, stored in a retreival system or transmitted in any form by any means, electronic, mechanical, photocopy, recording or otherwise, without the prior permission of the publisher, except as provided by USA coptright law

Scripture taken from the HOLY BIBLE: NEW INTERNATIONAL VERSION® NIV® Copyright ©1973, 1978, 1984 by International Bible Society. Used by permission of The Zondervan Corporation.

The "NIV" and "New International Version" trademarks are registered in the United States Patent and Trademark Office by International Bible Society

Illustrations by Rhonda Williams

First printing 2004

Printed in the United States of America

ISBN 0-9754017-0-X

Not as I Will, But as You Will

An Historical Novel of the Passion of Gethsemane

Let us help Jesus launch the Kingdom of Heaven on the Earth

Blessings
Kay Goto 3/27/2021

— Kathleen Goto —

To my loving and patient husband,
Hiroshi,
and my wonderful children:
Mei Nan, Shin Nan, Jin Nan,
and Akiko

Preface

Kathleen Goto's portrait of Jesus, or as she calls him here, Yeshua, is an intensely personal one. She takes you inside the mind and heart of this "first Son of God," the first of "many to come," and what's more, inside the mind and heart of his divine Father, the God who is the divine parent of all humankind. This is no longer the fearsome "Storm God" of the early Hebrew scriptures. This God takes an intense interest in the well being of all of his children, particularly his "Chosen Ones."

Done in flashback fashion, *Not as I Will, But as You Will* is a dialogue between the Angel Gabriel and Yeshua while in the Garden of Gethsemane, just up to the point of the betrayal by Judas. Yeshua relives his life, searching for an answer to the dramatic and terrifying choice that he must now make. One of the truly fascinating aspects of this telling is the family dynamics of Yeshua's mother, Mary, and her husband Joseph. The household that Yeshua grew up in is portrayed as not particularly happy or peaceful, in part, because of the circumstances surrounding his birth. His relationship with his cousin John is portrayed as initially quite joyful, yet over the years, a certain dissonance is seen and felt there, too.

Ms. Goto has meticulously researched both the standard Christian literature, as well as the applicable Hebrew literature, melding it with the *Divine Principle* of Reverend Sun Myung Moon, and other, more esoteric accounts of Jesus, his training and his mission. She then combines all of this into a felicitous and insightful account of those famous last hours of his life before his arrest.

In light of the current controversy surrounding Mel Gibson's film "The Passion of Christ," and the concerns about the perceived anti-Semitism of that account, it was thought best to state up front and categorically that the author here is quite aware of the best modern post-Holocaust scholarship on this subject. The author also has used Hebrew or Aramaic terms where and when possible in order to emphasize the fact that Yeshua was a practicing, devout Jew. In the case of quotes from the Gospel of St. John, the most polemic of all the gospels, the term, "the pious ones," was used in place of "The Jews" because it was felt that it more accurately fits the context.

Yeshua has to speak as he speaks, because he was not easy in any way on the "Jewish establishment" of the era. This in no way condones what has happened to the Jewish people over time. As is well known, the later "Christian establishment" has been just as guilty of distorting Jesus' message to some degree. In no way can the Jewish people of the present day be held accountable for these long-ago events, nor should they be.

It is hoped that this new telling will add to an increasingly deeper spiritual appreciation of Yeshua's great sacrifice as well as his vision for true peace throughout the world.

Reverend Paulina K. Dennis
Editorial Consultant and Theologian
Brooklyn, New York

Introduction

This is a story about the heart of Jesus. While using fiction to flesh out a human picture from the limited historical knowledge of the actual events of the time, the image that emerges of this passionate heart of unconditional love and sacrifice is absolutely real.

This version of the "greatest story ever told" is centered solely on the prayer of Jesus in the Garden of Gethsemane, as he asks God to spare his life. In a deeply emotional tribute to what perhaps has been until now the true veiled majesty of this complex and extraordinary figure, it brings to this event a new and fresh perspective. What other reason would he have had to pray such a prayer, other than the fear of death, the traditional explanation for it?

This question is answered in a recasting of the circumstances of the story, during these fateful few hours just prior to Jesus' arrest and crucifixion. Jesus—or Yeshua, the traditional Hebrew pronunciation of his name—is visited by Gabriel, an angel sent by God to comfort him, in the midst of his prayer. Yeshua has a dialogue with the angel, and combined with a series of flashbacks of past experiences reexamines his life and purpose.

These flashbacks for the most part are taken from biblical passages—primarily from the great discourses of Matthew and the Last Supper of John—with Yeshua's perspective of these situations related in his heartrending colloquy with the angel. Besides biblical passages—New International Version, unless otherwise noted—several unconventional sources are used for information about the life and thought of Jesus.

Why use a fictional backdrop to teach about Jesus?

As Aristotle expressed it, history teaches "how things are"; fiction teaches "how things could and should be."

The impact of this story of "how things could have been" is we are left with an unusually rounded, yet suprahuman, view of this greatest man who ever lived.

Contents

In The Garden of Gethesemane
— 1 —

The Early Years: Qumran, Miriam and John
— 33 —

Jesus and John—The Baptism
— 79 —

Temptation in the Wilderness
— 101 —

The Kingdom and the Twelve
— 115 —

The Sermon on the Mount
— 133 —

Parables of the Kingdom
— 151 —

Keys to the Kingdom
— 173 —

Three Days, Cleansing and Controversy
— 199 —

Miriam, the Last Visit
— 223 —

The Last Supper
— 239 —

The End of the Road
— 257 —

Notes
— 266 —

[Yeshua] went out as usual to the Mount
of Olives, and his disciples followed him.
On reaching the place, he said to them,
"Pray that you will not fall into temptation."
He withdrew about a stone's throw beyond
them, knelt down and prayed, "Father, if you
are willing, take this cup from me; yet not
my will, but yours be done." An angel from
heaven appeared to him and strengthened
him. And being in anguish, he prayed more
earnestly, and his sweat was like drops of
blood falling to the ground.

Luke 22: 39-44, RSV

Chapter 1

In the Garden of Gethsemane

"Oh, Jerusalem!" he cried, the words escaping in a breathless sigh to the unmindful city beyond.

> "Oh Jerusalem, Jerusalem, how often would I have gathered your children together as a hen gathers her brood under her wings, but you would not!" [1]

The chasm which separated him from that vision of downy bosom's embrace was a seemingly bottomless pit. In answer to his tender words, voices of the "vipers" and the "stiff-necked" echo across from this spiritual netherland of gloom to taunt him.

"Who are you to think you are the true son of the Unnamed One? We are sons of Abraham as much as you!"

While physically what lay between him and his heart's

Not as I Will, But as You Will   Chapter 1

desire was a mere valley with a parched creek running through it, in actuality it was a hostile, if intangible, abyss. Thorn-tangled ideologies, matured over history into impenetrable obstinacies, arrayed themselves against him. It was a struggle with the accepted concept of what the Jews were and their Law—how things are done—against, as he advocated, what should be done—building the Kingdom of Heaven on Earth, *haOlam haBa*. As different an outlook as achieving life is to avoiding death; or joy is to the absence of pain; or light is to the absence of darkness.

He healed the sick on the Sabbath and was severely censured for it by the religious leaders as a violation of the Mosaic Law.

"Which is lawful on the Sabbath: to do good or to do evil, to save life or to kill?" [2] he said to those religious leaders whose silence betrayed the limit of their understanding and their unwillingness to admit it. *"The Sabbath is made for man, not man for the Sabbath,"* [3] he explained, and their response was to slip away and plot how to get rid of him. He has brought new wine for old wineskins [4] that cannot seem to hold the contents. Now as his plans have gone awry, he must decide his next step.

This is the Garden of Gethsemane, two thousand years ago. Offspring of these same olive trees still stand even today. Twisted and gnarled, with some over a thousand years old, seemingly petrified, yet with new green shoots appearing unexpectedly. Trees known for their veritable indestructibility—cut them down to the root and they will grow right back, their strength and tenacity a reminder to him of the life he must live and pass on to those who come after him. They were often his only company in this orchard where he would come to pray, with the Golden Gate of the great Temple and the

– 2 –

In the Garden of Gethsemane

city of Jerusalem lying before him.

Spring is approaching. The faintly sweet scent of almond blossoms, the heralds of spring and an ancient symbol of rebirth, fill the air. The sparkling night sky, stretching with awesome expanse from horizon to horizon, is a metaphoric vision of eternity and a point of calm to his troubled thoughts tonight.

This is Passover night, "The Night of the Watchers." God commanded the Chosen People to keep watch during this night every year for Elijah, who will show them the coming Messiah. This was Yeshua Bar Yosef's watch, but his watch was different from others. His was reckoning with the bitter cup of death awaiting him at the hands of the Jewish leadership. He thought back to the past year's efforts. Why had the people not listened to him? He healed the sick, performed miracles, yet still they did not believe in him, understand who he really was and follow his leadership.

Yeshua watched, in lonely, tearful vigil, the starlit expanse over the city below. Tiny flames dotted the cityscape. People, he thought, maintaining the same vigil as he. Would that he could kindle those sparks into fires of faith; the outcome of tonight could be different! He could live to fulfill his mission of establishing the Kingdom.

The angular planes of his sun-darkened face were writhed in anguish. A strong man hardened to the life of the wilderness, yet tears flowed from those perceptive eyes. Intense eyes: generating hope in the faces of those he shepherded; but to those with foul motivations, they pierced the soul, as mirrors to its corruption.

The inviolable set of the jaw belied the tears; a confidence rooted in an implacable determination. This was a man who

– 3 –

Not as I Will, But as You Will   Chapter 1

was moved by emotions only when he allowed it. The great forehead and deep-set eyes held an arresting intelligence. The resulting face was a harmonized amalgam of emotion, intellect and will with an intensity so vivid—a coloration of truth, beauty and goodness—that it rendered those around him pastel by comparison.

He thought back to the past evening's events, a supper with those closest to him. A supper he had envisioned would be the last moment on earth he would have to spend with them. From this event a response had given him hope. At the end of the meal, after he had spoken deeply from his heart to them, some of the disciples expressed,

> *"Now you are speaking clearly and without figures of speech. Now we can see that you know all things and that you do not even need to have anyone ask you questions. This makes us believe that you came from God."* [5]

"You believe at last!" [6] Yeshua had answered. Finally, could it be true? A quixotic thought had begun to take shape in his mind. Perhaps it was not too late.

So he came to this garden, a place he often came to for solitary prayer and contemplation, with these three along with him. He expressed to them his sorrowful and troubled heart.

> *"'My soul is overwhelmed with sorrow to the point of death. Stay here and keep watch with me.' Going a little farther, he fell with his face to the ground and prayed, 'My Father, if it is possible, may this cup be taken from me. Yet not as I will, but as You will.' Then he returned to his disciples and found them sleeping. 'Could you men not keep watch with me for one hour?' he asked Peter."* [7]

– 4 –

In the Garden of Gethsemane

Yeshua looked over at the three forms lost in sleep under the branches of the old olive tree. His three main disciples, Peter, James and John—how he wished to somehow be able to rouse them. His hope in bringing them here to the garden was to be able to transfer to them his deep sense of responsibility to fulfill the Father's vision. Hope that they could inherit his heart of filial piety to the Father; hope that they could finally understand and embrace with him this great burden of regenerating faith in the lost sheep of Israel—such was the assurance the Father needed to see, to continue the present providence. Then, perhaps, his death would not be necessary as a ransom to Satan for the lives of this faithless generation.

True pain for him would not be that death, he thought, shuddering not from the chill outside but from the fear grasping his heart. His fear was not for himself. Surely he would willingly die the most torturous death if this assured the goal. His dread was for what would happen to his followers as well as the rest of the people of Israel in the event he would be killed.

"Because you did not know the time of your visitation, behold, your house will be left desolate," he had told his disciples. "Of the people's beloved temple, it will be destroyed— *I tell you the truth, not one stone here will be left on another; every one will be thrown down*," [8] he said to his disciples as they looked admiringly at the great Temple this past day.

Those prescient words haunting him now would come to pass in a mere forty years, when destruction of the Jerusalem Temple and the culture of Israel itself would be carried out by Rome. The Chosen People would be divided and dispersed throughout the known world. Their beloved city, the symbol of a culture of such monumental potential, would be leveled and the land strewn with salt, so that nothing would grow

– 5 –

Not as I Will, But as You Will   Chapter 1

there for generations.

The specter and terror of these future events passed before his eyes as he beheld, for the last time, the city he had loved so much. Maybe it was the potential he had loved more than what was really present. But soon all—past, present and future—would be wiped away, and he mourned for it like he would have mourned for the loss of his own child.

"Abba, what is Your will for me now? How can Your Kingdom still be built?" Sobs muffled his words, a jumble of prayer and lamenting reflection.

Elijah had come; the Messiah had come. Would that the city below knew that the visitation for which they were this evening watching for had arrived. But few could see. He was the one they were waiting for: the second Adam, the parent who had come to unite the lost, orphaned offspring of the first Adam. In their ignorance and rebelliousness, the people of Jerusalem were rejecting the very person they most longed for in their ancient collective heart.

"My Father, why have You lost faith in this plan to build the Kingdom of Heaven now? Wouldn't I, Your son, endure the worst living hell to make it work? Why do You ask me to throw it away uncompleted?"

"It will be especially hard for my children; they do not understand," he said, his voice faltering to a whisper, remembering the naive response of his followers to his disparaging words about the future.

"How can this be? These walls are so strong," was Peter's flippant response to the description of the coming destruction of the Temple.

"Would that you only knew the things that make for the

– 6 –

In the Garden of Gethsemane

Kingdom of Heaven," Yeshua had responded. "But, alas, they are beyond your grasp—and you shall suffer much before you finally come to understand them."

"The Kingdom of Heaven," he breathed the words soulfully; the words that had been a rallying cry to his disciples.

His thoughts were transfixed on the dream he had long cherished, recapturing the ideal of the restored Israel, an institutionalized dream of his people. The gateway to the establishment of the Heavenly Kingdom would have been the reorganization of the twelve tribes. The twelve tribes, established by Moses in the beginning of the history of Israel; disassembled by the interminable captivities and enslavement forced upon the Chosen People by enemy nations that overpowered them; then finally in their reestablishment, the prophetic sign of the end-times and the coming of God's Kingdom. The symbolic could become the reality, when certain spiritual conditions were met.

His mission, in one respect, was similar to the prophets, Who performed symbolic actions as precursors to future events as a warning to the people of the course of destruction the nation was headed down: Jeremiah smashing a wineskin,[9] Isaiah going nude in public,[10] Ezekiel reclining, observing the clay tablet with the image of Jerusalem inscribed.[11] All these actions foreshadowed the destruction and exile of the Chosen People, unless they changed from their ungodliness. It was an opportunity given by the Father; a crossroads where the people could change from the road leading to destruction to the road to the victorious Kingdom once promised them. Warnings, unfortunately, they had failed to heed.

Unless the people heeded the warnings, these symbolic gestures would unleash these future events, setting them inex-

~ 7 ~

Not as I Will, But as You Will   Chapter 1

orably in motion,[12] like a small stone tossed in the water sends ripples across a pond. In the same way that the prophets of old delivered symbolic actions as warnings of what may portend, his actions offered a hope of what the future may bring, if the people followed.

The Twelve Disciples he had chosen—one representing each of the twelve tribes—were the symbol of the restored twelve tribes of Israel, a restored, united Israel centered upon God. To fulfill this position, the Twelve must be absolutely united with him. Together they would become the catalyst to open the age of the Heavenly Family and the Heavenly Kingdom, a magnet the rest of Israel would irresistibly be drawn to follow.

The children of Israel would then become the first fruits restored back to the Father and a platform for the restoration of the rest of the fallen world. Would that they could know the time of their visitation, the time of their momentous opportunity, the hour that the past four thousand years of their history had been painstakingly preparing them for. Driven by this desperate certainty, Yeshua cried out for what was about descend on him and his people.

"This can't be! Yes, my course is set, but! 'Not as I will, but as You will,'"[13] he pleaded, the Father's loss of this opportunity uppermost in his mind. "I always knew my life must be a struggle, scrambling up the height of the mountain from ridge to rocky cleft, always ascending toward the summit even if never to reach it. My efforts at least would be investments toward that ideal, even if it was out of reach to me in my lifetime. I accepted that gladly. My hope was always that this heart could be inherited by my disciples, who together with me would build the foundation for the Kingdom. They would do greater things than I.[14] Yet time has run out, and still they

– 8 –

lack vision and zeal.

"They look for miracles instead, the Kingdom coming *'out of the clouds,'* [15] with no effort, as the Prophet Daniel predicted. All my parables—the Kingdom is like a mustard seed, like yeast in dough, like a vineyard, like salt—were to teach them that the Kingdom starts small and is developed and nurtured over time. Their faith and works were the nurturance, to bring it to fruition."

His voice lapsed into silence. They could not understand; he knew this now. They would fail without him. There must be a way for him to continue.

"The mission has failed," the Father had told him. "You must pursue the alternate course of death, or all will be lost." But what if there was no seed left to grow? Mustn't he stay to make sure the seeds of the Kingdom at least root? If only he could die—ten times, a hundred times, a thousand times—then succeed; it would be worth it.

He sought in prayer a release for the words inside him, crying out for a receptive mind to receive them. "Oh Father, they know so little about heavenly ways, about becoming godly individuals, having godly families, and such linkages that would make up the culture of Heaven that You are striving to build. Who will be their example to follow? Who will show them the culture of the Kingdom? Who will build the Kingdom of Heaven on Earth that we asked them to pray for, if I have to leave prematurely? To what unfortunate ends will my mission come to?"

He thought of the years of struggle that led to this moment. But what remained of them tonight was only a feeling he could not name, except that it was desperate, pensive, and solemn. It was the sum of so many mixed emotions: hope

– 9 –

Not as I Will, But as You Will   Chapter 1

for the destined course, despair at not having accomplished his original intent, even some relief that the years of struggle were almost at an end, but mostly pain at lost potential for himself and what he might have been able to accomplish if he only could continue.

"An angel from heaven appeared to him" [16]—the angel Gabriel, clothed in white with hair gleaming like sunlight. His visage was that of a man, but extravagantly bright. The voice of Gabriel, a gentle sea breeze on parched skin, was serene but commanding. "My Lord, it is I, Gabriel, messenger of the Father. How great is my blessing to be here to aid you in your hour of need. Your Father sees your pain, and has sent me to comfort you. You hold the fate of all of heaven and earth. As much as is possible, I will share this burden."

Yeshua replied, thankful for the presence of the angel, but suddenly unsure of his next step. "You come to me at my darkest time, and I am grateful, but this is a decision only I can make. It is not my comfort that concerns me. I mourn the fate of my people, which my death will seal." Yeshua fell silent; his face lowered in shadows. Gabriel watched and waited for the moment when he would be needed.

What followed was a heart-to-heart discourse—sometimes with physical words, but often an exchange of thought—with visions emanating from thought like the instantaneous emergence of a flower from a seed, as is the way of things of the spirit.

Moments passed and Gabriel spoke softly, capturing Yeshua's attention with penetrating eyes, deep pools of memories of the children of Adam. "So many have failed you. I have been a messenger between the Father and the children throughout their history. If only it were within my command

– 10 –

In the Garden of Gethsemane

to make them listen and fulfill their responsibility. It is you, the innocent—the most precious fruit of the Father's vineyard—that is now wasted for their failure.

"I was there when Adam and Eve fell, and sin and murder entered into the first family. The Father was cut off from His greatest desire, a relationship with His children. So far away from Him in heart they descended that they were separated by a great shadowy schism, through which He could barely perceive them. The angels were the only ones who could reach out to these fallen children and communicate with them. How sad we were for the Father. Through generations of men He waited for one man, Noah, who could finally respond to Him. Finally, with Noah, the Father had an obedient man, through whom He could begin to work.

"Still it was many generations more before a family could be found with the same quality of obedience. Through Abraham—born the son of an idol-maker—his son Isaac, and grandson Jacob, the Father had a family united with His will and the seed of His future Kingdom. Jacob's descendants were given the name Israel, 'he who strives with God,' which meant that they would be aiding the Father in His quest to restore all his children back to the fold. Hope was born for the Father and His servants. How hard we had worked for that day, trying to save mankind from self-destruction!

"From that ancestral root, for two thousand years the descendants were put through tribulation for one purpose— their obedience to the coming promised Lord. You are that person they suffered for, the one to mend this schism and redeem that original relationship lost between the Father and His children.

"Moses was your model, the leader to organize that fami-

– 11 –

Not as I Will, But as You Will   Chapter 1

ly, now a tribe, and educate them in the Father's ways and bring them into a land promised them. But in the world apart, tribes of evil had expanded to nations of evil. So now the Father needed a nation to be His base to reach out to the rest of the world.

"They were delivered out of slavery in Egypt into wandering for forty years in the desert of Midian. They were given the Tabernacle and the Law to follow as a symbol of this coming individual and of the behavior expected by the Father of His children. Their allegiance to the Tabernacle was transferred to the Temple, again a symbol of this coming redeemer.

"They were guided through this history facing direct harsh discipline and punishment immediately, whenever they were disobedient to the Father's direction. They were taught to cherish the Law more than food, like the very air they breathed, more than their life. Yet there was something that they were to cherish even more; which would come to embody that Law in his own body, in his own actions, example and leadership. The Law was not the end but the means to that end—the Father's true offspring.

"Finally they became a nation. They were given kings through Saul, David and Solomon, once again with the mandate to unite the people with the Father's will. You could have come then, my Lord, if the kings and the people had only united together and been humble to the Father's direction, trusting in the fact that it was He who, heretofore, nurtured them, protected them, educated them and gave them life.

"But the kings failed, and then the nation was chastised. The great Temple, which had become the center of their life, was destroyed, and they were captured, to sojourn many generations in enemy lands. Then the Father sent the great

– 12 –

In the Garden of Gethsemane

prophets to prepare them for the savior that they longed for. When their opportunity came, they must not fail again.

"All that preparation was for you to come, His only begotten son, who could intercede with the lost children and once again restore the parent/child relationship with Him lost by the first ancestors' failure. For you to succeed you needed this prepared nation to stand upon, united in heart with you, a horizontal model of brothers and sisters uniting the world to your parentage as you restored the first Adam's failure—as the true parent. You came for the world, not just for them. This was their stumbling block.

"As it was in Solomon's day, they expected to see the return of national glory through this figure. This vision was self-centered, which made them unable to embrace you the way you appeared; with none of the trappings they associated with power."

Yeshua shuddered, his thoughts captured in the dark embrace of desperation. "I am that intercessor, but I feel I too have failed—failed to teach them the course of a true son of the Father. I should have done more. As children of the Father they should first be concerned with that which is the concern of their parent. That is the suffering of the world, not their own salvation and blessing as individuals or as a nation—

Seek first the Kingdom of God and its righteousness and all else would come unto them.[17]

"But I failed to make them understand this."

Gabriel responded, gently, "My Lord, you have not failed. If they had truly listened to their prophets, they would have known you and followed you. I was there with the Prophet

Not as I Will, But as You Will   Chapter 1

Zechariah; his words were my words when he described you,

> 'He will take away the chariots from Ephraim
> and the war-horses from Jerusalem and the battle
> bow will be broken. He will proclaim peace to the
> nations. His rule will extend from sea to sea and
> from the River to the ends of the earth.'[18]

"The Prophet Isaiah's words were my words when he predicted,

> 'For to us a child is born, to us a son is given,
> and the government will be on his shoulders. And
> he will be called Wonderful Counselor, Mighty
> God, Everlasting Father, Prince of Peace. Of the
> increase of his government and peace there will be
> no end.'[19]

"You did not come only for the Chosen People, but for the entire world; to bring peace to the world, at the sacrifice of the Chosen. They are the Father's predestined workers of His vineyard, the Kingdom of Heaven.

"Isaiah further predicted,

> 'They will neither harm nor destroy on all my
> holy mountain, for the earth will be full of the
> knowledge of the Lord as the waters cover the
> sea. In that day the Root of Jesse will stand as a
> banner for the peoples; the nations will rally to
> him, and his place of rest will be glorious.'[20]

"Yet that could only be accomplished on the foundation of the nation's uniting with you, as the Father had prepared them to do," said Gabriel. "Alas, for you, the people confuse the scriptures, grasping that which is the most comfortable understanding. Yet, the Father knew there was always the dan-

– 14 –

In the Garden of Gethsemane

ger of failure."

"Finally, I spoke through the last prophet, Malachi, predicting dual possible outcomes at the time of your coming. This was a warning to the people. The Father knew that your appearance would not be easy for the people to unite behind. Therefore, as Malachi prophesied, the Father would send an Elijah who would prepare the people. Your cousin John—who was to take on the role of Elijah—would help prepare the people to receive you. This would be the *'great and dreadful day of the Lord.'*

"Great it would be, if the people could unite.

> *'But for you who revere my name, the Sun of*
> *Righteousness will rise with healing in its wings.*
> *And you will go out and leap like calves released*
> *from the stall, says the Lord Almighty.'*

"But terrible if they fail to unite with the Father's providence of the time. *'Or else I will come and smite the land with a curse,'*[21] was the Father's warning. Unfortunately for the Chosen People, because they did not revere or understand your presence, the curse now looms before them.

Yeshua's tear-filled eyes reflected the starlight, as he gazed over the sleeping city. "What can I do?" he lamented. "John was unable to fulfill his mission, and unfortunately since his death, *'the Kingdom of Heaven has suffered violence.'*[22] As you say, the curse is facing my people—and I can only say that if I could have united them, the outcome would have been great. But now it will be terrible. No matter what I do now, their future will be terrible."

Gabriel knelt before him. "Your disciples sleep away unawares of your pain. You should not be alone at this hour. You

– 15 –

are the great hope of the Father, the heavenly hosts and the world, the harbinger of the Heavenly Kingdom. The Father knows your pain, and it is His. Do not despair! The Will shall be accomplished! The people who fail will suffer; that is the law of the creation. But you have not failed. Take heart that you have performed your part and all is not lost. Your life has been a testament, an example for future generations, when they can finally pay attention. Through the base you have established, the Kingdom will eventually come. Visit with me your life and those you love. Bid them good bye in your heart! And let me help you find some comfort and direction."

The cool, succoring words of Gabriel blanketed his spirit, lighting the darkness, calming the pain, as the garden and the present moment receded in a swirling cloud of images from the past.

"The Father prepared everyone near to the event of your birth," said Gabriel, "for you, His special son, His great hope. Your cousin John's mother, Elizabeth, and his father, Zechariah, I visited to announce the birth of their son, the Elijah, and his mission as the prophet-bridge to the people, for the coming Lord. How thoroughly the Father planned to aid you in your heavenly responsibility. John could have made the difference between success and failure of your future mission. The Father knew that and planned greatly to influence him."

Gabriel raised his hands, and a vision opened of a September day in the Judean hills. It is the time of the olive harvest, and autumn has begun to color the scrub trees and sparse patches of grass around the small, sand dune-colored home of his relatives, Elizabeth and Zechariah. She is the matronly looking wife of a priest, and together they have been blameless and faithful all their lives in the sight of the Father.

– 16 –

In the Garden of Gethsemane

Yet they had been imprisoned in a long winter of barrenness, as they were childless and now of advanced age. On her face now is an expression of the most rapturous joy, for she has just discovered that she is pregnant.

> *"The Lord has done this for me," she said. "In these days he has shown his favor and taken away my disgrace among the people."*[23]

The scene then changes to the Temple in Jerusalem, where Zechariah is alone. He is assigned to Temple duties associated with the autumn Festival of Tabernacles, when the new olive crop is dedicated to the Lord. He is preparing the incense for burning as Gabriel appears, more majestically attired in this incarnation than here before Yeshua, but the face is the same. He speaks to him of the birth of his son.

> *"His name shall be John. He will be a joy and delight to you, and many will rejoice because of his birth, for he will be great in the sight of the Lord. He is never to take wine or other fermented drink, and he will be filled with the Holy Spirit even from birth. Many of the people of Israel will he bring back to the Lord their God. And he will go on before the Lord in the spirit and power of Elijah, to turn the hearts of the fathers to their children and the disobedient to the wisdom of the righteous—to make ready a people prepared for the Lord."*[24]

"He is Elijah, whom the Passover Watch looks for," said the angel, sternly, to the practical Zechariah, who obviously is skeptical of the words he is hearing. He shrugs.

"My wife and I are old. Who can believe such a thing is possible? Are you a demon sent to torment me?" Zechariah lamented. The angel motioned, and immediately Zechariah was struck mute.

"Because you do not believe, you will not speak a word until the birth of your son."

Gabriel then continued, describing the circumstance, "From these experiences, Zechariah and Elizabeth knew the important mission of their son. He was to be a person of singular responsibility, following in the tradition of another son of a barren woman of scripture, Hannah. One thousand years before Elizabeth was Hannah, also aged and childless. But by special heavenly dispensation, she gave birth to Samuel, one of the greatest of Israel's leaders and responsible for the anointing of King Saul. A similar mission John was meant to fulfill for you, the True King.

"Hannah knew the importance of her son. Immediately upon his weaning, she took him to the temple and dedicated him to be raised there. This so that he would be assured to be an instrument of the Father. John was equally a figure of predestined significance, sent from the Father with the one mission to testify to you and support you. He too was raised and educated in close proximity to the Temple."

"And your own parents, how much the Father prepared the way for them to embrace their special son's mission," said Gabriel. "Unbeknownst to Elizabeth and Zechariah, I also visited Mary, your mother and Elizabeth's cousin. I announced to her the precious news that she would bear you, the long-awaited *'son of the most high,'* the one *'to reign over the throne of his father David and the house of Jacob,'* [25] in a Kingdom never ending."

The story Yeshua had heard as a child, the scene surrounding the circumstances of his conception, opened in a vista

In the Garden of Gethsemane

before him. The winter in Galilee has given way to a riotous display of bright red anemones, purple iris and hyacinth, and yellow chamomile amid the wild oats and barley grasses. As the breezes of spring waft through them, the gently rolling hills and meadows are bathed in liquid color. Mary, Yeshua's mother, is at the well drawing water, when Gabriel, similarly garbed as with Elizabeth and Zechariah, appears before her.

> *"Greetings, you who are highly favored! The Lord is with you." Mary was greatly troubled at his words and wondered what kind of greeting this might be. But the angel said to her, "Do not be afraid, Mary, for you have found favor with God. You will be with child and give birth to a son. He will be great and called the Son of the Most High. The Lord God will give him the throne of his father David, and he will reign over the house of Jacob forever; his kingdom will never end."*

> *"How will this be," Mary asked the angel, "since I am a virgin?"*

> *The angel answered, "The Holy Spirit will come upon you and the power of the Most High will overshadow you. The holy one to be born will be called the Son of God. Even Elizabeth your relative is going to have a child in her old age. She who was said to be barren is in her sixth month. For nothing is impossible with God."*

> *"May it be to me as you have said," she replied. Then the angel left her.*[26]

Yeshua looked at the young woman in the vision, so full of hope and faith. He thought sorrowfully of their later life in the dusty, cramped dwelling in Nazareth. She always strug-

Not as I Will, But as You Will   Chapter 1

gled to help her son's mission, but at the same time she had to maintain her large family and serve her husband, Joseph—to whom by this time she was married. Mary's face, Yeshua remembered, was always rimmed with sadness and pain, which resonated with the pain he endured in his family life growing up. The suffering she quietly endured, he knew, was that she could do no more for her son.

Gabriel said gently, "Your mother is true to you in her own way, but a woman's life, as you know, has little power. Her suffering your whole life has been a desire to help you, but also the inability to act beyond her husband's behest. Thus, it was foretold to her by the holy man Simeon, upon your consecration to the temple as a baby.

> "'This child is destined to cause the falling and rising of many in Israel, and to be a sign that will be spoken against, so that the thoughts of many hearts will be revealed. And a sword will pierce your own soul too.'[27]

"This foretold the great trauma that was descending upon your family; the trial Israel itself would experience in coming to terms with you, the heir to David and the Father's champion to establish His earthly reign. What the Father wanted, and what the people wanted, was different; thus you came in a way that was not expected.

"Joseph, your earthly father, I also visited in a dream. He could not understand how his bride could be pregnant by the Holy Spirit; and I turned his heart from thoughts of 'divorce,' to see your mother's travail as a blessing from the Father. Yet he was never quite sure about you. You were never his son. And when the other children came along, unfortunately, as they were his own, they were foremost in his heart."

– 20 –

In the Garden of Gethsemane

Gabriel's words confirming the sense of dull antipathy he had always felt from his father, Yeshua reflected on how he had always felt he was competing with him for his mother's heart. For most of his memory, Joseph had won out. His mother's family concerns had long since given way—from heavenly things and the role of the first son in the future—to earthly needs.

"What have visions to do with the price of cedar and pine?" Joseph would angrily say. The dream of the angel's appearance to Joseph had long since faded—probably forgotten by the time Yeshua was old enough to remember.

The unspoken source of embarrassment in their family's home life as he was growing up was that Mary had been pregnant before Joseph and she were married. And though Joseph pretended to believe that Mary's pregnancy was from the Holy Spirit, he obviously had doubts. His affinity toward his own natural children to the exclusion of Yeshua was the rule rather than the exception. Yeshua suspected that the reason they stayed in Nazareth and had not moved to Jerusalem, where both his parents' families dwelled, was because of this old scandal that still smoldered among his relatives.

The memory of a long-forgotten experience in his childhood came to him. He had awakened in the early morning light to see the face of his father gazing at him. The gaze was that of a stranger, not a father; eyes of antipathy, beholding an outsider, not a son. He shuddered at the feeling that had swept over him at a tender enough age to be barely a memory, the feeling of being unwelcome in his own home.

He shook his head, closing his thoughts to this painful memory. He pondered how, as a boy, he had longed to live in Jerusalem, near to the holy Temple. There he could have

– 21 –

Not as I Will, But as You Will   Chapter 1

grown up close to his cousin John, the person he loved most in his family. Even at a young age they shared an affinity for things of the spirit to a much greater degree than other boys their age, preferring communing with nature and going to the Temple to playing children's games with friends. At times, he remembered, he would run away from his family to the Temple. Here, he felt, was his true home while growing up.

Gabriel waved his hand, transforming Yeshua's thoughts into a vision. It was a twilight scene in the distant past of Joseph and Mary standing at a campsite, distraught about Yeshua, who was nowhere to be found. He had not been seen since they left the Temple in Jerusalem, a day's journey back. They had joined the mass of other devout families making the return trip to Nazareth from the yearly Temple pilgrimage for Passover. They had just realized that probably Yeshua—twelve years old at that time—must have stayed behind at the Temple. With the day's journey back and another day looking to find him, it was three days before they finally caught up with their maverick son.

Yeshua remembered that incident, when his parents finally found him.

> When his parents saw him, they were astonished. His mother said to him, "Son, why have you treated us like this? Your father and I have been anxiously searching for you."
>
> "Why were you searching for me?" he asked. "Didn't you know I had to be in my Father's house?" But they did not understand what he was saying to them.[28]

Yeshua said, "I realized at that time that only I could be responsible for my education and preparation for my future

– 22 –

In the Garden of Gethsemane

mission. My parents had no comprehension of my needs. The Father only was my guide; I went where He bid."

Even though he tried to be obedient in most things, this became an impediment to their family's livelihood. Their eldest son would never show an interest in learning the family carpentry trade. Yeshua would go off for long walks—trips to the mountains or to meet up with his cousin John—without telling them. His explanation to them would be, "I am about my Father's business." His mother, he knew, was in the middle, trying to deal with both commitments: her extraordinary son's needs and her family's. But even she grew exasperated with his independence, behavior unlike any other Jewish boy of his time, in a culture where a child's life was totally family-directed. For Yeshua's part, he did not behave this way out of rebelliousness. To the contrary, he often felt alone and isolated but was driven by some internal spiritual compass to prepare for his future mission.

Gabriel spoke to what Yeshua was not willing to admit: that others could have been there for him but weren't. "While blame has no value except in understanding, you must understand where others failed by creating a drag on your potential to soar; it was like having broken feathers on an eagle's wings. Sorrowfully, Lord, you who were blameless must bear the burden of their neglect.

"Your parents and John's parents should have better understood the important missions their children had. They were prepared as such to unite to raise the two of you together, in the Temple. You should have been raised in Jerusalem. John's family should have helped your family, and by so doing, help quiet any rumors. His father was a respected priest. John should have been encouraged by his family to serve you and support you—he the Elijah, to you, the Son of

Righteousness. Those families, for their own reasons, apart from the Father, divided. What resulted was like a division of mind and body—you and John, the Messiah and Elijah—sowing the seeds of failure from early on."

Yeshua thought back fleetingly to those family members, what they could have done that they failed to do. But it was not in his character to cast blame. "Maybe my earthly father Joseph could have embraced my mission more, and supported my mother to do the same. Maybe Elizabeth and Zechariah could have prepared John more to understand his position. But I am the one responsible for success or failure, not them," he whispered with intractable decisiveness, moving beyond the thought.

Gabriel responded feelingly. "You are truly the Father's only begotten son. I am honored to serve you."

"John and I had our own opportunity to unite, centered on the mission," said Yeshua, as his thoughts turned wistfully to memories of his boyhood. He had decided that his parents could not help him make ready for the mission he knew intuitively the Father was preparing him for. He determined to go about it himself, wherever it led him. That was the beginning of those steps of self-education, cloistered retreats to nature and places where people of all kinds congregated, living textbooks the Father led him through in preparation for his coming time to lead.

His thoughts turned into a vision of one of his

In the Garden of Gethsemane

favorite spots for meditation and prayer: the summit of Mt. Tabor, a few miles from his home, which surveyed an area which was steeped in the history of his people. The mountaintop granted a sweeping view of the width of all Israel, from the Mediterranean Sea on the west to the Sea of Galilee on the east. He spent many hours, even days, on the gently rounded and forested summit that looked over the valley below, where the Kishon River ran through it. This was the scene of one of the most victorious events in the history of the Chosen People. Deborah, the great woman judge, and her general, Barak, and his army ran down these slopes and defeated the Canaanite general Sisera. It was an instance of Divine intervention, where the usually small stream was swollen, and overflowed its banks, causing the enemies' chariots to become stuck in the mud. There, the Israelite army, on foot, could capture them.

This valley was also the crossroads of the ancient international highway that passed through Israel. A ways to the west was the impregnable fortress city of Megiddo, built initially by King Solomon to house the horses and chariots of his vast army at the zenith of Israel's power as a nation. The city oversaw passage along the ancient trade route through Israel called the "Way of the Sea" prophesied by Isaiah[29] to be the route where the coming "Righteous One" would appear.

In a manner now becoming familiar to Yeshua, Gabriel waved his hand toward the horizon and Yeshua's thoughts became a vision. The image appeared of a giant caravan passing through the valley below. His boyhood fascination came in view before him in a sweeping panorama of colorful fabrics, animal smells, the cacophony of voices, brays and grunts of the animals and billowing dust. These were the traders, pilgrims and travelers in seemingly miles-long trains of laden

Not as I Will, But as You Will

Chapter 1

camels, mules, horses and donkeys. He remembered fondly these mobile metropolises that were always friendly to an affable Greek-speaking boy willing to hire on to perform simple tasks. They would often allow him to travel with them.

They journeyed through Israel on the Via Maris, a Roman-made road that cut diagonally through Israel from north to south. To the north they journeyed to Damascus to join with the Great Silk Road traffic through Syria, Babylon, Persia and on to the exotic lands of India and China. And to the south of Israel, to the most important Roman port of that age, Caesarea, and the sea routes to Greece and Rome; and farther south to destinations in Egypt and the spice routes to Arabia. It was for him, in his boyhood, a colorful fluid and constantly changing train of higher education: of diverse languages, of international culture and religion, and international politics traversing practically his back yard.

He learned the differences in peoples and cultures, but also the sameness—same hopes, same dreams, same struggles. The same love of truth, beauty, goodness and family; and the commonness of basic moral ideals shared by all the diverse cultures he met. Through these caravans, the Father taught him to appreciate not just his own people but the world, the rest of the Father's family. He thought about the Father's words from Isaiah, about the mission of the nation of Israel. From the earliest age, he knew it was his mandate to bring this about,

"A house of prayer for all nations."[30]

Yeshua mouthed silently the words, "A house of prayer for all nations," looking at the angel who hovered protectively beside him. "That's really what the Father wants," he mused, "not for me to die." He spoke not expecting an answer but

In the Garden of Gethsemane

reacting in bewilderment at the colliding demands of the juncture he was confronted with. Gabriel nodded silently, knowing his position was only to support Yeshua in the decision he had to make.

Yeshua looked back to the scene of the caravan and thought again of those days of his youth, of John, who often joined him in those days of adventure. John and Yeshua, like twin sides of a raging river, moved in tandem through their life, sometimes close, sometimes far apart, but inexorably tied to each other because of their shared passion, their faith. Their families moved in different circles. John's being a priestly family meant he was raised in Judea, in the backdrop of the Jerusalem Temple. Yeshua's family, however, lived a more parochial life in the countryside of Nazareth in Galilee, two to three days' journey away.

Yet they found ways to meet, hitching rides on the caravans between the two districts, out of a venturesome need for a common outlet for their shared devotional search. John was emotional, charismatic and dynamic, true to his namesake, the Prophet Elijah, whose spirit he was prophetically to inherit. Expectation was high for his future from the priests of the Temple. Yet, like his cousin, he knew they were not leading him; God was leading him. And he had to find his own way of serving the Lord. Yeshua was equally intense but more internal, more thoughtful, less emotionally reactive.

Yeshua thought how John and he had shared an unnamed clarity of their future goals and how they must necessarily intersect. Intuitively they deemed it necessary to support each other to keep on track, and to be undistracted from that destiny; a concern that didn't seem to be foremost in the minds of those family members and acquaintances around them. With the stewards of the Temple, John was often in trouble

Not as I Will, But as You Will   Chapter 1

for his independent-minded ways. But with more support from his family and the religious establishment, he was accorded more deference for his ways than was Yeshua.

From the perspective of outward preparation and dynamic ability, it appeared that John was the divinely chosen leader. As his parents were of advanced age when he was born, he was practically raised in the Temple and was fawned over as a natural for future pastoral leadership.

Yeshua, on the other hand, came from the simple prosaic background of a tradesman's family in the countryside, far removed from the political and social center of Israel. Yeshua was raised by a simple carpenter, albeit one of noble lineage. While Joseph, Yeshua's father, was a descendant of King David, he was in no way connected to the former dynasty of Israel's leadership. Such families had been scattered and fragmented with the Babylonian and Assyrian captivities of the leadership. Nonetheless, there was the miraculous angelic appearances at the time of his birth, proclaiming his special identity as the long-awaited Davidic King.

But God's ways are not people's ways, so it was hard to correlate that premonitional destiny of Yeshua with the reality. He was a boy without a natural father—in a society where familial relationships were supremely important. How easy was it for the local people to believe that Yeshua's mother was truly pregnant by the Holy Spirit? To a practical, earthy people such as the Nazarenes—simple people, mostly farmers— this was something better not even dealt with, if believed at all. He was just Yeshua, the carpenter's son. All such capricious hearsay was to be seen manifest; then, perhaps, believed.

Yeshua thought of how little time he spent in ministry in Nazareth in later years, because of the contempt born of

In the Garden of Gethsemane

familiarity that the people there had for him. When teaching the people in the synagogue of his hometown, people would be amazed by his words. But someone would remark, sarcastically,

Isn't this the carpenter's son? Isn't his mother's name Mary, and aren't his brothers James, Joseph, Simon and Judas? Aren't all his sisters with us? And they took offense at him. "Only in his hometown and in his own house is a prophet without honor," he had told them. And he did not do many miracles there because of their lack of faith.[31]

In those days of his youth, if it hadn't been for his relationship with John, he would have found no support whatsoever for the special spiritual destiny he was driven to pursue every waking. It was only when he could escape with John—to seek, to dream, to scheme of those heavenly things that only they seemed to be interested in—that he found an outlet.

It led them to places that shocked their parents and the Temple priests, like traveling with caravans to visit cultures as far removed as Persia. This was of special interest to Yeshua, who wanted to understand the identity and faith of the wise men who had been led by the Spirit came from there with gifts to his family at the time of his birth. He was not interested in the personages of these men as much as their spirit and desire to move beyond their own faith to embrace another faith, and the greater cause of the world beyond their own culture. To him it was an example of what he must do as well.

John was most interested in another exploration they pursued; the Essene community of Qumran, in the desert of

– 29 –

Not as I Will, But as You Will

Chapter I

Judea, where they dwelt together as teenagers after John's parents died. There they could touch more deeply the fundamental precepts and roots of their own faith with highly devout priests and monks, shunning the outside world for a communal spiritual quest.

From Yeshua's thoughts there manifested a panoramic view of the desert he loved, lying before him. The Judean desert, the ancient land of sojourning of his ancestors: the land of Joshua and Caleb, the great judges Samson and Samuel, the kings David and Solomon, and the prophets. All fought and died for this tiny piece of land, parched and useless to eyes less sensitive to its beauty. But the feminine embrace of the gently rolling hills, mesmerizing in its invariability, had often beckoned him in times of transition when he was seeking solitude and reflection.

Just northeast was ancient Jericho—a name that bequeathed to its inhabitants a thirst for God's will—an area as varied as the desert was uniform. It encapsulated the expansive temperament of that Will: in the stark reddish cliffs, the abundant green vegetation along the Jordan River, and the expanse of the deep furrows of the wilderness valley between. All this was compacted within an area of thirty miles from the Holy City of Jerusalem—the world digested to a capsule area.

Yeshua reflected on all the experiences he had had here in this area, with people who had affected his life deeply. Near here is the Essene community of Qumran, where John had resided since shortly after the death of his parents. As a young man he had joined the strict order, the *Yahad* (unity of the brethren), as the community referred to themselves. While Yeshua had lived with them for a short time, he never could commit to their viewpoint, so he remained on the outside. The *Yahad* community saw themselves as the inheritors of the

– 30 –

In the Garden of Gethsemane

tradition of the Levites, the priestly line of Israel: heralding the eminent coming of a priestly messiah, superior in their view to the kingly Davidian messiah of traditional expectations.

Yeshua would visit John, and they would travel the desert lands together: from the river, as far as hilly Hebron, Abraham's burial place, due south of Jerusalem. They were drawn there during the heat of the summer for the lush grapes ripening on the vines. Metaphors to describe the human situation abounded from the grapevines. He often would fall back upon these metaphors in his ministry.

> "I am the vine; you are the branches. If a man remains in me and I in him, he will bear much fruit; apart from me you can do nothing." [32]

The life-giving sweetness and energy of the grapes to a body parched and lifeless with the desert heat was analogous to the life the Father sought to bring to the Chosen People through His son.

It was on one such trip of Yeshua's to the Essene community to visit John that he first became fully aware of Miriam, daughter of the family John had lived with since joining the community. Yeshua swept his hand across his eyes in a stab of anguish as this thought pushed its way into his mind. Of all avenues of thought for him at this moment, this was, perhaps, the most painful; the final hitting home of what the sacrifice of his life meant beyond just the moment of death. His future hopes for a life with her—a family—were dashed. This was a greater pain, a greater loss, than his own death.

Not as I Will, But as You Will

Chapter 2

The Early Years: Qumran, Miriam and John

With a powerless shrug of his shoulders he allowed the memory to come to the forefront of his mind. John and Yeshua were eighteen years old. John, the elder by six months, was anxious to enlist his cousin in the spiritual life of his adopted community. They had spent a couple of years there together formerly until Yeshua left to travel to distant lands. Yeshua had not been back in more than a year. Now he had returned as he had promised he would. But when Yeshua arrived, before meeting John, he couldn't resist a visit to the desert bluffs and wadis where the colors of spring had draped the otherwise drab landscape in intermingling patches of soft lilac and blazing yellow. He felt the land was beckoning him, displaying proudly her new garments for him to admire.

There was a certain well and a small stream shaded by date palms where shepherds of the region would bring their flocks to be watered. It was also the water source for most of the villages surrounding Qumran and thus a gathering place for gossip and news for all the women of the community. Then he saw *her*, standing alone to the side. Miriam.

Miriam

It was her eyes that had first attracted him; as always, it was what Yeshua saw first in people, as he was overly sensitive to someone less encumbered with self-absorbed fears, doubts or guilts. This time, however, the familiar eyes held a different quality as she waved in recognition. And his recognition of her was subsumed by a new awareness of her; and, it appeared, of her toward him. He had known her ever since he had been visiting John at Qumran. Her self-possessed and guileless greeting, he mused, had warmed his heart as no other person's welcome could.

He cautiously approached her in response, aware of the fact that she was now a young women and he was an unattached young man; and they were expected to maintain a certain distance between them.

Miriam was the daughter of the family who had adopted the thirteen-year-old John after his parents had both passed away. Her father was brother to Zechariah, John's father. She had become the sister John had never had growing up and he became her elder brother. While Yeshua lived at the compound, she had two elder brothers and she would follow them around, the kid sister always trying to enter their world. But today the glance she sent him was not meant for her brother.

– 34 –

The Early Years: Qumran, Miriam and John

When last he had been at Qumran, she had seemed a child. But looking back, he remembered her absolute integrity, and an inquiring faith together with such determination that it had led them on merry chases to escape her inquisitiveness. All these qualities would be important in anyone that he would seek as a wife. She was then about fifteen, just blossoming into womanhood, with only those life-infused eyes clearly visible under the blue cloth of her headscarf and veil blending into the neutral-colored, long, flowing traditional robes of the women of that community.

At the time, he said little to her other than a brotherly hail, but inside his emotions were boiling with desire to speak to her and express his newfound joy at seeing her. So much so that he was conflicted, taken aback by his feelings of attraction. It was a feeling he had wanted to reject, but something told him he had to deal with it. His future course of life had to be with the right mate, and the Father would lead him to that one person. He must be sensitive to the purpose of those

feelings, he reminded himself, to lead him to the prepared person his heart could identify.

He knew the social code—especially severe among the Essenes—demanding that he not communicate with an unattached young woman like this, except through the parents, his parents to hers. Any whisper of scandal associated with a girl could destroy her reputation and her chances of ever being married, making her a social outcast with little hope of survival once separated from her parents.

His own notorious reputation in the Qumran community aside, that of an outspoken and rebellious firebrand, he did not even consider the possibility of his parents being such a go-between. His parents had long-since left him to his own devices. His mother showed no interest in finding a proper mate for him, the eldest son. Here again, the status that he faced in his own community of Nazareth was colored by the old rumors of his illegitimacy. Without family support, he was looked on as an outcast, a poor prospect for marriage material.

Yeshua grimaced, remembering his thoughts at the time. His mother—how deep had been his frustration over her failure to find him a spouse, as was her duty. It was highly irregular for a young man to have to find his own spouse in Jewish society. Even later on in his ministry this frustration erupted full-blown at a wedding he had attended with his family in Cana.

When the wine was gone, Yeshua's mother said to him, "They have no more wine," encouraging him to use his unusual abilities to materialize some more wine. Her request had annoyed him on one level because he did not like to use his spiritual powers for matters that bordered on merely enchant-

– 36 –

The Early Years: Qumran, Miriam and John

ing the crowd. Though still resistant to it, he now acknowledged, there was another reason for his irritation.

"Dear woman, why do you involve me?" he had told her. *"My time has not yet come."*[1] How could she have shown more interest in a neighbor's wedding than in preparing for that of her own son? Whether his mother's assistance would have made any difference in a marriage proposal to Miriam's family, he would never know. Now he must make his mark in the world, to prove his eligibility and win the family's support for her to be his spouse.

He was a warrior on the front line of battle, faced with the choice of a marriage before battle—when he would risk leaving helpless dependents with his death—or waiting until the battle was won. He could celebrate the victory with his wedding feast, honored by the kingdom he had conquered by love. Silently, he had determined to look forward to that victory celebration and marriage supper, rather than dwell on the loneliness. These thoughts returned to him as he remembered this chance meeting, which had started a fire and longing in his heart that today was still unquenchable—and now would remain so forever.

Gabriel told him, "Your situation grieves the Father terribly. The scriptures predicted the glorious mission of the 'Son of David' who would rule over the throne of the House of David. This should have been political leadership as well as spiritual leadership of his people. The Father's heart was that you would have been born in the house of the monarchy of Israel. Your scion should number as the grains of sands, as your ancestor Abraham was promised.

"The Father originally intended there would be an unbroken line of the sovereign rule of the House of David for all

– 37 –

Not as I Will, But as You Will   Chapter 2

time. But, as the Prophet Samuel told King Saul, '*You acted foolishly, you have not kept the command the Lord your God gave you; if you had, He would have established your kingdom over Israel for all time. But now your kingdom will not endure.*' [2] So, broken and dispersed, the political leadership of Israel floundered and all but disappeared. Today, a puppet of the Roman Empire is in the position of that monarchy, without any connection to the House of David. That is the tragic situation you were born into, lineage-less and destitute, a sovereign in exile, at the bottom of the society you were destined to lead."

Yeshua nodded; his face was taut, a bulwark against despair, as a door in his life, shut with unbearable pain, had once again opened. Miriam was a symbol, a reminder of what could have been—what ultimately needed to be—if he were to fulfill his objective. But wrestling the thought from his mind, he reminded himself of his pledge he had maintained to the Father and his mission. That insecurity of his place, his position, would never dominate him. He knew who he was, and where he had to go to fulfill the mission the Father had predetermined for him. Up to now he had, with an inviolate self-confidence, embraced whatever future challenges he would have to overcome to fulfill it. Even life as a celibate warrior, spilling his blood for the sake of the kingdom, if this was the choice that must be made.

He harbored no resentment nor did he fix blame for the choices and values the Chosen People had made over the years, which had relegated him to be born at the bottom of the society rather than the top. But this bleak destiny now meant the suffering of others, not just himself. And he found himself for once in his life stymied, hesitant to face it. It was a new feeling, this irresolution that he was grappling with.

The Early Years: Qumran, Miriam and John

"They have been their own worst enemy," Yeshua said finally, pondering Gabriel's providential perspective of his position. Either they will dominate the world with love, and God's Kingdom will come. Or they will be dominated—and ultimately destroyed—by the evil world that opposes the very notion of a godly kingdom.

"Oh Israel," he said mutely to the sleeping city beyond, framed in the moonlight, his voice lowered to mask the emotion. "There is no middle ground for you. Much has been given you, and much is expected. *Because you are lukewarm, He will spit you from His mouth.*"[3]

A calm, purposeful dignity entered his voice, as he began to speak words torn from the most secret place in his heart. Words he had longed to speak to an ear who could hear and digest them. So far he could find no such earthly counterpart. But Gabriel, he realized, was such an ear, even if words would be spoken for no other reason than for Heaven to have a record of them.

"So much has the Father prepared for the success of His providence at this time—so much will be lost if we fail. To dominate Rome for Heaven's sake would be the next step, once the twelve tribes were assembled and God's nation secured in His ways. The way was prepared through Caesar Augustus' reign and his *Pax Romana,* uniting the world in trade, communication and culture. Like the spokes of a wheel emanating from the center, I envisioned that the road to peace and the Kingdom of Heaven on the Earth would be routed through the Roman Empire. It is why Rome exists, for this purpose. To this extent, Augustus' 'peace' was guided by God. The Chosen People and Rome's destiny are intertwined by divine intervention."

Looking again to the city, he continued, "The Roman soldiers call me in jest the 'King of the Jews,' meaning that I am some kind of mad, crazy person—and my people, by association, are the same. I mourn the loss of opportunity to show who we really are. We, the chosen nation of Israel, are the ones the Father has entrusted with this great and holy mission, to bring peace to the world. Of course I want to have the chance to challenge life as my forebear David had.

"He, as a warrior king, was victorious over his foes; so I, as the king of peace, would be victorious over mine. I have such confidence to succeed, if time allowed me the chance. I long for the chance to live a victorious life, and, like David, survey the fruits of it in my old age, bathed in the Father's gratitude and satisfaction, as well as that of my people. Who would not desire, if given the choice to see their lives brought to fruition, fulfilling their potential, whether it be great or small. Such is the desire of human life, as is God's, whom we reflect.

"But if this moment is lost, all preparation culminating at this time will also be lost. Without being dominated with love, Rome will collapse into evil, and the Chosen People will be taken with them—lost forever as God's elect. Would that I could have even talked about these things to my disciples. But in the short time I have had with them, I know they are not ready. They are still children, unprepared for the next step."

Gabriel said, gently, as if Yeshua's heart was a tiny wounded bird encircled in his hands, "They should have known you. The Prophet Malachi, the last of the prophets, sought to impress upon the people that what they did would affect your fate. *'But for you who revere my name, the sun of righteousness will rise with healing in its wings.'*

"Malachi's prediction of the *'great and terrible day'*[4] of the

– 40 –

The Early Years: Qumran, Miriam and John

Lord was a warning. Great will be the day if they are faithful. Then the son will indeed rise and together he and the people would be victorious. But terrible if they are not faithful and obedient—terrible for the prophesied son, and eventually for the fate of the people. Terrible would be the fate of the son who is supposed to rise with healing in his wings. He would be rejected by a people of little faith. He would be like an unwelcome reminder of their contrariness and they would have to destroy him to justify their actions. Then in their weakness and division, they would suffer the same fate by the world.

"The result was that you who were destined to be the greatest leader of Israel's history began from the lowest position—almost that of a pariah. Rather than being born in a king's palace, you were born in an animal's manger."

"I guess I have always known this," Yeshua said thoughtfully, "but I had accepted the challenge because I was aware that the most painful sorrow was the Father's. I could never complain about my situation, for the reality of it hurt the Father more. My position was always to comfort the Father—to say, 'Don't worry. I'll succeed anyway.' My determination was to make this day 'great' for the Father, regardless of the handicapped position I was starting from."

Yeshua smiled grimly at the sanguine confidence he had held, desiring beyond hope that this goal was still possible. Unconsciously, he closed his eyes and turned his thoughts back to that scene at the well, when he had been confronted with his feelings for Miriam. Similar thoughts, he remembered, had converged in his mind, blunting his response to her welcome. He knew she couldn't understand his reticence, and he would do nothing to dispel it. Maybe she was the one for him; the future would tell. For now, initially their eyes met

– 41 –

Not as I Will, But as You Will — Chapter 2

and communicated something magnetic between them, something understood that they both desired.

At that moment John had come running through the plaza shouting, "There you are! I've been looking all over for you," "I heard you were here." The tenuous, shimmering thread between them had evaporated as Yeshua turned to greet John. John took him by the hand and led him away, voicing his desire for what he wanted to do with him during this visit. As he left, Yeshua had glanced over his shoulder at the vibrant eyes, barely visible under the headscarf, noticing her awareness of him as he walked away. His prayer as he left, he remembered, was that they could meet again, when he could be less equivocal. He had dared not hope when or if that would ever happen; it was too overpowering a distraction for him.

Observing his thoughts, the bittersweet walk in distant memories, Gabriel said, "She would have been the one for you. She felt it from that meeting." A vision appeared, but it was one in which Yeshua was observing Miriam's thoughts.

Miriam watched the two figures walking away. The past two years had opened up new eyes in her to the soft-spoken, independent young man with the inviolately perceptive eyes. She had missed him terribly when he left and had wondered if he would ever know how she felt. But those eyes had certainly found her today and as her feelings had erupted upon seeing him, they needed no probing to know her desire. She knew he knew and to some degree reciprocated, although she found his reluctance disquieting. Had John warned him away from her?

John had suspected her new interest in Yeshua by her continued questioning about him and perked-up ears whenever he became the topic of conversation in the family. She

– 42 –

The Early Years: Qumran, Miriam and John

recalled his response was not particularly supportive of her blossoming interest. In the tradition of many of the leadership of Qumran and a path followed by many of Israel's great prophets, John had already decided upon a life of abstinence, and he thought Yeshua had as well. Although, he admitted, they hadn't spoken about it recently.

Then he spoke directly to her thoughts, in a tender, serious tone of brotherly advice "Miri, Yeshua has a greater mission that all else in his life is subservient to. You must be prepared for that. I don't want to see you hurt."

She had bowed her head so he could not see her expression, but he evidently felt it. She smiled now when she thought of John's final comment. He had remarked, teasingly, "But if I know my determined little sister, she's going to go her way, regardless, and my brother Yeshua better watch out." Her response had been a confident smile—the same she wore now—which said to him he was right. He had shrugged in resignation.

My father will be aghast, she thought, no longer smiling. Yeshua was very controversial in the compound, because he disagreed with basic tenets of the community. This had put Yeshua's relationship with her family at an arm's length. While Yeshua was still welcome to stay with them when he came to visit John, this strain probably precluded any possible relationship between Yeshua and her. Besides, she was supposed to be formally betrothed next month.

But she had been in a very rebellious mood about her betrothed. He was too strict, too insensitive to deal with her strong will. She would never fit in the box of tradition that their community put women in. Women had a greater part to play than their traditions allowed, she contended. They

– 43 –

should be partners to their men, not servants. And she intuited that Yeshua agreed with her. Her eyes followed the departing duo, just in time to meet Yeshua's backward glance. Her eyes caught his, and she knew then she would marry no one else.

Yeshua smiled wistfully, sadly, the smile of pained remembrance. "I know what it's like, that longing for someone that so consumes your thoughts, so electrifies your heart with hope for the future, that it fills up an emptiness that until that moment you didn't realize existed. I had to run from it, because I knew that it had too much power over me. Yet they are natural desires that are the most beautiful part of human life. They are made to be all consuming, because they are meant to bind you to one another eternally—the birth of a small unique world you create together, made up of the connection of your family and relationships with the world. I knew that desire and longed every day from that time I met her for the opportunity to fulfill that desire." He sighed, then went on.

"Our meeting came a few years later, after I had returned to Israel from my journey to the East. I was traveling with John after he left the Qumran community. We taught and preached together in the desert region nearby. It was at one such gathering that she appeared. I had not seen her since the last time I was at the compound, five years earlier. I couldn't take my eyes off her. I know—and I guess she knew—that I was talking most of the time to her."

A scene of the Judean Valley near Jericho manifested itself. Dusk was descending, but light still reflected on the reddish-brown cliffs and the purple and mauve clouds of the glorious setting sun of the desert. It was a small mixed group, old and young, men and women gathered on the rock-strewn valley

The Early Years: Qumran, Miriam and John

with Yeshua sitting informally in a rock speaking to them. An old woman sitting near the front was shoved aside by a young man seeking a better position. Yeshua spoke, his attention directed at the young man:

"It is not good for a son to push away his mother, that he may occupy the place which belongs to her. Whoever does not respect his mother—the most sacred being after his God—is unworthy of the name of son.

"Hearken to what I say to you: respect woman, for in her we see the mother of the universe, and all the truth of divine creation is to come through her.

"She is the fount of everything good and beautiful, she is also the germ of life and death. Upon her man depends in all his existence, for she is his moral and natural support in his labors.

"In pain and suffering she brings you forth; in the sweat of her brow she watches over your growth, and until her death you cause her greatest anxieties. Bless her and adore her for she is your only friend and support on earth.

"Respect her; defend her. In so doing you will gain for yourself her love; you will find favor before God, and for her sake many sins will be remitted to you.

At this point Yeshua became aware of a familiar presence in the crowd. Miriam was sitting unobtrusively, just part of the crowd. Consciously or not, his gaze kept returning to her.

"You have read, he began, 'that at the beginning the

– 45 –

Not as I Will, But as You Will

Chapter 2

Creator [made them male and female] and said, [For this reason a man will leave his father and mother and be united to his wife, and the two will become one flesh]? So they are no longer two, but one. Therefore what God has joined together, let man not separate.'[5]

"Love your wives and respect them, for they will be the mothers of tomorrow and later the grandmothers of a whole nation.

"Be submissive to the wife; her love ennobles man, softens his hardened heart, tames the wild beast in him and changes it to a lamb.

"Wife and mother are the priceless treasures which God has given to you. They are the most beautiful ornaments of the universe, and from them will be born all who will inhabit the world.

"Even as the Lord of Hosts separated the light from the darkness, and the dry land from the waters, so does woman possess the divine gift of calling forth out of man's evil nature all the good that is in him.

"Draw from her—this temple—your moral force. There you will forget your sorrows and your failures and recover the love necessary to aid your fellow men.

"Suffer her not to be humiliated, for by humiliating her you humiliate yourselves, and lose the sentiment of love, without which nothing can exist here on earth.

"Protect your wife, that she may protect you—

The Early Years: Qumran, Miriam and John

you and your household. All that you do for your
mothers, your wives, for a widow, or for any other
woman in distress, you will do for your God." [6]

John approached Yeshua when he finished speaking and the
people started to disperse. "Your speech about women
encourages them to be present. As a rabbi, you should not
teach women. They will cause you to stray, to lose your focus
in your prayers. They have a place, of course, but not in worship."

Smiling the usual smile he had for John and his theologi-
cal sparring, Yeshua said, "God created man in his image—
man and women, He created them in his image. Therefore,
both man and woman reflect Him." But he saw that John had
a point he wanted to make and wasn't listening to anything
else.

Yeshua said, in an offhand way, "We'll talk later," and he
walked away. John and he were like brothers—close and com-
bative, engendered by their family ties as well as their passionate advocacy. Yeshua did not want their disputations to be so
public.

His thoughts turned to that familiar face, which had
become the focus of his talk. It was curious that she had chosen not to make John aware of her presence. He remembered
the last time he had seen her by the well outside Qumran. The
same eyes, but now having taken on a new cast: the innocent,
curious eyes, beguiling in their lack of guile, were now open
and humble to a force he recognized that was perhaps moving
them both together for heaven's purpose. They had recognized
each other immediately, and a curious ethereal interplay took
place between them during his speech. He mused, worriedly,
that it must have been as apparent to others as it seemed to

Not as I Will, But as You Will   Chapter 2

him that he was speaking to her during most of the talk. He looked around to see if she was still there.

The crowd was dissolving, as it was nearing mealtime. Yeshua did not see her, but he felt that she would seek him out if given the opportunity. And it would not be in a crowded throng such as this. He slipped away up a path into a fragrant hilly glen of scrub pine and short brush. He rested on the rocks and watched the feast of colors of the descending sunset. But his thoughts were on this young woman.

He had broached the subject of Miriam with John after the last time they had met. He asked innocently if she was betrothed, not explaining any purpose to his question. John picked up on his reasoning, however. "She is their only daughter, and you know my uncle's attitude toward you," said John with a questioning glance at the end of his comment. "You're not looking at her seriously, are you? She's betrothed for several years now to the son of one of the head rabbis." Yeshua pursued this line of thought no more.

After John's remark, Yeshua had avoided seeing Miriam at that time, letting providence find a way for them if it was meant to be. He understood that betrothals in the community sometimes extended over a period of many years, as young pious priests sought to delay marriage and family as long as possible for the sake of spiritual pursuits. Many at Qumran shunned marriage completely opting for a celibate life. They were known for this practice outside the community, as it was a highly unusual practice in the strong family-centric culture of his people.

Sitting in the clearing, thinking back to his last encounter with Miriam, Yeshua shrugged, shaking his head; he knew his reputation in the settlement. He was a firebrand, an outspo-

– 48 –

The Early Years: Qumran, Miriam and John

ken detractor. John was always standing up for his cousin in the compound, because Yeshua would never keep quiet during scripture study. He had been respectfully asked to leave when he was living there with John five years ago. He was indeed an unlikely marriage prospect for the daughter of one of the rabbis.

He heard footsteps and turned to see who was approaching. Those eyes—it was she, as he knew it would be. His breath stopped, knowing what this moment could become, yet knowing that the time was not yet right—if it ever would be. Many women were drawn to him. He was used to dealing with that. But what he saw in her eyes was a reflection of what he knew to be in his own. This was something different—a special attraction, born not just of physical desire but of some greater destiny, a feeling that he sensed impelled her as well. He knew he should pay attention to this special attraction he felt.

She approached hesitantly, as if she did not know exactly why she was here but came because of some will not her own. Their eyes met, but her glance lowered respectfully. He was looking at her with the faint trace of a smile. It was not a look of the approach of the unfamiliar, but of a subject of familiar contemplation. As if he were seeing this moment as long-expected, intensively awaited, but something he had not yet come to terms with in his mind. When she raised her eyes and smiled back, it was the same smile as his. And he knew she knew what his expression meant: uncertainty, intrigue, perhaps, but absolute uncompromising integrity to be maintained for whatever the future might hold.

"Forgive me for disturbing you... my brother." She hesitated at how to address him, as if her old way didn't seem appropriate now. "Your words touched me deeply. Nowhere does

– 49 –

Not as I Will, But as You Will

Chapter 2

anyone speak such words of comfort to women." She knelt on the grass a little ways before him, and continued, "Where does such wisdom come from? You know my father is a teacher of the ancient scriptures; yet I have not heard this in his teachings."

Looking down at her expectantly, Yeshua replied—not answering her question, yet speaking to the boiling quandary behind it that had brought her here. "The Father has made half the human race male and, half female. Male and female are like a lock and key. A women holds a great treasure behind a lock and only a man has the key that opens it, to reveal that treasure."

Then he spoke directly to the situation between them, wasting no words. "Little sister, I have not seen you since last I was at the community. It was a special moment by the well that has not left my thoughts since. You have grown up. Your presence today gladdened my heart—though, perhaps, John will not be happy? He's a very protective elder brother."

Miriam looked at him, again hesitating—at a loss for how to continue. Finally, recovering her thoughts, she said, "Yes, he does not know I am here. Is he the reason you left the community last time, avoiding me?"

Yeshua replied, "Yes, and you risk too much, coming here. I cannot allow you to proceed without recognizing the cost."

"I know, but this is my choice. My family is my responsibility. Forgive me for imposing. I have wanted to speak to you, ever since seeing you that time at the well. But my feeling for you does not demand a response. I want to learn more of what you speak. I am hungry for such words. My community, as you must know, will not teach women such things. Our presence in prayers and study is thought of as a distraction to

– 50 –

The Early Years: Qumran, Miriam and John

men's meditation. But you do not mind for us to be there and listen. You can't imagine how grateful I am for that."

Yeshua nodded and smiled gently, "Yes, I know, I am always in conflict with the scribes and priests about it. Remember the words of the Prophet Malachi, *'Has not the Lord made them one? In flesh and spirit they are His. And why one? Because He is seeking his offspring.'* [7] Your Heavenly Father knows that women protect the most precious jewels of all within them—the next generation. This the Father reveres above all other treasures, and He would have me educate them, to dedicate that fortune to Him."

He gazed fixedly at her; she returned his look with that expression of open, guileless curiosity that was so attractive to him. There was a moment of charged silence, of shared uncertainty and expectation between them.

"Rabboni... yes, that's what you are... why is it that you are such an age, and have not yet found your treasure—you who appreciate the value of it so much?"

Looking away from that scene, Yeshua said, almost sadly, to Gabriel, connecting to his thoughts at that time, "The perceptiveness of her question struck me speechless. I knew this was not a moment that should be taken lightly. That her words were not just hers, but the Father's, speaking through her to me. Part of the preparation for my mission, should the people fulfill their responsibility, would be to find a wife and establish the model for the family—as I first must establish the model for individual relationship with the Father and person-to-person relations. Each to be in its own time.

"The Father's deepest desire is to see husbands and wives that reflect His image in their love to one another; as they show His love as a parent toward their children. Giving Him

– 51 –

Not as I Will, But as You Will   Chapter 2

the opportunity to experience familial love with objects perfectly reflective of his nature. And ultimately, the lineal descendants of the Father would have been manifested through such families—the very thing that Adam and Eve were unable to provide. This would be the model and the fulfillment for the Kingdom of Heaven. Only I, the Second Adam, the first-born fruit of the Father's lineage, could truly establish this model." He returned his attention to the vision before him.

With eyes closed, Yeshua waited to regain breath and composure pulled out of him from the emotional impact Miriam's question held for him. Finally he opened his eyes and looked at her. Candidly he spoke; he knew his voice was too stressed, too passionate, for his words to be anything but completely honest. He knew somehow the honesty was needed and appropriate to this moment, a moment forced upon him by forces beyond his will. "That is my deepest pain—and the Father's deepest pain. I don't know if I can or will ever be able to fulfill that role."

Miriam look startled. "But surely, after what you just said, you do not believe in the role of some rabbis never being married, as the Qumran *Yahad* teach."

Yeshua answered softly—the softness a heaviness of emotion weighting down the words, "It has not yet been decided if I am to be. There are some who for the sake of building the Kingdom of Heaven must be as eunuchs, never marrying, never having children; but it is not really the Father's desire and it makes Him sad.

"He sees each of us as incomplete without our partners. At the beginning He, the Creator, '*made them in his image, male and female,*' and when they are brought together, they are no

– 52 –

The Early Years: Qumran, Miriam and John

longer two, but one. From them come the Father's greatest treasure, children. Therefore, each family itself is a diamond of many facets, many characters, itself and its parts each unique expressions of the Father's character."

Miriam exclaimed "Where do such words come from? They ring so true, but yet at the same time they are so new to my ears."

Yeshua said,

> *"They ring true because, as a newborn child in the night recognizes the mother's breast, so people held in the darkness of error recognize instinctively their Father, in the Father whose prophet I am."*[8]

"I have been sent by the Father with a new message. I am the one the prophet Isaiah predicted.

> *'A shoot will come up from the stump of Jesse; from his roots a Branch will bear fruit. The Spirit of the Lord will rest on him—the Spirit of wisdom and of understanding, the Spirit of counsel and of power, the Spirit of knowledge and of the fear of the Lord.'"*[9]

Miriam moved closer to Yeshua, kneeling on the grass close to him. As she spoke, the abruptness in her voice was a confession spun from an overflow of emotion. "I know nothing of the prophecies, whether you are whom you believe you are or not. I only know what I feel when I am near you. If it is true that you are to be one of those eunuchs for the sake of the Kingdom of Heaven, then perhaps I must be too.

"I have watched you from afar all these years since first I laid eyes on you. I could not get you out of my mind. I could not accept another man since seeing you, although many have

– 53 –

Not as I Will, But as You Will   Chapter 2

sought my favor. I made it a point to serve your cousin, John, at mealtimes, and would ask about you in veiled questions. Tell me what I should do with this desire. Is it not your desire as well? I know what I saw in your eyes when I approached you this evening?"

Yeshua said, "You, I think, the Father does not want to be childless. What you saw, you saw. But it cannot be acted upon. So you see, this is my pain, my quandary. I cannot ask you— anyone—to wait for me when there is no certainty that I will be able to be their husband."

"What will determine your course?" she asked simply.

Yeshua looked at her face, burning in his memory the picture of her tear-stained cheeks, bright, earnest, responsive eyes—mirroring his own pain and loss. It was an image he would treasure in his mind, to draw upon at times when he needed a goal, a hope for the future.

It was a few moments before he trusted the tenor of his voice to answer her without cracking with emotion. "My course will be decided by the lost sheep of Israel. If they respond to me, I will be victorious and can rise to lead them. If they show faithlessness to me, and will not respond, my course will be death. It is so prophesied—glory or suffering and death."

Miriam reached to touch him, but he gently moved her hand away. "I cannot—we cannot be. Believe my eyes, the feeling you saw, but until the time is right, that memory is all you and I can have. I cannot determine your course, whether you will wait or not."

"I will wait. Can I see you?" she asked, her voice impassioned but set, ready for any answer to come.

– 54 –

The Early Years: Qumran, Miriam and John

Again Yeshua had to wait moments for the palpable storm in his thoughts to pass. He spoke quietly, with controlled passion. "No, you must not. For both our sakes, you must stay away. When I know, I will come to you. Until then, do not try to find me. It may be a few years before I know." Then he touched her outstretched hand, allowing himself and her that one electric connection, a shimmering filament of pathos for them to carry in their memory over the coming years of separation. "Promise me," he said gently, "you will prepare for both possibilities. You must make a life with someone else, if I cannot be there for you."

"I cannot say that." She breathed the words, barely audible.

Yeshua nodded and sighed—he knew no words to respond. He rose, looking around, noticing the darkness descending in the grove. "Come, you must leave before me," he gently urged.

As she rose, he put his hands on her shoulders and looked into her eyes. "The Father has sent you. Trust in Him. You are His daughter. He will guide you as to what to do. Believe what you see in my eyes; they can only speak the truth. If there is to be anyone, it will be you. But my life is not mine to determine. I have a greater responsibility which has yet to unfold. Thank you for your faith, for your love. Your image, as you were tonight, will be my precious companion during these coming years of trial. You have my heart, but I have nothing else to give. Pray for the people to respond and for my success. Then there will be a time for us."

Miriam nodded, her expression crisp, clean, decisive, but the bright sparkle of tears betrayed the emotion within she was trying to suppress. "I understand; I will wait here for you. I will pray for you," she replied simply, with a hushed finality.

Not as I Will, But as You Will   Chapter 2

She left quickly, knowing that for both of them, no more words could be said.

Tears flowing, Yeshua's head lowered to retreat from Gabriel's view. When he looked up his face was tightened to stem the flood of tears. "What have I done?" he whispered. "What have I done to the Father's desire to have the seed of the Kingdom of Heaven from my own body carry on my legacy? He sifted through countless generations of lineage to arrive at my birth, his restored Adam, to start a new pattern for the human race.

"My bride, who would have become His Bride, the restored feminine that He and the world have never been able to experience. That which has never existed but could have started with us, the family the Father could dwell in the midst of, as mind is to body. The Kingdom of Heaven on the Earth would have started from this.

"Alas, what of my hope—and hers? All hopes are dashed by this course descending upon me." The tortured words faded to an inaudible murmur.

Gabriel nodded and waited respectfully. Only Yeshua alone could resolve this agony within himself.

JOHN

Yeshua finally raised his head and looked at the angel, grateful for his quiet, consoling company. Finally, with a deep sigh, and a shrug of his shoulders—in an attempt to escape the emotional turmoil—he abruptly changed the subject and again began to speak about John.

"John and I did not see each other for several years after I

– 56 –

The Early Years: Qumran, Miriam and John

left Qumran. I remember meeting him after that separation. We were so glad to see each other. My return to the homeland saw much change among the people. *Many seemed to be filled with despair, forsaking the Laws of Moses in favor of the customs of the Roman vanquishers in hopes of winning favor with them.*[10] There was even much disarray among the *Yahad*. John was disillusioned with the community, finally admitting that certain points I had made about their narrow viewpoints were indeed right. They were becoming more and more isolationist and thus increasingly irrelevant to the future of the people of Israel."

As Yeshua spoke, a vista opened of a clearing shaded by willows and papyrus reeds, of a bend in a now tranquil Jordan River. A thicket of fragrant oleander concealed its banks and the characteristic foliage-rich green color of the water was visible. This was a favorite spot of John's for baptism. Yeshua and John sat cross-legged among the scrub brush in the warmth of the clearing.

"Suffering does not have to be part of God's will for the redeemed, as the *Yahad* teach," Yeshua told John. "God would rather have faith and obedience in the people than see them endure misery. Remember what the Father told the Prophet Ezekiel:

> *"Say to them, 'as surely as I live, declares the sovereign Lord, I take no pleasure in the death of the wicked, but rather that they turn from their ways and live. Turn! Turn! From your evil ways! Why will you die, O house of Israel?'*[11]

"In all the prophecies of the end-times there is an element of *if*: If the people believe and are faithful, then blessings will come, but if they are unfaithful and disobedient, they will

Not as I Will, But as You Will   Chapter 2

bring destruction upon themselves. Men always have the element of responsibility, of faith and obedience, in determining the outcome in their lives, both individually and as the Chosen nation," Yeshua said. "This is the message that the Chosen People must hear at this time, because now is the time when that determination is being wrought, whether blessing or curse will befall this nation."

John nodded in agreement. "Now is the time of the fulfillment of scriptures; the Kingdom of Heaven is at hand. What we need," he concluded, "is repentance on the part of the Chosen People for their deviation from God's will, so that the blessing of the Kingdom can be bestowed upon them. The problem is the *Yahad* shuns reaching out to those who are lost in sin, seeing them as part of the congregation of perverse men whom they, the true Israel, must separate from. Their view of human life is that it is irrevocably predestined. I can't agree with such a callous and discriminatory attitude toward a majority of God's Chosen People. I can't accept that sinful behavior is a predestined absolute."

Yeshua's animated expression showed he was intrigued by John's statement; it was a departure from his perspective when Yeshua had last seen him, a step away from the extreme narrow orthodoxy of the community's beliefs. "Yes, John," he said, "that's it; I agree."

"Well, wait a minute," John said, "I don't necessarily agree with you. You're too radical. You think everybody can be saved, even those outside of Israel. The Psalmist says, God will bring about a time when the wicked will vanish from the earth, never to be remembered—no mention of being saved.[12] Another scripture says:

> *"His kingdom will appear throughout creation.*

– 58 –

The Early Years: Qumran, Miriam and John

*Satan will be no more, and sorrow as well. The
angel appointed chief will avenge them against
their enemies. The Heavenly One will arise from
his throne and travel forth with wrath for the sake
of his children. The earth will tremble and be
shaken to the core. The mountains will be leveled
and the hills shake and collapse. The horns of
the sun will be broken, its light will dim, turn
dark; the moon will not give her light and will
be turned to blood. He will appear to punish
the Gentiles, and He will destroy all their idols.
Then you, O Israel, will be happy because God
will exalt you, and bring you near to the heavens.
And you will look down from above and see your
enemies in hell. And you will see them and rejoice
and give thanks and praise to your creator.'*[13]

"I don't believe all can be saved."

"But John, all at least must have the *chance* to be saved," said
Yeshua. "Remember the words of one of the same Psalmists
saying, *'He shall bring the pagan nations to serve under His
yoke; and he shall purify Jerusalem, making it holy as of old: so
that nations will come from the ends of the earth to see his
glory.'*[14] In other words, The Lord does not want to destroy
the pagans but to bring them under His loving yoke.

"He wants his people to purify Jerusalem by making it
holy as of old, so that our God can exalt His people as the
lamp to the world, to draw the world unto Him. The Father
wants all His children to return to him. All of the world are
the potential sons and daughters of God, because all of them
descended from Adam and Eve, the first begotten son and
daughter of God. The fact that they are born in a fallen state
of separation should not condemn them from ever knowing

– 59 –

their true parent, the Father in Heaven. But, so much of the Father's plans depend upon us, the Chosen People's response to Him."

John replied in mock offense, "You sound like the Sadducees, believing the past and future are determined strictly by the choices that we humans make in obedience or disobedience to our God; not those that He makes. You make Him sound impotent."

Yeshua spoke with a more serious tone, trying to raise the discussion above the level of just dialogue and argument. He had an important point to make—to convince John to work together with him in his mission, to renew the pact they had shared as youth. "You call that being a Sadducee? I call it being responsible to God for what we understand. If I understand more than someone else about God's will, then I am more responsible for fulfilling that will. To those who have much given, much is expected.

"Of course the Father is not impotent; but rather He gives us—His children—the opportunity to participate in restoration, to inherit His sovereignty. Why else would the Father ask every generation to view, as if he, himself, came forth out of Egypt—that he himself is chosen as the Father's representative. *And you shall tell your son on that day, it is because of what the Lord did for me when I came out of Egypt.*[15] The Father sought through the Chosen People to create not just a national culture, but a direct progeny who shared His zeal for shaping heaven on earth—sons and daughters, not followers.

"You know this mandate for our national identity traces especially to the pledge given by the Father to King David through the prophet Nathan. David was to be king over the house of God's people.

The Early Years: Qumran, Miriam and John

*"Now therefore thus you shall say to my servant
David, 'Thus says the Lord of hosts, I took you
from the pasture, from following the sheep to be
prince over my people Israel... The Lord declares
to you that the Lord will make you a house. When
your days are fulfilled and you lie down with
your ancestors, I will raise up your offspring
after you, who shall come forth from your body,
and I will establish his kingdom... , and I will
establish the throne of his kingdom forever. I will
be a father to him, and he shall be a son to me.
When he commits iniquity, I will punish him
with the rod of men, with the blows of the sons of
men; but I will not take my steadfast love from
him... And your house and your kingdom shall
be made sure forever before me; your throne shall
be established forever.'* [16]

"And each succeeding king received the pledge from
Heavenly Father,

*'You are my son, today I have begotten you. Ask
of me, and I will make the nations your heritage,
and the ends of the earth your possession. You
shall break them with a rod of iron, and dash
them in pieces like a potter's vessel. Now therefore,
O kings, be wise; be warned, O rulers of the
earth.'* [17]

"Indeed, they were God's anointed sons, sharing in His
restoration providence."

John responded, "Yes you are of the House of David, and
I of the priestly line of Levi. That is why we must obey our
calling, but the House of David has failed. They are too far

– 61 –

Not as I Will, But as You Will   Chapter 2

out of position to ever obtain power again."

Yeshua quietly replied, "We used to share a belief in the restoration of the throne of David. Even Zechariah's prophesy at your birth said as much—spoke about your future role in bringing back the restored House of David's leadership.

> *"'Praise be to the Lord, the God of Israel, because he has come and has redeemed his people. He has raised up a horn of salvation for us in the house of his servant David (as he said through his holy prophets of long ago)... And you, my child, will be called a prophet of the Most High; for you will go on before the Lord to prepare the way for him, to give his people the knowledge of salvation through the forgiveness of their sins, because of the tender mercy of our God, by which the rising sun will come to us from heaven to shine on those living in darkness and in the shadow of death, to guide our feet into the path of peace.'*[18]

"You are the returning Elijah. We used to speak about it and agreed it was our shared pact to take responsibility for the return of heaven's sovereignty of my ancestor David. And you have the ear of the temple scribes and priests; they respect you greatly. What changed your thinking? Has the *Yahad* changed your thinking that much?"

John retorted, "My thinking is my own. I don't know that I am Elijah, but as Elijah did, so must I. I am the voice of one crying in the wilderness to prepare the way of the coming Lord. The House of David has lost the blessing of the Lord because they abandoned His will to apostasy. It is the House of Levi—my descendants—and the Pious Ones, who kept faith with the original will of the Lord and his priesthood

– 62 –

The Early Years: Qumran, Miriam and John

and did not embrace the heathen's puppet government put over us to control us, like a leash on a dog. They will be the ones to see the Kingdom emerge and judge this faithless generation. Israel needs no king; our God alone is our king. This the *Yahad* are correct about. Our God only gave the people a king when they demanded it. The Law of Moses must be restored and our people wrestled from the Hellenistic horde that seeks to swallow them up."

"Worldly politics, John, is not the answer to the situation. Neither side has the answer; they only further divide the people. The answer is that our God is looking for the foundation of a united people to work through. This is God's appointed and anointed time. This is the time when the Father will work through the foundation of a united, faithful people, just as he worked in the days of Moses, when the people united behind him. Also in the days of the judges—of Gideon, Samson and Samuel—and the monarchy of David and Solomon, when the people united around God's chosen representative, the nation could prosper. Our land, our kingdom was the greatest in the world, more powerful than any other. What was different at that time? Wasn't it that we were a united people, united with the Father's representative, united as a people with the same design and desire.

"The chosen people's unity around God's will is what will make the difference, not any actions by individuals. A pious remnant such as the *Yahad* fasting and praying in the wilderness, supplicating to the Father on behalf of the people of Israel, will not be enough. You yourself like to chide the Pharisees and Sadducees that they should produce fruit in keeping with repentance. And not to think they can say to themselves, 'We have Abraham as our father.' I tell you that out of these stones God can raise up children for Abraham',

– 63 –

Not as I Will, But as You Will   Chapter 2

you tell them.' [19] What else is their fruit but leading and teaching the Father's remnant to follow and obey His will?"

"Yes, leadership," said John, "but around the Torah. They must follow the leader that leads them to follow the commandments, to take upon themselves the yoke of the commandments. Then they are fulfilling their role as children of Abraham."

"But John," said Yeshua, "There are two yokes that must be embraced in fulfilling the commandments. They must be distinguished because they represent both faith and works, as integrally related parts, as the mind is to the body. The yoke of the kingdom is the first commandment:[20]

"Shema Y'srael, Adonai Elibenu Adonai ehad. Hear, O Israel: The Lord our God, the Lord is one. Love the Lord your God with all your heart and with all your soul and with all your strength." [21] To love God is to love God's will, and to be faithful at all times to that. That is separate from all the other commandments. When you are faithful to the Father's will, then you must follow the remaining commandments—the second yoke—in pursuing that will. This is like the mind working with the body, doing actions which only bear fruit in goodness and righteousness. When you pursue only the second yoke, with no emphasis on the first commandment—it is a body working without the mind, which is ultimately fruitless."

John said, testily, "the question is, what is the will of the Father. Who knows the will—only you?" Is everybody else abandoning the yoke of the kingdom, because they do not agree with you? Who determines what is God's will?"

Yeshua smiled patiently but responded adamantly, "The one who understands the Father's heart. Who else but the son

– 64 –

The Early Years: Qumran, Miriam and John

understands the Father's heart? That is what you look for, for the son to understand the Father's heart and thus the Father's will. Am I that son? That is for you to decide. But consider this, no matter how pious, how faithful is the faithful son, the father still mourns for the prodigal sons that have strayed and his pain and longing for them can never be supplicated until they are brought back into the fold. A truly pious and faithful son will try to return the lost siblings to the fold rather than trying to fill the place of the lost in the heart of the father."

John looked at Yeshua curiously. He sensed that this was more than just dialogue for Yeshua. He was perceiving a more serious desperation behind Yeshua's smile and his words this time. John realized now that something was different about Yeshua from that time five years ago when they had last been together. He would be silent; he motioned for Yeshua to continue.

"The Father seeks a united family centered around his elect; that is all that is needed for His coming Kingdom to be established," said Yeshua. "As he worked centrally through Moses, the patriarchs, the judges, King David, and the prophets, he will work today with his anointed ones—anointed ones, you and I."

John replied, pointedly, "Anointed ones! You have more faith in me than I have in myself. We are adults now; time to put away childish dreams."

Yeshua moved to his knees, his eyes shining, his hands outstretched and animated. "The Father's heart, my brother, follow the Father's heart! Anointed means just this: you understand the need and will take responsibility for it. Those who don't understand cannot take responsibility. Remember the heart of the Father expressed in the 'Song of the Vineyard,' by

– 65 –

the prophet Isaiah:

> 'I will sing for the one I love a song about his vineyard: my loved one had a vineyard on a fertile hillside. He dug it up and cleared it of stones and planted it with the choicest vines. He built a watchtower in it and cut out a winepress as well. Then he looked for a crop of good fruit, but it yielded only bad fruit. Now you dwellers in Jerusalem and men of Judah, judge between me and my vineyard. What more could I have done for my vineyard than I have done for it? I looked for good grapes, why did it yield only bad?'[22]

"'What more could I have done for my vineyard than I have done?' the Father asks. Don't you find His heart reflected; doesn't it move you to tears to act? He mourns the lack of good fruit in the vineyard as a loss of the whole vineyard. He longs for the reclaiming of it in total. Would he be satisfied with the few vines bearing fruit without the many?

"The prophet Ezekiel writes of Israel as a baby daughter, abandoned, despised by others, that the Lord found in the wilderness, covered with the blood and dregs of birth. He picked her up, washed her off, and held her to His bosom. He poured out His heart, energy and zeal to raise this daughter with the greatest finery of clothing, adorned her with jewelry and gave her the finest of foods to eat. She grew beautiful to see, and He prepared her as a bride, covering her nakedness with the corner of His garment.[23]

"But the daughter was ungrateful to all that the Lord did for her. She prostituted herself with other suitors, degrading her body and offering it to all who passed by, the Egyptians, the Philistines, the Assyrians and the Babylonians. So the

The Early Years: Qumran, Miriam and John

Lord abandoned her to them. They ravaged her, discarding her when they finished with her." [24]

Then Yeshua said, changing tone abruptly, "John, you are a Levite. Beware the Levite pridefulness. You think you are doing the right thing by rebuking idolatry and immorality. You look to your ancestor Phinehas, Aaron's grandson, as the model, when he received the blessing from God for your clan to be the priestly clan. But remember the prophet Malachi's admonition to the tribe of Levi, *"If they do not listen and if you do not set your heart to honor my name. I will send a curse upon you and I will curse your blessings. Yes, I have already cursed them because you have not set your heart to honor me."* [25]

"What is listening to God and honoring the will of God? I believe it is not enough to do only what in Moses' time was doing God's will. What is meant by doing the will of God? Is it only showing what is wrong action, or is it to show truly what is right action. You preach repentance and baptism for the coming kingdom. How can the Kingdom of Heaven come if we do not know what is right action on the foundation of that repentance and baptism? You wait for God to come and bring the Kingdom. I say that God waits for us to fulfill some portion of responsibility for the Kingdom to be able to come."

"Yeshua," John says exasperatedly, "that is blasphemous. How can the Almighty Un-named One be dependent upon us? How can He be almighty, if He needs our effort? Who are we but clay in the potter's hands? How can the clay influence the potter? Your vision is folly! He causes the rain to fall or the sun to shine regardless of our efforts. In the same way He will bring the Kingdom in the fullness of time, with or without our efforts. Isaiah says as much:

– 67 –

Not as I Will, But as You Will   Chapter 2

> *"'Their descendants will be known among the*
> *nations and their offspring among the peoples.*
> *All who see them will acknowledge that they are*
> *a people the Lord has blessed.' I delight greatly*
> *in the Lord; my soul rejoices in my God. For*
> *he has clothed me with garments of salvation*
> *and arrayed me in a robe of righteousness, as a*
> *bridegroom adorns his head like a priest, and as*
> *a bride adorns herself with her jewels. For as the*
> *soil makes the sprout come up and a garden causes*
> *seeds to grow, so the Sovereign Lord will make*
> *righteousness and praise spring up before all*
> *nations.'* [26]

John continued heatedly, "We will determine if we will be a part of that kingdom by our preparation, our obedience to His laws and our purification of ourselves internally and externally before Him—like properly prepared soil can enable the seeds to sprout when the time is full."

"John," remonstrated Yeshua, smiling grimly at his cousin's exasperation. "We used to spend hours discussing what the heavenly kingdom would be like, and one thing I thought we had agreed upon was that it would be a dynamic interface between God and mankind and the creation. You've been around the *Yahad* and their deterministic views too long. Man has free will; that is our blessing or our curse depending upon how we use it. We can use it to love one another and serve one another, to love our Father in Heaven and serve Him; or we can use it to do the opposite, to hate and destroy.

"What the Father cannot do is make us love when we would prefer to hate, to serve when we would prefer to covet or destroy. He can only implore us to make the right choices with our free will; to love and not to hate, which He has been

– 68 –

The Early Years: Qumran, Miriam and John

doing throughout history through our testaments and the prophets' words. When we do that—such a small part of the Kingdom of Heaven, but an absolutely essential part—then He can do His part to bring about the Kingdom. Remember Psalm 133:

> *'Behold, how good and how pleasant it is for brothers to dwell together in unity. It is like the precious oil upon the head, coming down upon the beard—even Aaron's beard, coming down upon the edge of his robes. It is like the dew of Hermon coming down upon the mountains of Zion. For there the Lord commanded the blessing, life forever.'* [27]

"Dear brother, you know what I mean. The metaphor of the sanctifying precious oil so saturating the head and beard and dripping down on the robe is like absolute total consecration of the Chosen People to the Father though this action. The dew falling on Mt. Zion as heavily as it does on Mt. Hermon would yield such tremendous fruitfulness of the land. This symbolism shows the ultimate success possible for the Chosen People if they would have such brotherly unity.

"How good and pleasant it is when brothers live together in unity! For there the Lord bestows His blessing, even life forevermore. How much more clear can it be what the will of the Father is, and what can draw His blessings to us? Don't you see this is the Father's will for us—the way we listen and honor Him—and contribute to the coming Kingdom? What more would parents want from their children? Are earthly parents so different from our heavenly parent?"

John stood up and walked across the clearing; the view of gathering clouds was suspended above him over the river's edge. "I wish I had your hope. Our people are so divided and quarreling, how can you make them unite?"

"John," said Yeshua, following him over to the river's edge, "just believe and follow me and my hope will be yours. *'Seek first His kingdom and His righteousness, and all these things will be given to you.'*"[28]

He touched John's shoulder lightly. "Remember Jacob's dream? He had a dream in which he saw a stairway resting on the earth, with its top reaching to heaven, and the angels of God were ascending and descending on it. And the Lord blessed him and said, your descendants will be like the dust of the earth, and you will spread out to the west and to the east, to the north and to the south. *'And all peoples on earth will be blessed through you and your offspring.'*[29]

"In traveling to other lands, these words have come back to me again and again. We are to be the bridge between earth and heaven, light and dark, for the peoples of the earth. That was the blessing that Jacob was given. And the prophets of old, Jeremiah, Ezekiel and especially Isaiah came with the predictions of the universal kingdom to be established on the foundation of the restored throne of David. Remember, Isaiah spoke about the peacemaker, the herald of this universal kingdom:

> *"How beautiful on the mountains are the feet of those who bring good news, who proclaim peace, who bring good tidings, who proclaim salvation, who say to Zion, 'Your God reigns!' Listen! Your watchmen lift up their voices; together they shout for joy. When the Lord returns to Zion, they will see it with their own eyes.*
>
> *"Burst into songs of joy together, you ruins of Jerusalem, for the Lord has comforted his people,*

The Early Years: Qumran, Miriam and John

he has redeemed Jerusalem. The Lord will lay bare his holy arm in the sight of all the nations, and all the ends of the earth will see the salvation of our God."[30]

"I see it as possible to accomplish, and now is the time the Father wants to fulfill this prophecy. And I understand now that this is my mission, to help our people fulfill their position in advancing 'the salvation of God to all the nations.'"

"My brother, the Father—our Father—is just waiting for our response, for our demonstrating our allegiance to Him and His word. Our people were given this task by the Father to our ancestor Jacob, to help the world creeping on the earth but still imbued with a desire for heaven. We are the acacia tree in the desert, connecting earth and heaven through its outstretched branches and roots. The Father needs for us to waken to our responsibility. That is His will!"

John threw up his hands, smiling, and acquiesced. "Welcome home, brother. It is good when brothers dwell together in unity, even if we can't always agree on what exactly that unity means. It's good to have you back. You do indeed make me think. So, tell me," he said, laughing, "what other new apostasies have you been dabbling in for us to argue about. You've been away so long in parts unknown. I'm almost afraid to ask."

Yeshua's attention returned to the present. Glancing at Gabriel, he said, "John was truly happy to see me, as if a part of our old relationship was returning.

"He said, 'We will still disagree on how the Kingdom will come. But at least we both agree that now is the time for its fulfillment—now!' His eyes betrayed his happiness even though his voice yielded only grudging acceptance of the

– 71 –

Not as I Will, But as You Will   Chapter 2

renewed compact we were making.

"I told him about my travels in the eastern regions, in Persia, India and Nepal, what I learned and how it applied to our ministry to the Chosen People. I had spent six years traveling to the seats of the major religions to study their faiths: India for the Hindus, Tibet for the Buddhists, and Persia and the Zoroastrians. I learned the essence of these beliefs and gained acceptance and followings in all those regions.

I told John, "Even among the heathens there are traditions where there is virtue and courage for the good and a will for something more than they have. The pursuit of goodness for goodness' sake is exalted, even when there is no hope of reward. In a sense, this is a greater good then we the Chosen People possess, because we act with the hope of reward at the end. This is because we are chosen by the Father and will receive the Father's blessing if we succeed.

"We must value the good in others and the way the Father is working to raise up all peoples to ultimately know Him and pursue His Kingdom on Earth. The Father can work through all that have a desire for good, even be it someone like Caesar Augusta, who in many ways represents much that is evil. Even he has a will for peace and pursues it among the diverse peoples of his republic."

I suggested to John that we should work together evangelizing. I said the people needed exhortation to not despair, because the day of their redemption from the yoke of sin was near. We, by our examples, must confirm the people's faith in the God of their fathers." [31] John agreed, at least for a time. The formula we followed was simple, John exhorted them to repentance of their present sins; and I gave them hope of the new age to come.

– 72 –

The Early Years: Qumran, Miriam and John

Following his thoughts, the scene before him changed to a rock and scrub brush strewn hillside of Judea. Mud and stone huts, the same gray-beige color as the surrounding countryside, were scattered in the distance. It was an area Yeshua recognized near Jerusalem, skirting one of the small outlying villages. It was one of the instances when John and Yeshua were together teaching. Yeshua, resting casually on a stone crag jutting out of the hillside, was speaking to a small group, with the people sitting on the sparse grass before him.

> *"Weep not, oh, my beloved sons! For your griefs have touched the heart of your Father and He has forgiven you as he has forgiven your ancestors. Hear His heart in his words expressed.*[32]
>
> *"Forsake not your families to plunge into debauchery; stain not the nobility of your souls; adore not idols which cannot but remain deaf to supplications.*
>
> *"Fill my temple with your hope and your patience, and do not adjure the religion of your forefathers, for I have guided them and bestowed upon them of my beneficence.*
>
> *"Lift up those who are fallen; feed the hungry and help the sick that you may be altogether pure and just in the day of the last judgement which I prepare for you."*[33]

One in the crowd asked cynically, how they should thank their Heavenly Father, since the Roman intruders had robbed their temples and destroyed their sacred vessels.

Yeshua responded,

> *"Enter into your temple, into your heart;*

– 73 –

Not as I Will, But as You Will — Chapter 2

illuminate it with good thoughts, with patience and unshakable faith, which you owe to your Father.

"And your sacred vessels! They are your hands and your eyes. Look to do that which is agreeable to God, for in doing good to your fellow man, you perform a ceremony that embellishes the temple wherein abides Him who has created you.

"For God has created you in His own image, innocent, with pure souls and hearts filled with kindness and not made for the planning of evil, but to be the sanctuaries of love and justice.

"Therefore I say unto you, soil not your hearts with evil, for in them the Eternal Being abides.

"When ye do works of devotion and love, let them be with full hearts and see that the motives of your actions be without hope of gain or self-interest."

"For actions so impelled will not bring you nearer to salvation but lead you to a state of moral degradation wherein the state of lying and murder pass on for generations down.[34]

"Remember what the prophet Isaiah says.

"He gives power to the faint; and to them that have no might he increases strength. Even the youths shall faint and be weary, and the young men shall utterly fall: But they that wait upon the Lord shall renew their strength; they shall mount up with wings as eagles; they shall run, and not be weary; and they shall walk, and not faint."[35]

— 74 —

The Early Years: Qumran, Miriam and John

The people, mostly farmers, simple, unaffected, far removed from the temple hierarchy and temple politics, listened intently to Yeshua's words.

John confronted Yeshua quarrelsomely after the meeting, "You emphasize too little their private steps to salvation. That for their body to be a temple it must be cleansed, must be purified, with repentance for their sins—private disciplines that will keep their sinful tendencies in check and prepare them for the coming of the kingdom. If they neglect such actions, it is better they should go to the temple."

Yeshua replied, patiently, "There is new truth, John. I have come with new wine. Your wineskins are old, cracking, and will lose the precious contents. You must renew your container for truth or you will miss the value of new words.[36] *The Kingdom of God is not coming with signs to be observed; nor will they say, 'Look, here it is!' or, 'There it is!' For behold, the kingdom of God is in your midst."* [37] He paused. "The kingdom will be in the community of faithful, in their love and caring for one another, reflecting their love and caring for their Heavenly Father and His responding love to them."

"When the Father is in me, am I not His temple? Do I have to go to the temple to feel the Father's presence? Every since the beginning, His presence can be felt in the things that He has made.[38] Why do you go to the desert? Isn't it to be more able to feel the Father's presence? At that moment, is your body not His temple? But what value is that temple to the Father if He cannot use it—use *you*—as an instrument to build the Heavenly Kingdom? Preparation for the Kingdom is more a community activity than an individual's. It is by their love, inner-directed by the love of the Father, that they will be recognized, by Heaven and by the world."

– 75 –

Not as I Will, But as You Will

Chapter 2

John, exasperated, exclaimed, "That is blasphemy, Yeshua! The Kingdom will come, and we who are diligent to His commandments will be able to enter therein. Those who are not obedient will not be able to enter."

Yeshua put his hands on John's shoulders, his expression fervent and embracing. "John, remember the prophet Jeremiah, what the Father told him:

> *"The time is coming," declares the Lord, "when I will make a new covenant—NEW COVENANT—with the house of Israel and with the house of Judah. It will not be like the covenant I made with their forefathers when I took them by the hand to lead them out of Egypt, because they broke my covenant, though I was a husband to them," declares the Lord.*
>
> *"This is the covenant I will make with the house of Israel after that time," declares the Lord. "I will put my law in their minds and write it on their hearts. I will be their God and they will be my people. No longer will a man teach his neighbor, or a man his brother, saying, 'know the Lord, because they will all know me, from the least of them to the greatest,' declares the Lord."[38]*

Said Yeshua thoughtfully, "That is the relationship I am bringing to the Chosen People—a new relationship, more intimate with the Lord God, as a Father is to a son, not as a servant is to a master. Believe in me, have faith in me for just a while and you will understand!" His voice was taut with emotion, almost pleading—the cracks in their relationship, like bleeding wounds in his spirit, were hurting.

Yeshua's gaze now strayed as he pondered that moment,

– 76 –

The Early Years: Qumran, Miriam and John

because it was to foreshadow the eventual parting of the ways between them. "John and I had become close again," he mused, "but I could not change his attitude about certain points and they continued to be a barrier to our unity. I felt then the possibility that I would have to move forward without him and I felt a desolate and lonely foreboding about it."

At that, Yeshua fell sadly silent.

Not as I Will, But as You Will

Chapter 3

Jesus and John—The Baptism

The waning moon suddenly brightened, emerging from a cloud. Gabriel had retreated into the shadows, leaving Yeshua alone with his thoughts. The brightness illuminated the still, sleeping city beyond the valley below where he had loved and served the people. The walls of the temple loomed like a rampart, a spiritual and physical barrier to the city and the people he was trying to save. The actual barrier was the priests within, who should have been his allies in the restorative providence he was commissioned to fulfill. This city that the Father loved so much would have to pay for the sin the priests were about to commit by in capturing and executing him. He closed his eyes to not see, but nothing could remove the vision in his mind of the smoldering ruins of the city. The scene he visualized would transpire within two generations—knowledge as certain to him as that this night would be followed

Not as I Will, But as You Will   Chapter 3

by morning.

He glanced across the width of the city. To the north to the Bethesda pool, where the disabled, blind, lame and paralyzed gathered. He thought of the paralyzed man he had healed there, and later received grief from the scribes and Pharisees for healing on the Sabbath. They would now kill the healer, rather than have him upset their comfortable traditions, no matter how mortally ill in spirit and in need of healing they themselves were—*"Blind guides! Straining a gnat to swallow a camel."* [1]

To the west, to the palace of the duplicitous Herod—blind guides, the words echoed—the cabal of the political maneuverings of Herod and the hypocritical orthopraxis of the temple priests, whom the wily fox had hand-picked for their loyalty to him. This self-serving attitude that allowed them to commit the right actions in the letter of the law with totally wrong, destructive motivation was the battleground Yeshua had been fighting on all these months here in the city. The battle was now lost. The people would now suffer for their leaders' lack of leadership. Yeshua shook his head in sad resignation.

To the south, to the old city, the City of David, where his ancestor dwelt. David had made mistakes, but never ones of the arrogance and hypocrisy this generation of leaders displayed, he mused. He could be forgiven for his mistakes and still be used by the Father because he could be humble, admitting his mistakes and coming to the Father in prayer and repentance. This ability is lost in these leaders, making them deaf to the Father's direction. Again, as always, it will be the people who will suffer for their faithlessness.

To the mount behind him, and the Judean desert beyond

Jesus and John—The Baptism

where he had spent so much time with John in the desert and the Jordan River valley. "John, how I miss you!" he whispered; the memory of John's death was still too painful.

In his thoughts he visualized the Jordan River and the ford where the river narrowed, at summertime when the water was low and was easily crossed. It was always a meeting place for John and him. The river was special to them, as it was to all people of Israel. It flowed through Israel like a spine, spreading its lifeblood through its tributaries into the otherwise parched, arid lands of Israel. It was the spiritual birthing place of so many of the chosen people's leaders, from Jacob to Joshua to Elijah, and the boundary of the Promised Land given to the Chosen People by the Father. He could hear the words of Deuteronomy, the promise given to the Chosen People by the Father that would forever frame this tiny piece of land in the minds and hearts of its progeny.

> *"Hear, O Israel. You are now about to cross the Jordan to go in and dispossess nations greater and stronger than you, with large cities that have walls up to the sky. The people are strong and tall— Anakites! You know about them and have heard it said: 'who can stand up against the Anakites?'" But be assured today that the Lord your God is the one who goes across ahead of you like a devouring fire. He will destroy them; he will subdue them before you. And you will drive them out and annihilate them quickly, as the Lord has promised you."* [2]

"If God went before us, how could we fail?" he mused, his mind wandering down paths of ancestral memories, "This was the unspoken pride of my people, if often a misplaced pride." This ancestral presence, the passion, of Jacob, who was

– 81 –

Not as I Will, But as You Will

Chapter 3

also called Israel, the future of a people; Joshua, the anointed successor to Moses; Elijah, who would return someday— could that have been John? The vision of the prophet-priest was so strong and anticipated at the river's edge. And especially now with the fever-pitched expectation of this time as the last days, as foretold in the Holy Scriptures. The religious-minded Jews, weary from centuries of vicissitudes, were looking for the promised deliverance, the coming of the anointed one, the *Mashiah* (messiah). In the far distance, near where the mouth of the Jordan empties into the Dead Sea, were the stark grey-yellow stone mountains of the Essene community of Qumran, a religious order whose very purpose for existence was to prepare for the imminent end days.

The scripture so often referred to in prayers and liturgies at Qumran came to mind:

> *"The heavens and earth will listen to His*
> *Messiah and none therein will stray from the*
> *commandments of the holy ones. Seekers of the*
> *Lord, strengthen yourself in His service! All you*
> *hopeful in your heart, will you not find the Lord*
> *in this? For the Lord will consider the pious and*
> *call the righteous by name. Over the poor His*
> *spirit will hover and will renew the faithful with*
> *His power. And he will glorify the pious on the*
> *throne of the eternal Kingdom. He who liberates*
> *the captives, restores sight to the blind, straightens*
> *the bent. And the fruit will not be delayed*
> *for anyone. The Lord will accomplish glorious*
> *things which have never been, for he will heal the*
> *wounded, revive the dead and bring good news to*
> *the poor."*[3]

The prophetic announcement was from Isaiah and the lat-

Jesus and John—The Baptism

ter part was an especially descriptive reference to the work of the messiah. Yeshua and John had often referred to it in ministering.

"The Spirit of the Sovereign Lord is on me,
because the Lord has anointed me to preach good
news to the poor. He has sent me to bind up the
brokenhearted, to proclaim freedom for the captives
and release from darkness for the blind." [4]

Isaiah also spoke portending the return of Elijah, the one to prepare for the coming messiah. This was the role foretold to be John's mission at his birth, *"A voice of one calling: 'In the desert prepare the way for the Lord; make straight in the wilderness a highway for our God.'"* [5]

Fervent memories swirled around Yeshua of those times, when this spirit was the uniting force between John and him, the early days of their dual ministries at the Jordan. "Repent, for the Kingdom of Heaven is at hand!" was the call to passers-by that brought them in swarms to their gatherings. The desire for the coming kingdom was a shared palpable energy that was fueled merely by being voiced by pilgrims at the river's edge. Expectation was great for the time of its fulfillment.

They were living out their childhood dreams of ministering together. John was the charismatic one, wearing belted camel skins—not unlike Elijah of old—and eliciting faithfulness in the crowds by evoking another era, when fire and brimstone followed faithlessness and material blessings followed faith.

Left alone to his thoughts, Yeshua spoke them—a memory, a desire, a prayer or a plea, the object being all of these. "At that time, even John was inspired with the prospect of being the spearhead of this movement to reassemble the tribes, to recapture the former glory of Israel. Isaiah 40 was the hope shared by us, even if there was disagreement on how the end times would manifest and from where the promised messiah would come. Israel's suffering course was finally coming to an end and her time to shine was before her.

"Comfort, comfort my people, says your God.
Speak tenderly to Jerusalem, and proclaim to her
that her hard service has been completed, that her
sin has been paid for, that she has received from
the Lord's hand double for all her sins."[6]

Gabriel returned from the shadows. His face, excited, was like another light source besides the moonlight. It had brightened as he engaged in the progression of Yeshua's thoughts.

Gabriel said, "Do you know how much all of heaven was with you at this time? Through so many ages the angelic realm had waited for the moment of fulfillment of the Father's plan—when finally His son could be received and the glorious prophetic fulfillments begun. Now the Son of David and Elijah were together; the glorious victory was coming to pass. Our hopes were alive, palpable."

Yeshua glanced at him, noting the change in his expression. The thought had not occurred to him of how much the angelic world too must have been cheering them on, adding to the supernaturally enlivened atmosphere of that time at the river's edge.

Yeshua said with an ever-so-slight wistful smile, "Yes it was such a hopeful time. Preaching repentance for the coming judgment at hand was the opening way to start people thinking of remaking, reordering their lives in preparation for the coming providence of the Father, the establishment of the

Jesus and John—The Baptism

Kingdom of Heaven on the Earth. We preached and ministered to the crowds that gathered on both sides of the Jordan River. John baptized for forgiveness of sins in his own Qumran-inspired way of ritual immersion. I spoke of the coming kingdom, and how they could be a part of it. We captured attention from afar, drawing people from Jerusalem and beyond."

As he spoke, the scene materialized of a morning on the shore of the Jordan near Bethany. John and Yeshua were together in the Jordan. John had his hands raised, his face entranced, as receiving a vision. He said in a loud voice to many gathered near him, gesturing to Yeshua:

> *"Look, the Lamb of God, who takes away the*
> *sin of the world! This is the one I meant when I*
> *said, 'A man who comes after me has surpassed*
> *me because he was before me.' I myself did not*
> *know him, but the reason I came baptizing with*
> *water was that he might be revealed to Israel."*
> *Then John gave this testimony: "I saw the Spirit*
> *come down from heaven as a dove and remain on*
> *him. I would not have known him, except that the*
> *one who sent me to baptize with water told me,*
> *'The man on whom you see the Spirit come down*
> *and remain is he who will baptize with the Holy*
> *Spirit.' I have seen and I testify that this is the*
> *Son of God."* [7]

Yeshua nodded in remembrance, "I had just returned from a trip to Galilee. It was the time for John, representing the Age of the Prophets, to baptize me, symbolically bestowing the blessing of the prophets upon me and opening up the new age that we were just beginning. Something I knew but he wasn't yet aware of. I went to the Jordan to be baptized by him. John

– 85 –

Not as I Will, But as You Will   Chapter 3

had a very deep spiritual experience at that moment about my mission. He at first tried to deter me, saying, 'I need to be baptized by you, and do you come to me?'

"I told him, 'Let it be so now; it is proper for us to do this to fulfill all righteousness.' Then John consented and baptized me. As soon as I was baptized, at that moment heaven was opened, and he was given direct testimony to follow me." [8]

Following his thoughts, the scene changed to the following day. *John was there again with two of his disciples. When he saw Yeshua passing by, he said, "Look, the Lamb of God!"* [9]

"Those two disciples, Simon and Andrew, were the foundation of the twelve disciples. They came directly from John's witness to me. If only that inspiration could have lasted; if John could have continued to bring people to me to help expand my influence among the priests and scribes, the power base of the religious community of Israel. John's vision of me, however, did not sustain his faith in me. Even at that time John had the seeds of doubts about his position, despite the fact he was being given direct spiritual testimony about my mission."

As Yeshua spoke, the scene before him changed to a short time later at the same spot on the shore, when John was visited by a conflagration of Jerusalem priests, sent by the priests at the temple. John had just finished immersing in water a family for baptism when, as he stepped away from the water, he was suddenly surrounded by the priests. Their words were inhospitably blunt in their questioning. John was taken aback and slow to answer.

They asked John, "Are you the Christ?"

"I am not the Christ," he replied.

– 86 –

Jesus and John—The Baptism

They asked him, "Then who are you? Are you Elijah?"

"I am not," he told them.

"Are you the Prophet?"

He answered, "No."

Finally they said, "Who are you? Give us an answer to take back to those who sent us. What do you say about yourself?"

John replied in the words of Isaiah the prophet, "I am the voice of one calling in the desert, 'Make straight the way for the Lord.'" [10]

"Why then do you baptize if you are not the anointed one, nor Elijah, nor the Prophet?"

"I baptize with water," John replied, "but among you stands one you do not know. He is the one who comes after me, the thongs of whose sandals I am not worthy to untie." [11]

Yeshua said, "When John told me this, it surprised me the answer he gave. John saw his position as teaching in the same spirit and power as Elijah, but fell short of claiming he was Elijah.

"I told him, 'But, you *are* Elijah! You are a witness to this providence that the Father is working. It doesn't mean you are the physical presence of Elijah. If you believe in me, then you are the Elijah who can testify to them of my position. You are testifying as Elijah would testify if he were here. That is what the voice crying in the wilderness does, testifies to the workings of the Father to those who are less sensitive to the Father's voice.'

– 87 –

Not as I Will, But as You Will   Chapter 3

"John had seemed obviously perplexed, taking my words in, but showing in his expression that he lacked commitment. His commitment to being Elijah meant his commitment to me—which was the problem."

Yeshua continued, "Believing in me was actually the real problem, secondary to my words. "John's heart was absolutely desirous to serve the Father. He must have been conflicted deeply over this call to action to unite around the true center, God's chosen instrument—which was me. When it came to the familiarity of me, his cousin, being that chosen one—even with Heaven's testimony reinforcing it—John had doubts.

> *"John told his followers, 'I baptize you with water. But one more powerful than I will come the thongs of whose sandals I am not worthy to untie. He will baptize you with the Holy Spirit and with fire. His winnowing fork is in his hand to clear his threshing floor and to gather the wheat into his barn, but he will burn up the chaff with unquenchable fire.'"* [12]

"His concept that the one coming would be more powerful, whose sandals he would not be worthy to untie, created an unreal expectation that I could not live up to. And feeding that doubt was probably the desire to keep his position and his followers and to not have to be second to someone else. To truly follow me, he would have to bring his following to me and become my first disciple. Then as my first disciple, bridging to the people that I had difficulty reaching, particularly the priests and scribes. He started, but was unwilling to follow through and finish. In the end, perhaps, his pride at being here in the spirit and power of Elijah was as Elijah the leader, not Elijah following the messiah, especially the messiah, his cousin—his illegitimate cousin in the eyes of many."

– 88 –

Jesus and John—The Baptism

Gabriel said, "As a student of the scripture John should have been aware of the Father's use of people who seem unlikely choices from the point of common sense. If you look in your lineage—and even at times in his—among the forefathers of your lineages are people who seem curiously out of place. King Solomon was born illegitimate from Bathsheba, at the time David's concubine. Tamar seduced her father-in-law Judah, disguised as a prostitute, to providentially continue the line of Abraham, when Judah's sons failed to have offspring by her. Your situation is not so unusual, from the point of view of the providence of the Father."

Yeshua replied, "Yes those are situations not often discussed. But I was not the one to remind him of it.

"The priestly leadership, on the other hand, had begun putting pressure on John to reject me. They saw me as a threat to their hold on the people. Their promises to John of legitimacy for his own ministry were becoming more and more appealing. This tension was, I believe, the final divide between us, leaving us both at the mercy of conquest by the secular world, which it was actually our shared mission to change and resurrect."

Gabriel added, thoughtfully, "John was gaining power and authority, for the purpose of testifying to you. That was why the Father brought the people to him. But he misread his position. He thought because more people came to him than to you that he must have the greater mission. You came from humble beginnings, so the Father knew someone with great power to influence had to lead the people to you. That was John. Look and see."

A scene familiar to Yeshua appeared, the springs of Salim in the northern Jordan Valley, where John would often bring

Not as I Will, But as You Will   Chapter 3

his followers to use the running water for baptism and the cool rocks surrounding as a setting for preaching. John was approached by a few of his disciples who asked him, "Rabbi, that man who was with you on the other side of the Jordan, that you testified about, he is baptizing, and everyone is going to him."

Yeshua's attention was captured by the question, as well as John's answer, as he looked on the scene

John replied, cryptically:

> *"A man can receive only what is given him from heaven. You yourselves can testify that I said, 'I am not the (Christ) but am sent ahead of him.' The bride belongs to the bridegroom. The friend who attends the bridegroom waits and listens for him, and is full of joy when he hears the bridegroom's voice. That joy is mine, and it is now complete.*
>
> *"He must become greater; I must become less. The one who comes from above is above all; the one who is from the earth belongs to the earth, and speaks as one from the earth. The one who comes from heaven is above all. He testifies to what he has seen and heard, but no one accepts his testimony."* [13]

His attention returning to the present, Yeshua said, sadly shaking his head, "The bridegroom's friend should share in the joy and experience with the bridegroom, not separate and watch from a distance. How little he understood his true value! Here was when our relationship finally started unraveling. Tension and fights erupted more and more between us. John would always look back to the past for truth, never see-

Jesus and John—The Baptism

ing the possibility of new truth. But I had come to fulfill the truth, to raise it to a higher level.

"John would look to the Ten Commandments as ultimate law. But I told him, there are only two commandments, *'Love the Lord your God with all your heart and with all your soul and with all your mind and love your neighbor as yourself.'*[14] Then, you would fulfill all the commandments—you no longer need the ten. John looked to separate from the world to serve God. And those he baptized, he taught to do the same. That would have been perfectly right in a different context, at a different time. But God is demanding different attitudes at this time. I tried to teach him the need to look outward to connect to the world, to the knowledge of the world, the peoples of the world—which I understood I must do to ultimately lead them all. Sometimes I think, if only we had had more time…"

Gabriel, his voice hard and implacable, replied, "You mustn't defend him. He made his choice by his actions. It was false humility that said, 'he must become greater, and I must become less,' meaning you must increase in popularity and he must decrease in popularity. If he had united with you, both he and you would have increased in popularity, he as your first disciple and you going on to fulfill your mission as the future king. Sadly for all, he was conflicted as to the purpose of his popularity, yielding to a misplaced sense of humility.

"Shortly after that time he cut back on public ministry and became embroiled with the intrigues of Herod's court, which was his downfall—imprisonment and beheading shortly after at the hands of King Herod. Why should he care about the defilement taking place at the hedonistic court of Herod, when the defilement of the nation was unfolding, with the rejection and destruction of God's son imminent? This was

Not as I Will, But as You Will   Chapter 3

something which he could have directly impacted, had he stayed and supported you."

Yeshua nodded, accepting Gabriel's words with lowered eyes, the words scalding his heart. The scene changed to another familiar memory of Yeshua's, a gathering in Galilee at the synagogue of the twelve and other onlookers. Yeshua remembered the occasion, when some of John's disciples were in the crowd listening to his teaching. They came with a message from John in prison. *John's disciples asked him, "Are you the one who was to come, or should we expect someone else?"*

Yeshua seemed obviously stunned, but catching himself, replied, *"Go back and report to John what you hear and see: The blind receive sight, the lame walk, those who have leprosy are cured, the deaf hear, the dead are raised, and the good news is preached to the poor. Blessed is the man who does not fall away on account of me."*

Yeshua spoke of the cryptic words. "My words were a code known well to John, reflecting back to Qumran and the messianic expectation that John knew was fulfilled in those words, but that now, undeniably, I had brought to fulfillment through mirroring these in my accomplishments. It was a painful reflection that John should know without being reminded. Indeed, the tragedy I felt was that whether John understood or not, it was too late for him. His fate was set; he would not make it out of the prison. The only concern was John's disciples, that John lead them to me."

As John's disciples were leaving, Yeshua began to speak to the crowd about John: *"What did you go out into the desert to see? A reed swayed by the wind? If not, what did you go out to see? A man dressed in fine clothes? No, those who wear fine clothes are in kings' palaces. Then what did you go out to see? A*

– 92 –

Jesus and John—The Baptism

prophet? Yes, I tell you, and more than a prophet. This is the one about whom it is written: 'I will send my messenger ahead of you, who will prepare your way before you.'" [15]

Interjecting, Yeshua said, "I had to speak to the question that many had approached me about, "if you are the Lord, where is the Elijah who is prophesied to come before the Lord?"

The scene continued. *"I tell you the truth: Among those born of women there has not risen anyone greater than John the Baptist; yet he who is least in the kingdom of heaven is greater than he. From the days of John the Baptist until now, the kingdom of heaven has been forcefully advancing, and forceful men lay hold of it. For all the Prophets and the Law prophesied until John. And if you are willing to accept it, he is the Elijah who was to come. He who has ears, let him hear."* [16]

Yeshua's attention returned to Gabriel. "How painful were those words for me. They were a condemnation I had painstakingly avoided making but was forced to make by the circumstances. Least in the kingdom is a reproach from Heaven on John's position in the Father's providence. By his actions be became a block to the Kingdom of Heaven, rather than a stepping-stone. The result of a failure of leadership has such broad effects. It would be most felt by the innocent, the flock, with no power of influence on their future. Those innocents were dependent upon the leadership, whose failure placed future desolation in their path from the fiery judgment incurred."

He continued, thoughtfully, as if reminding himself of what brought him here, "No matter what John and the Jewish leadership did or didn't do, these people—the Jewish faithful—still had a great part to play if they were willing. Their condition of faith and obedience in me could make up for the failure of that leadership and still fulfill the conditions for Israel's restoration. I would not let them get away with the thought that, 'If you and John are not together, then you must not be the chosen one—we do not have to follow you.' I continued preaching to the gathering, trying to make them see their responsibility dissociated from what the leadership does."

Yeshua returned his attention to the scene and his words to the gathering:

> *"To what can I compare this generation? They are like children sitting in the marketplaces and calling out to others: 'We played the flute for you, and you did not dance; we sang a dirge, and you did not mourn.' For John came neither eating nor drinking, and they say, 'He has a demon.' The Son of Man came eating and drinking, and they say, 'Here is a glutton and a drunkard, a friend of tax collectors and "sinners." But wisdom is proved right by her actions.*

> *"Woe to you, Korazin! Woe to you, Bethsaida! If the miracles that were performed in you had been performed in Tyre and Sidon, they would have repented long ago in sackcloth and ashes. But I tell you, it will be more bearable for Tyre and Sidon on the Day of Judgment than for you.*

> *"And you, Capernaum, will you be lifted up to the skies? No, you will go down to the depths. If the miracles that were performed in you had been performed in Sodom, it would have remained to this day. But I tell you that it will be more*

Jesus and John—The Baptism

bearable for Sodom on the Day of Judgment than for you."

In tearful prayer Yeshua concluded his remarks to the small group:

"I praise you, Father, Lord of heaven and earth, because you have hidden these things from the wise and learned, and revealed them to little children. Yes, Father, for this was your good pleasure. All things have been committed to me by my Father. No one knows the Son except the Father, and no one knows the Father except the Son and those to whom the Son chooses to reveal him. Come to me, all you who are weary and burdened, and I will give you rest. Take my yoke upon you and learn from me, for I am gentle and humble in heart, and you will find rest for your souls. For my yoke is easy and my burden is light." [17]

Tears falling in remembrance, Yeshua said, "The leadership of Israel had failed, but the Father still held out hope to them, the simple faithful. Even now I still harbor that hope, however misguided it might be—even if the Father has finally given it up—that the Chosen People can unite with me, bridging the chasm of faithlessness that emerged because of the arrogance of Israel's religious leadership. If the Father has given up, I have not!" he said, his voice calmed to a whisper but unyieldingly emphatic.

Yeshua rose and returned to his sleeping disciples, trying in vain to rouse them. "'Simon,' he said to Peter, "are you asleep? Could you not keep watch for one hour? Watch and pray so that you will not fall into temptation. The spirit is willing, but the body is weak." [18]

– 95 –

Not as I Will, But as You Will   Chapter 3

Peter nodded groggily, and murmured something unintelligible, obviously sleeping. The stupor they had fallen into seemed under a hostile will, a spiritual possession of sorts. Powers and principalities of good and evil seemed to have met in this garden this evening, Yeshua reflected.

Yeshua returned to his position. "I had hoped that bringing them with me, I could make them understand. I know the Father's heart. He would change, even at this late hour, if I could show faith among them. As the Father told the Prophet Jeremiah, '*If at any time I announce that a nation or kingdom is to be uprooted, torn down and destroyed, and if that nation I warned repents of its evil, then I will relent and not inflict on it the disaster I had planned.*' [19] When the people of Nineveh repented of their sins, God spared them. If Sodom and Gomorrah had repented—if Abraham could have found even one righteous man—they too would have been spared.

"What more can I do? They are like young children, who enjoy my company and my miracles, like a child's game, but are incapable to see and share, with eyes of a dutiful son, their parent's—my—anxiety. But if they don't understand, they will suffer so much more when I am gone. They are my children, how can I abandon them to this fate. They must be given a chance, still."

Gabriel shrugged, relaxing his sternness, the hint of a bewildered smile flickering across his face. Yeshua's capacity for forgiveness and perseverance suddenly had moved beyond his comprehension.

Gabriel said, "True, it is not too late in the Father's eyes. But from tonight the final decision must be made. Even now your opponents plot your destruction. They are coming," he cautioned, darkly.

– 96 –

Jesus and John—The Baptism

A scene now appeared, familiar to Yeshua, the smooth-paved square adjacent to Herod's palace. The palace's marble stairs descended to the stone wall that separated the palace from the town square, and the intense fragrance of roses, pomegranates and cypress from the palace gardens beyond the wall seemed to settle on the square, like an almost palpable cloud. In the dim lamplight radiating from the palace terrace above, small groups gathered, mostly out-of-town holiday visitors reuniting with old friends.

Nearest to their sight was a group that stood out from the others, with longer beards and sideburns and the priestly garb of the temple. They were, Yeshua recognized, members of the Sanhedrin, engaged in some kind of heated debate. A few were familiar to Yeshua, especially Caiaphas, the high priest that year and president of the Sanhedrin, and Annas, Caiaphas' father-in-law. The topic of discussion was Yeshua's imminent arrest.

Annas was trying to temper Caiaphas' fire to proceed with Yeshua's arrest forthwith.

"We must wait until after the Sabbath, or else the many people gathered here who have listened to him will rebel and bring the Roman guards upon our heads. Wait till after they have left and the city quiets down. Then we can act."

Caiaphas waved his hand, annoyed, an unconscionable act to his elder but one betraying the tension between them over this issue. "I will not wait. It is all arranged. He will escape again, as he has done in the past."

Annas, his voice showing annoyance at the disrespect shown him in front of other members of the council, countered, grabbing Caiaphas' arm. "Be reasonable! You take this too personally. Your jealousy of this rabble-rouser's influence

– 97 –

Not as I Will, But as You Will   Chapter 3

is too apparent. We must be wise. Besides, we must free one person for the Sabbath. Dare we challenge Pilate's will on who will be freed for the Sabbath? You want Barabbas freed, but given the opportunity, he will ask for this one to be freed instead, in his mind a crazy dreamer of little political threat to him. Barabbas murdered a Roman guard and has sworn to fight the Romans.

"You push too far, Caiaphas! Beware of Pontius Pilate. He despises us. He blames the priesthood for the riots. There have been too many of late, causing him to have to even take up residence here, which he hates. You know, he looks for every opportunity to bring tighter military rule. He would break the back of the priestly rule we enjoy. Think of the future, and what this may bring upon us."

Caiaphas pulled away from Annas' grip, "Yes, Pilate looks for opportunity and will find it anyway. He hates us and will find many more reasons to torment us. He would love to see this blasphemer Yeshua Bar Yusef released to stir up the people and profane the faith. Then he can step in and knock us down. But God will hear us; maybe even the almighty Caesar will hear us and recognize Pilate's evil scourge of us!" His voice rose to a crescendo, capturing the emotions of the others.

Annas responded, aware of the demagoguery Caiaphas was using in mentioning Pilate's name, "You have complained too much to the emperor already. He will not be happy to hear of you shielding known rebels from death. You are strengthening the Procurator's hand. Where now we have a small dettachment of Roman soldiers, we will soon have a Roman legion to tame us."

The murmurs of the group grew angry in response to Caiaphas' mention of the hated Procurator, Pilate. Annas,

Jesus and John—The Baptism

shaking his head, shrunk to the side, aware that the sentiment of the others was moving against him to Caiaphas. "You have your way, Caiaphas; may it not be the path to destruction," he said, resignedly.

Yeshua said quietly, "I know they come. Tonight I'll decide." Almost against his will, thoughts of John reasserted dominion in his mind. He spoke, pushing the words out through the pain.

"Truly, John was a great loss to my mission. Many people followed him. Those men at the very least feared and respected John, knowing his influence among the people. They could never ignore him but had to listen to him and consider his words. Even the Sadducees and Pharisees respected him, so he would have been a bridge to them as well for me."

Yeshua shook his head, looking behind him to where he had left his disciples. "They were my foundation, once John was gone—unschooled, simple, good-hearted people, but incapable of intellectually grasping what a cleric such as John had the capacity to understand easily."

Gabriel, nodded at his answer, grimacing at the thought of the crushing responsibility Yeshua was shouldering for the success or failure of his mission—still unwilling to give up. He could only marvel at Yeshua's patience and loyalty, to remain here, knowing the mortal peril set to descend upon him. His decisions, Gabriel realized, had long ago transcended personal desire.

Yeshua continued, "It was still so hard for me to give up on John, even when I realized he had left me. I went to the wilderness of Jericho to pray and reassess my mission, still thinking there might be some way to bring John back. I wonder, is it weakness in me or strength, that tenacity that will not

– 99 –

Not as I Will, But as You Will — Chapter 3

allow me to let go of those I love and believe in?"

Gabriel smiled gently. "It is the Father's love, too. Never has He given up on the children of Adam, despite countless generations of their inability to respond to His love. Instead they place Him in the position of the servant to their needs rather than the Father at the head of their lives. You are the Father's son. This love is something the angels—ourselves only servants—cannot share or understand.

Yeshua nodded with a wry, taciturn expression. "Admittedly, it is certainly not practical. Satan took this opportunity in the wilderness to strove with me, personally trying to make me lose hope and give up altogether."

Chapter 4

Temptation in the Wilderness

A vision of the Judean wilderness opened before Yeshua, as he recalled the forty-day fast following his separation from John. During that time he had traversed barren terrain from the wadis and ravines to steep cliffs in a spiritual quest. Before them was the pinnacled summit of a cliff overlooking the valley below and the ruins of ancient Jericho—oldest of cities, conquered by Joshua when the Chosen People first entered Canaan. Rising above the ledge to the summit were sheer, rocky cliffs, stark and bare of vegetation. In the early morning sunlight shadings from ruddy brown to rusty orange reflected on the cliffs behind, breaking up the gray shadows of the stony world surrounding.

Yeshua recognized a dark cavern in the side of the cliff as a place he had withdrawn to for a time for shelter, meditation and prayer. The view from this summit, where he had spent

Not as I Will, But as You Will — Chapter 4

many hours and days, surveyed much of the ancient world beyond the Jordan River valley hugging the cliffs below.

As he observed the familiar scene of the sun rising to the east over the Jordan River valley, revealing in radiating red splendor the desert expanse before him, Yeshua said: "As I contemplated this view, my thoughts traveled to the distant lands beneath that horizon and felt strongly the connectedness I had to it. Out there beyond the desert is the birthplace of the *kingdoms of this world.* The original Garden of Eden, where the first Adam and Eve, disobedient to the Father, brought sin, separation and conflict into this world and whose sons, Cain and Abel, brought murder.

"There is Ur, near ancient Babylon, where Abraham, the son of an idol maker, was called by the Father to spawn a new race of man, one that is obedient to the Father's will—a relationship as different as a sheep's relationship to the shepherd differs from goats. From him came two sons, Isaac and

Temptation in the Wilderness

Ishmael, and two nations; but yet still nations apart and warring. All this I had come to embrace and restore; first the sheep—the Chosen nation—and then the goats, the rest of the world.

"I had come to the mount, as Moses had come to Mt. Sinai, to seek guidance from the Father. Still my thoughts were much about John—symbolically the shepherd's staff, meant to unite the flock around him. John as the descendant of Aaron—the priestly counterpart to Yeshua as Aaron was to Moses—was making the same mistake as his forefather.

"Both had failed to maintain faith in God's chosen leader, being too familiar and critical. Moses and Aaron were brothers, as John and I were... like brothers. *The son can do nothing by himself; he can do only what he sees his father doing, because whatever the father does the son also does.*[1] Aaron should have had faith in Moses, waiting on Moses in his absence. The son must learn from the mistakes of the fathers, and my prayer was for a way to reach John before he made the same mistake.

"It was Aaron who led the people to build an idol of a golden calf at the foot of Mt. Sinai when Moses did not return when expected. Aaron and the people were forgiven for their faithlessness to Moses only by the petition of Moses to God."

> *"I have seen these people," the Lord said to Moses, "and they are a stiff-necked people. Now leave me alone so that my anger may burn against them and that I may destroy them. Then I will make you into a great nation."*
>
> *But Moses sought the favor of the Lord his God. "O Lord," he said, "why should your anger burn*

– 103 –

against your people, whom you brought out of Egypt with great power and a mighty hand? Why should the Egyptians say, 'It was with evil intent that he brought them out, to kill them in the mountains and to wipe them off the face of the earth?' Turn from your fierce anger; relent and do not bring disaster on your people. Remember your servants Abraham, Isaac and Israel, to whom you swore by your own self: 'I will make your descendants as numerous as the stars in the sky and I will give your descendants all this land I promised them, and it will be their inheritance forever.' Then the Lord relented and did not bring on his people the disaster he had threatened.[2]

"I felt there was a way to renew John's faith in me without him having to pay the price for his disobedience. If John could have united with me, his life would not have ended so unexpectedly as a victim of his own rashness. While Moses was on the mountain, Aaron led the people to rebel out of ignorance of the Father's true will. At the moment when he was most needed in the Father's providence, Aaron's descendant John would also fail, out of ignorance and a false pride in his own position. Aaron, because he changed his heart, could be forgiven; I hoped for the same with John."

Gabriel said pensively, provocatively—opening up an avenue of thought he himself was obviously uncomfortable with—"You know, my Lord, you have the same choice as Moses did. If the Father were faced with the choice of losing you and your lineage and the rest of fallen mankind's lineage—the Chosen People and the rest of the world—He would choose you in an instant. It would be like Noah and his family after the flood judgment. This much claim Satan has

Temptation in the Wilderness

on the children of Adam, after the failure this time of receiving you. That was your other alternative."

Yeshua shook his head violently. "How can the son do less than the father? It has never been an alternative for me! Of course I know this possibility! But, as Moses before me, how could I live with myself if my choice caused the deaths of all I loved? The Father has always left the choice to me, but I know His true desire. As you say, He never really gives up on His children, no matter how long they tarry in sin and denial of their true nature and value.

"It is why I never allowed myself to have a family until I was sure that I would succeed. I don't even want the choice offered to me of this. This way my choices are clean and clear. Either I succeed, or by my sacrifice in redemption, the hand of Satan would be stayed toward fallen mankind. And the way would be opened for a second try—a second chance at success of my mission by someone else."

Yeshua turned his attention back to the scene of the vision. He remembered that moment of confrontation with the ultimate power of darkness and shrank slightly at the memory. He said, "I had been drawing near to the end of the forty days and was at a point when my hunger, fatigue and disillusionment were the greatest. Satan came personally and tempted me to show doubt or disloyalty, in order to wrestle the position of Lord over Creation from me.

"Satan knew my vulnerabilities; he knew this was the time I was most exposed to failure. I had to summon all the strength of will I possessed to overcome, even though his trials were so simple and obvious to me. He tested my faith and obedience to the core of the message of Moses; my faith in God's continued aid and sustenance[3] and my humility and

– 105 –

Not as I Will, But as You Will   Chapter 4

steadfastness to God during trials.[4] In general, he tried to challenge my faithfulness toward the One God of Israel, disdaining false gods—or false ways to success."[5]

A feeling emanated from the scene of a lurking malice in the air—a hostile will asserting itself. Yeshua kneeling in prayer in the gray-shadowed, stony environs, appeared small, vulnerable and alone. Satan appeared in the personage of a benevolent angel. The dark, fearsome wave of despair and confusion that enveloped Yeshua was almost tangible now to Yeshua as Gabriel watched off to the side. Shaking with the intensity of the moment, Yeshua faced up to him. The angel's countenance, while mild, showed shadowy eyes with a hard steely, glint—mesmerizing as a snake's, hiding a secret intent. With oily smooth words, he pretended to comfort Yeshua, proffering a way out of his suffering circumstance.

> *"If you are the Son of God, tell these stones to become bread."*
>
> *I answered, "It is written: 'Man does not live on bread alone, but on every word that comes from the mouth of God.'"*[6]

Yeshua said, "If I had deemed bread more important to me than the will of God at that moment, I would have already lost and never would have received the answer I had been fasting and seeking for the past forty days. Then the devil took me, in the spirit, to the holy city and had me stand on the highest point of the temple."

> *"If you are the Son of God," he said, "throw yourself down. For it is written: 'He will command his angels concerning you, and they will lift you up in their hands, so that you will not strike your foot against a stone.'"*

– 106 –

Temptation in the Wilderness

I answered him, "It is also written: 'Do not put the Lord your God to the test.'"

The devil showed me all the kingdoms of the world and their splendor. "All this I will give you," he said, "if you will bow down and worship me."

I said to him, "Away from me, Satan! For it is written: 'Worship the Lord your God, and serve him only.'"

"Then the devil left me; and you and your angels came and attended me." [7]

Yeshua, silent for an extended moment, then went on. "That moment on that mountain was reminiscent of tonight. Satan can often use our best intentions, our love, to confuse us and derail us from the Father's will. I could not give up on John, just as now I cannot give up on my disciples—he used my love to confuse my will. I finally had to realize the Father was asking me to abandon John to whatever fate lay in store for him. That was most painful, as is tonight and this decision. Always, the agonizing question, even for me, is whether God or Satan speaks behind an inspiration. At times I feel like I am balancing on the blade of a dagger, battling demons with flaming swords to wrestle answers—to see clearly the path to follow."

Gabriel sighed deeply, as if he were experiencing the moment equally intensely with Yeshua. He said, "Yes, always, Satan's greatest weapon is confusing good and evil. Of course, he was the angel of the greatest intellect who was chosen by the Father to educate His children, Adam and Eve, his first victims.

"My heart resonated with your pain that day, but you had

– 107 –

Not as I Will, But as You Will
Chapter 4

to choose to deny Satan's temptation before we could come and minister to you. As we were there with you, we were there with Adam and Eve, the original parents of humankind. I have seen Lucifer's works throughout history. I saw the pain he caused the Father by tempting His children away from Him—Lucifer the angel of light, thrown down to the earth by God to became like a snake in the grass with only evil, predatory and selfish intent for his human charges.

> *The great dragon was hurled down——that ancient serpent called the devil, or Satan, who leads the whole world astray. He was hurled to the earth and his angels with him.*[8]

> *The Lord God said to the serpent, "Because you have done this, Cursed are you above all the livestock and all the wild animals! You will crawl on your belly and you will eat dust all the days of your life."*[9]

"The angels with Lucifer are thus denied the love of God. Crawling on their belly means they would become miserable beings, unable to function properly or perform their original purpose. Eating dust means they feed off the evil intentions of humanity—separated from the source of love and goodness—like eating food that is poison.[10]

"What a dichotomy we face! I, Gabriel the messenger, who must offer you the cup of this destiny, find also my hand holding back. I suffer with your loss to the providence of our God, the Father!"

"How the Father has mourned his lost children, watching them fall deeper and deeper away from Him into the self-imposed suffering from their unprincipled behavior, led by this false adopted Father! A father with no good intent for

– 108 –

Temptation in the Wilderness

them and who only had power because the children gave it to him.

"And those first two grievously flawed parents gave birth to children who, like they, were far from the Father's will for them. With the elder killing the younger, thus violence toward one another was introduced as early as the first family of the human race!

"I was there with the Father through all His efforts with succeeding generations. He searched to find a root of goodness that He could work with among the poisonous invasive weeds that had sprung up and taken over His Garden.

"I was there with Moses and helped him receive the Ten Commandments that guided this chosen root. Receiving and following the commandments was like the first step of a long climb for humankind out of the realm of being and behaving like animals toward the goal of becoming human beings and the Father's children once again.

Gabriel continued, "I was there with Daniel when this same chosen root fell once again into disobedience and was forced into the suffering of captivity and abandonment until they repented of their sins.[11] I was there to give them some remnant of hope and encouragement to stay the course. I led them to know that the end was in sight, and that their Lord would finally come to complete their salvation if they could just maintain faith and obedience to their mandate as the Chosen People.

"You were to be that end, the one they suffered for, waited for, the second Adam, the one to restore that failure of the first Adam. You became the temple for the Father that the first Adam failed to fulfill. Yet that is not your only mission. The second Adam was not only meant to become the perfected

– 109 –

Not as I Will, But as You Will   Chapter 4

temple and dwelling place of the Father but also to restore Adam and Eve's position as parents—that would have been you and your bride. Furthermore, the Kingdom of God is to come through those first parents establishing the model for dominion of love toward the rest of humanity and the creation, an example from which all will model their hearts and actions.

"Thus, the first parents were to exemplify perfection of heart, as a living temple of the heart of the Father; then to establish the example of the family of love with God at the heart of their relationships; the world of truth, beauty and goodness would have been a naturally evolving consequence from that original root. Sadly, indeed, for the Father has to answer the question of who will now do that?

"You, the savior human history waited for—who would die a thousand deaths if it were to bring about the kingdom—now are faced with dying the seemingly meaningless death of a thief on a cross, at an age where your whole life's potential is ready to burst into bloom. I fear that if I had to make the decision for you, I could not advise you to do this. It is truly up to you to take on this destiny. It is almost too grievous for me to imagine."

Yeshua looked at the angel, feeling excruciatingly the pain in his mind that his loss would bring to the Father and to the angelic world. His face quivered sorrowfully, his hand passing over his face in a sign of sad resignation. As if once and for all closing the door to this cherished dream that would never be realized—the dream he and John had at one time shared, but from this wilderness time on he had shouldered alone in exhausting forbearance. His shoulders seemed bent and stooped as if the burden were a palpable weight of the lost potential that ultimately had such far-reaching effects on all:

– 110 –

Temptation in the Wilderness

the Father, the angelic world, the Chosen People, and past, present and future generations of the world.

He remained silent and bent for several moments, his body convulsing in sobs. Finally, his voice faltering to a whisper, he said, "John was beheaded at the hands of Herod less than a year later, too young, too soon to see such a bright star of heaven eclipsed before its full potential light could be manifest. And I was alone, truly alone, like one bank of the river without the other. At that point I felt like the seemingly unstoppable dynamic power of our youth was decimated in a flood of unspent, unfocused, wasted potential." He again fell silent, still gently shaking and sobbing.

Then Gabriel truly understood the deep pain of loss Yeshua felt for John when they separated. The loss and ultimate death of his brother, friend and comrade and how this time to mourn, which Yeshua had never allowed himself before, now was needed to close this chapter in Yeshua's life. Gabriel said, "Then you had to start over, by yourself, building your own foundation of faith with the people, when John would no longer help you and be a bridge. What a great loss. He developed such a strong following, but he would never bring that over to you, as he was meant to do."

Yeshua wept, a long and sorrowful release—when words were no longer enough to quell the pain.

Moments or hours later, Yeshua knew or cared not, he spoke, in a tone of respectful finality of this brother he loved, "John's death was just such a tragedy. *HaSatan*, the adversary, took the opportunity, the moment of disunity between us, to invade and take his life. John believed in what we were doing, the need for the restoration of the twelve tribes, in preparation for the coming Kingdom. But through his confusion

— 111 —

Not as I Will, But as You Will   Chapter 4

about his part in it, Satan had that momentary opportunity to seize him. His loss to the Kingdom is great and sorely missed. Yet the Kingdom could still move forward, if the people united with me. At the loss of John, I focused totally on that one hope, the faith of the simple people."

He breathed deeply, looking down into the Kidron Valley below, and the road to Jericho that led back to that mount of memories in the wilderness.

He continued, wistfully, *"Since the days of John the Baptist, the Kingdom of Heaven has suffered violence, and men of violence take it by force.*[12] But, still those men of violence are my only hope."

Yeshua's thoughts turned to words he had shared with some of his disciples on this last trip to Jerusalem. He said, "Conscious of John's failure—a failure of embracing leadership and all its ramifications, good or difficult—I made it a point to teach my disciples about true leadership."

Following his thoughts, the scene changed to a discussion with James and John as they rested along the roadside of Judea.

James and John asked him, *"Teacher, let us sit on your right hand and upon your left in your glory."*

Yeshua reproached them gently, *"Whoever wants to become great among you must be the servant, and whoever wants to be first must be slave of all. For even the Son of Man did not come to be served, but to serve."*

A young man had come up to them. He asked him, *"Good teacher, what must I do to inherit eternal life?"*

Yeshua told him, *"You know the Commandments: 'Do not*

Temptation in the Wilderness

murder, do not commit adultery, do not steal, do not give false testimony, do not defraud, honor your father and mother.'"

"Teacher," he declared, "all these I have kept since I was a boy."

"One thing you lack," he said. "Go, sell everything you have and give to the poor, and you will have treasure in heaven. Then come, follow me." At this the man's face fell. He went away sad, because he had great wealth. Yeshua had then said to his disciples, *"How hard it is for the rich to enter the kingdom of God!"* [13]

Thinking now of these words, he said to Gabriel, "John was like this rich man, but the riches he was not willing to give up were not material riches. To John, riches were the people's acclaim of him as their leader.

"I went into the wilderness to counter a spirit of hopelessness I felt after I knew that John would be unable to fulfill his responsibility. All I could see was the goal. Food, drink, clothing, shelter were irrelevant to me; my only desire was to find with certainty the next step. I determined to die there of exposure and deprivation if I could not find a way to accomplish my mission. The way opened up to me after Satan's temptations were vanquished.

"For a short time I remained in Judea. Then came the news that John was imprisoned in Herod's fortress of Machaerus, east of the Dead Sea. I returned to Galilee, *To Capernaum, which was by the lake in the area of Zebulun and Naphtali— to fulfill what was said through the prophet Isaiah:*[14]

> *"Nevertheless, there will be no more gloom for*
> *those who were in distress. In the past he humbled*
> *the land of Zebulun and the land of Naphtali,*

but in the future he will honor Galilee of the Gentiles, by the way of the sea, along the Jordan—

"The people walking in darkness have seen a great light; on those living in the land of the shadow of death a light has dawned.

"You have enlarged the nation and increased their joy; they rejoice before you as people rejoice at the harvest, as men rejoice when dividing the plunder.

"For as in the day of Midian's defeat, you have shattered the yoke that burdens them, the bar across their shoulders, the rod of their oppressor.

"Every warrior's boot used in battle and every garment rolled in blood will be destined for burning, will be fuel for the fire.

"For to us a child is born, to us a son is given, and the government will be on his shoulders. And he will be called Wonderful Counselor, Mighty God, Everlasting Father, Prince of Peace."[15]

"Alone, I began the long arduous journey to fulfill that scripture, one side of the river without the other, but still I began."

Chapter 5

The Kingdom and the Twelve

Yeshua looked around the garden at the source of a faint scent on the breeze wafting his way, the gentle, subtle fragrance of almond blossoms. Spring is coming soon, he thought. He loved spring most of any time of the year, because it was when the whole earth came back to life. "Spring in Capernaum," he thought; "I'll never see it again: the orchards of almond trees in bloom, the olives, date palms and grape vines; soon all will be budding."

This was the city by the lake in Galilee, where he made his home and had begun his public ministry, after leaving the wilderness. It had been less than three years, he realized, but it seemed like another age ago. He loved this city, where he had the opportunity to meet so many kinds of people coming through on the trade routes that converged here. His thoughts went to when he first settled in Capernaum and started his mission there. His first memory was of meeting up once again with the brothers Andrew and Simon, now called Peter, the same Peter languishing over by the old olive tree.

They were the followers whom John, moved by the spirit had, told to come to him. As he was walking along the lakeshore he saw them, for the first time since he had left them at the Springs of Salim. It had been a joyful moment, a sign from heaven that this was indeed to be the starting place of his new ministry. He spoke of that memory.

"After leaving Judea, as [I] was walking beside the Sea of Galilee, [I] saw two brothers, Simon, [I] called Peter, and his brother Andrew. They were casting a net into the lake, for they were fishermen. 'Come, follow me,' [I] said, 'and I will make you fishers of men.' At once they left their nets and followed [me].

"Going on from there, [I] saw two other brothers, James son of Zebedee and his brother John. They were in a boat with their father Zebedee, preparing their nets. [I] called them, and imme-

The Kingdom and the Twelve

diately they left the boat and their father and followed [me] [1]—
The sons of Thunder was my name for them because of their
passionate natures, but now their voices are muted and they
languish with Peter, deaf to my pleas."

"These three," he continued, "are the best of my followers,
my inner circle, who were always with and with whom I shared
the most my thoughts, my hopes, my dreams." He breathed
deeply, sighing disquietedly as he rose to walk toward the spot
where the three slumbered.

Gabriel said, as his eyes followed Yeshua, "My Lord, they
are still asleep. The spirit has overpowered them. They cannot
respond."

Yeshua replied, standing, pacing indecisively between
where they were reclining and his position: "From John to the
fishermen, indeed the Kingdom of Heaven had suffered violence and men of violence take it by force of faith—denied
the strength of character based on spiritual discipline and the
long-steeped tradition of the better prepared priestly class.
But they were my foundation and I poured my heart into
them to educate them." He finally relaxed back down, thinking back to another spring morning a year ago.

At that time, Yeshua had called together the seventy-some
young men who had been following him for a special purpose.
The memory flowed into his consciousness as it simultane-
ously appeared before him, of the gently rolling hills of the
countryside surrounding his beloved city-of-the-lake. The
scene was a certain rocky mountain crest that yielded a striking view of the broad expanse of the lake. This was a place he
often would escape to for peace and solitude. This time he
had prayed on this mountain all night over the designation of
the twelve from among his followers.

Not as I Will, But as You Will   Chapter 5

"These twelve represented the twelve tribes of Israel, symbolic of restoring those twelve tribes lost during the period of exile in Israel's history. It was such a struggle choosing the right men from the limited numbers of my followers. If the heart is there among them to fulfill this role, the Father can use this symbolic value to build upon to bring it about in actuality.

"But it is a great or terrible pronouncement dependent upon whether they have this heart *'I have come to bring fire on the earth, and how I wish it were already kindled!'*[2] If it were, they would take this fire of truth to the four corners of this country, creating a righteous inferno in the hearts of the Chosen People for the Father's will. But it had to be first kindled in the hearts of these twelve.

"The Chosen People have been very greatly blessed by the Father in knowing His Will and being His chosen instruments. *'That servant who knows his master's will and does not get ready or does not do what his master wants will be beaten with many blows. But the one who does not know and does things deserving punishment will be beaten with few blows. From everyone who has been given much, much will be demanded; and from the one who has been entrusted with much, much more will be asked.'*[3]

"*'My people, who are called by My name'* was what the Father called us to King Solomon. We are a breed apart, especially prepared for this moment. The heart of a Jew has deep, tenacious roots like the acacia tree in the desert weathering storms and drought with the deepest of taproots—taproots connected directly to the Father enabling them to gain water, life and sustenance where others can't. We can dominate the landscape wherever we are and, as the acacia tree, provide shelter for the weary, worn and homeless wandering in the desert

– 118 –

The Kingdom and the Twelve

of this world. That's how we can draw the world into the Kingdom.

"But our strength can also be our weakness. From this same taproot, which is the source of strength, comes a thirst for justice and the law, a tortuously absolute justice that can lead us to honor law over love. If their hearts are not harnessed to the Father's parental heart, and His love of goodness, they can be twisted to serve evil, even by their virtue.

"The Father spoke directly to King Solomon, *'When I shut up the heavens so that there is no rain, or command locusts to devour the land or send a plague among my people, if my people, who are called by my name, will humble themselves and pray and seek my face and turn from their wicked ways, then will I hear from heaven and will forgive their sin and will heal their land.'*[4]

"There is the other side of the promise, the curse, if we fail. If the twelve, and thus the people of Israel, do not recognize the time of their visitation, their blessing, *'the kingdom of God will be taken away from them and given to a people who will produce its fruit.'*[5] I spoke to them as the prophets of old spoke, giving the good news of what they could expect, but always with the caveat of *if*. *'If you have faith as a grain of mustard seed, you can move mountains... You will sit to judge the twelve tribes of Israel,'*[6] IF you can demonstrate the faith the Father is asking of you."

Gabriel listened quietly, attentively, a sounding board for Yeshua's reflections, ever mindful of the decisive moment approaching him. Come what may, Gabriel knew Yeshua would have to leave this garden committed to death on the morrow. He knew the decision had already been made in Heaven. Gabriel could say nothing to spur his decisiveness,

Not as I Will, But as You Will   Chapter 5

realizing, with Yeshua, the choice was not the struggle but finding a victory in his choice that could be a hope for those left behind.

Yeshua continued speaking, the lake scene before him releasing a flood of memories of his thoughts that night on the mountain, when he had envisioned the future centered around these twelve. "Symbolically, they were the pebble in the water whose waves were the spiritual condition for me to claim the throne of David.

"Of course this assignation to begin with is symbolic. The great prophets would embody their pronouncements in small acts signifying the larger event they foreshadowed, setting in motion the essential act by the symbolic seed they sowed. Isaiah walked naked as a symbol of the future when Israel would be stripped of everything they valued, including even their land, and enslaved to their enemies. Jeremiah smashed the flask, as symbol of the breaking apart of the nation.

"But, also, on a practical level, I had to balance the diverse attitudes of the people of Israel with the backgrounds and personalities of these men so as to represent all Israel. I had to find the right men who, at this critical juncture in Israel's history, could be a unifying core from which to expand outward to the four corners of Israeli culture.

"Now was the time when so many small groups were competing for the heart of the people. Much of the leadership, traditions and culture had been lost through the years of the Babylonian and Assyrian exiles when the cream of Israel was held captive in distant lands. As well the recent domination by the Greeks, where Greek language and culture had been forced on us and our own common language suppressed.

"The Romans, heretofore, had maintained a gentle domi-

– 120 –

The Kingdom and the Twelve

nation, looking for the dominant rabbinical tradition they could lift up and work through to direct the rebellious but religious-minded people of Israel. This they rightly saw was the key to maintaining cohesiveness in this difficult to control people. Aside from the main traditions of the Pharisees, Sadducees, and Essenes, there are many small religious groups, such as mine, challenging for position and recognition within the broad reach of the Jerusalem Temple community.

"The group at this time who could gain the greatest following among the people would be lifted up by the Romans as representing the interests of the people of Israel. My ultimate goal was reaching out to the world. And the vehicle I see prepared by the Father for that is the Roman Empire.

"Going to Rome would be the next step in my vision of kingdom-building, after I could unite my own people. Rome must come under the one God's will, an instrument for peacemaking by its adoption into the family of God. It was prepared by the Father for such a role.

"Our community, the Diaspora, encompasses not only the whole of Israel, but also the vast network of communities of Jews spread throughout much of the known world. They often pilgrimage from those far-removed places to come together on holy days at the Jerusalem Temple, which is the heart of the faith of our people. They would be the veins for the transference of this new blood of the family of God to the extremities of the world.

"The prophet Ezekiel says the temple will be the dwelling place of the Father on earth. *'Son of man, this is the place of my throne and the place for the soles of my feet. This is where I will live among the Israelites forever.'*[7]

"Then, as prophesied, Israel would become the center of

– 121 –

Not as I Will, But as You Will

Chapter 5

this earthly kingdom of peace. The prophet Zechariah foretold, *'This is what the Lord Almighty says: "In those days ten men from all languages and nations will take firm hold of one Jew by the hem of his robe and say, 'Let us go with you, because we have heard that God is with you.'"'*[8]

"'They will neither harm nor destroy on all my holy mountain, for the earth will be full of the knowledge of the Lord as the waters cover the sea.'[9] said the Prophet Isaiah.

"Gabriel," he said, turning abruptly to the angel, his face betraying his inner turmoil. Drawn, contorted lines of tension furrowed the surface like deep scars—a mask of pain. "I cannot forget this vision nor the opposite alternative, if this vision is not realized! One of these two destinies will be realized in our time. Such is the time that is upon us. I cannot abandon any little hope there might be for the restoration of my people's position and the fulfillment of their mission."

Gabriel, his own face mirroring the pain he saw, said, "My Lord, Isaiah's warning to Israel falls now upon you. He knew your potential so well, as well as the risk to you. He said of you, *'He was despised and rejected by men, a man of sorrows, and familiar with suffering. Like one from whom men hide their faces he was despised, and we esteemed him not.'*[10] Would that those three could see your face now, which is the exact expression of those words! Would that change their heart? I wish desperately to have that hope in them that you still hold.

"If only even these three could have absolute faith and absolute obedience to you and your direction, they can fulfill this symbolic condition. This would be the fire kindled that could be spread to the four corners of the earth, the fire of truth and love.

"If they could only have such faith, at that point would

– 122 –

The Kingdom and the Twelve

come a cloud of witnesses from Heaven, as has never been seen on earth before. The passed-away prophets and forefathers, as well as the angels, would descend to inspire the people on earth and speed the providence to success." [11]

"Yes," said Yeshua, thoughtfully—his mind grasping at every possibility—"It could be that the three could represent the twelve, as the twelve represent Israel: and as they go, so goes Israel, in the Father's eyes. With the right heart, even the smallest condition of faith the Father can use."

Gabriel spoke, reaching earnestly for some chance for Yeshua, "Solomon's kingdom, as promised by God to his father David, could have been the root of the Kingdom of Heaven in his time if he had only been faithful. The twelve tribes were scattered after the failure of Solomon's kingdom. But the prophet Isaiah predicted, *'In that day the Root of Jesse will gather the exiles of Israel; he will assemble the scattered people of Judah from the four quarters of the earth.'*" [12]

"The Prophet Micah foretold, *'I will surely gather all of you, O Jacob; I will surely bring together the remnant of Israel. I will bring them together like sheep in a pen, like a flock in its pasture; the one who breaks open the way will go up before them; they will break through the gate and go out. Their king will pass through before them, the Lord at their head.'* [13]

"This has to happen; if not now, then when?" Wistfully, softly, Gabriel continued, capturing Yeshua's attention by an emotional intensity matching Yeshua's in serendipitous excess. "You were truly to be that king, that prince—the progeny of David—entering in the Eastern Gate of the Temple—for whom, as the Prophet Ezekiel foresaw, [14] that gate was specially prepared, by the Father's commandment. That temple is where the throne of the Father would be and the place where

– 123 –

Not as I Will, But as You Will   Chapter 5

the soles of His feet were to live among the chosen people forever."[15]

The note of cold reality then returning to his voice, he said, "But the remnant—the twelve even—must follow you for you to take that position, for the symbolic to become substantial. The sheep must recognize their shepherd or they are alone and helpless fodder for the wolves."

Yeshua responded, "But the faith of three men can be the beginning of this. You said it yourself. Their obedience to me could become that symbolic act that sets in motion the machinery of change, as a pebble striking the water creates great circles of disturbance, a seed planted that will grow into a mighty tree. In its smallness it symbolizes the might of God that can be unleashed by small acts—the uniting and restoration of the nation of Israel, by the faith of three. And, from that seed, then the twelve may still come. Success really depends upon how perfectly they can follow and unite with me."

Gabriel nodded, knowing what Yeshua's answer would be even before he spoke, but grasping for some way to comfort him with a fate that Gabriel saw inexorably descending upon them. "My Lord," he said, "is it not too late for them to respond?"

Yeshua shrugged painfully, lifting his palms in exasperation. "They have not yet failed; give them this time still. My hope in bringing these three here tonight was that it was not too late. The Father always hopes for, up to the last minute, a change of heart. Jeremiah says: *'If at any time I announce that a nation or kingdom is to be uprooted, torn down and destroyed, and if that nation I warned repents of its evil, then I will relent and not inflict on it the disaster I had planned. And if at anoth-*

– 124 –

The Kingdom and the Twelve

er time I announce that a nation or kingdom is to be built up and planted, and if it does evil in my sight and does not obey me, then I will reconsider the good I had intended to do for it.'[16]

"Did not the Father relent to Jeremiah after promising destruction to Israel for its sin, saying, *'Tell them everything I command you; do not omit a word. Perhaps they will listen and each will turn from his evil way. Then I will relent and not bring on them the disaster I was planning because of the evil they have done.'*[17]

"Ezekiel says, *'say to them, as surely as I live.' Declares the Sovereign Lord, I take no pleasure in the death of the wicked, but rather that they turn from their ways and live.'*[18] His heart is the heart of a Father, not a judge. He is looking for a chance to forgive his children—any sign that they have had a change of heart. Abraham needed to find only ten righteous men to save Sodom from fire and brimstone. I had some hope at our Last Supper together that these three—especially Simon-Peter—could understand and help the others to understand their mission.

"If they don't, even my death will not bring the condition for the restoration of the twelve tribes. I fear the loss completely of the foundation of the nation the Father has worked to establish all these past generations with the chosen people; *that the kingdom of God will be taken away from them.*[19] I have to pursue any hope."

Gabriel nodded, "Yes it is true. After this loss, the kingdom will be long in coming. From the days of Adam until now were many generations. I cannot fault you in trying up to the last moment to find a way to save this star-crossed generation."

Yeshua shuddered; his intensity of thought was reflected in

Not as I Will, But as You Will   Chapter 5

the glisten of sweat on his body, chilled by a sudden cool draft. "These twelve, is there still a way to reach them—even these three here in the garden with me to begin with?" He pondered this, as a vision opened before him of that morning on a mountainside in Capernaum. The sun was rising, cascading gold against the backdrop of the mountainside, the morning he chose the twelve disciples.

The scene unfolded, with Yeshua calling the twelve chosen disciples to him out of the large group, which gathered on the hillside to listen to him speak.

> *"These are the names of the twelve apostles: first, Simon (who is called Peter) and his brother Andrew; James, son of Zebedee, and his brother John; Philip and Bartholomew; Thomas and Matthew the tax collector; James son of Alphaeus, and Thaddaeus; Simon the Zealot and Judas Iscariot..."* [20]

Remembering this special moment, Yeshua looked at the faces of the twelve newly chosen to fulfill this position. He had blessed them and given them authority to drive out evil spirits and to heal every disease and sickness. He had demanded of them to forsake all, even homes and families, an unheard of demand in the family-centered climate of post-captivity Israel. It was what their culture clung to, having lost everything else of value. To leave your family was an incomprehensible, shocking thing, leaving you no roots to fall back upon. Yet, that is what these twelve had done at his urgent demand. That much they had united with him in spirit. "Dare I have hope they can still fulfill?" he wondered, echoing the thoughts he had had even then, as he spoke to them that day.

> *"These twelve [are] sent out with the following*

– 126 –

The Kingdom and the Twelve

instructions:

"Do not go among the Gentiles or enter any town of the Samaritans. Go rather to the lost sheep of Israel. As you go, preach this message: 'The kingdom of heaven is near.' Heal the sick, raise the dead, cleanse those who have leprosy, drive out demons. Freely you have received, freely give.

"Do not take along any gold or silver or copper in your belts; take no bag for the journey, or extra tunic, or sandals or a staff; for the worker is worth his keep. Whatever town or village you enter, search for some worthy person there and stay at his house until you leave.

"As you enter the home, give it your greeting. If the home is deserving, let your peace rest on it; if it is not, let your peace return to you. If anyone will not welcome you or listen to your words, shake the dust off your feet when you leave that home or town. I tell you the truth, it will be more bearable for Sodom and Gomorrah on the Day of Judgment than for that town.

"I am sending you out like sheep among wolves. Therefore be as shrewd as snakes and as innocent as doves. Be on your guard against men; they will hand you over to the local councils and flog you in their synagogues. On my account you will be brought before governors and kings as witnesses to them and to the Gentiles.

"But when they arrest you, do not worry about what to say or how to say it. At that time you will be given what to say, for it will not be you

Not as I Will, But as You Will

Chapter 5

speaking, but the Spirit of your Father speaking through you.

"Brother will betray brother to death, and a father his child; children will rebel against their parents and have them put to death. All men will hate you because of me, but he who stands firm to the end will be saved. When you are persecuted in one place, flee to another. I tell you the truth, you will not finish going through the cities of Israel before the Son of Man comes.

"A student is not above his teacher, nor a servant above his master. It is enough for the student to be like his teacher, and the servant like his master. If the head of the house has been called Beelzebub, how much more the members of his household!

"So do not be afraid of them. There is nothing concealed that will not be disclosed, or hidden that will not be made known. What I tell you in the dark, speak in the daylight; what is whispered in your ear, proclaim from the roofs. Do not be afraid of those who kill the body but cannot kill the soul. Rather, be afraid of the One who can destroy both soul and body in hell.

"Are not two sparrows sold for a penny? Yet not one of them will fall to the ground apart from the will of your Father. And even the very hairs of your head are all numbered. So don't be afraid; you are worth more than many sparrows.

"Whoever acknowledges me before men, I will also acknowledge him before my Father in heaven. But whoever disowns me before men, I will disown

The Kingdom and the Twelve

him before my Father in heaven.

"Do not suppose that I have come to bring peace to the earth. I did not come to bring peace, but a sword. For I have come to turn a man against his father, a daughter against her mother, a daughter-in-law against her mother-in-law—a man's enemies will be the members of his own household.

"Anyone who loves his father or mother more than me is not worthy of me; anyone who loves his son or daughter more than me is not worthy of me; and anyone who does not take his cross and follow me is not worthy of me. Whoever finds his life will lose it, and whoever loses his life for my sake will find it.

"He who receives you receives me, and he who receives me receives the one who sent me. Anyone who receives a prophet because he is a prophet will receive a prophet's reward, and anyone who receives a righteous man because he is a righteous man will receive a righteous man's reward. And if anyone gives even a cup of cold water to one of these little ones because he is my disciple, I tell you the truth, he will certainly not lose his reward."[21]

"Then he called the crowd to him along with his disciples and said: 'If anyone would come after me, he must deny himself and take up his cross and follow me. For whoever wants to save his life will lose it, but whoever loses his life for me and for the gospel will save it. What good is it for a man to gain the whole world, yet forfeit his soul?

*Or what can a man give in exchange for his soul?
If anyone is ashamed of me and my words in this
adulterous and sinful generation, the Son of Man
will be ashamed of him when he comes in his
Father's glory with the holy angels."* [22]

Yeshua winced at the thought of the trial-laden months between then and now, and at the prescience of the words he had uttered to them. They suffered persecution with him because they were following someone outside the mainstream of the Jewish religious community. He knew, for all their faults, they had truly been up against the powers of that community—and of Hell arrayed in spiritual battle—to stop them, to stop him by defeating them.

He stood up, abruptly. *Then he returned to his disciples and found them still sleeping. "Simon," he said to Peter, "are you asleep? Could you not keep watch for one hour? Watch and pray so that you will not fall into temptation. The spirit is willing, but the body is weak."* [23] There was no response from any of them. They slept deeply, their bodies limp, nestled against the trunk and protruding roots of the tree. The gnarled old olive tree's twisted branches shadowed their faces with a spider web pattern in the moonlight.

Yeshua returned to his position on the grassy mound. Gabriel, watching his face as he returned, spoke exactly to the thought in Yeshua's mind. "A web of confusion is exactly the way Satan holds their minds. Their conscience is tied up in knots of confusion, fear and hopelessness—their spirits too encumbered to respond."

"Yes," said Yeshua, "Satan's web binds their spirit; they still sleep. They are losing their vision of the Kingdom. It is what I have tried most to make them understand, what I spoke of

The Kingdom and the Twelve

over and over again, the coming Kingdom of God," he said. "It gave them hope in the midst of all our difficulties. I knew they were ignorant of scripture, so I spoke to them as you would children, with stories and parables.

"Their identity as the Chosen People is in their blood and in their culture. If they do not know scriptures, then they know the stories their fathers told to them as children, passed on from father to son for generations. They know of Abraham, Isaac and Jacob who were given the blessing of multiplying as the stars. And Jacob was given the name Israel, which means, 'he struggles with God,' He and his descendants were to be God's partners in overcoming the world of sin.

"They know of the twelve tribes and the importance God placed in Israel being organized around them. Moses established the twelve tribes in the wilderness at the foundation of our nation. And though destroyed through Israel's captivity and exile, their reestablishment was a sign of the end times and the Father's renewed covenant with the chosen people as His partners in establishing the Kingdom.

"From this, they should have understood their cherished position to the Father, as those chosen descendants representing those tribes. It was a blessing that they were chosen to participate in the messiah's struggle with Satan, to bring about the long-promised reign of the Father. But, obviously, they did not understand. What more could I have done to make them understand, to make them more serious? *This generation will be held responsible*[24] for their failure to respond to the Father. After all their preparation, when He needed them, they were not there. Alas, I despair to know what more I can do now."

Gabriel drew his arms around Yeshua, comforting him.

– 131 –

"Your words will always be with them. Some day they will think back to them and understand," he said gently.

In concert with his words the vision of the surrounding hills of the Sea of Galilee appeared. He remembered the circumstances well of this moment from the recent past.

Chapter 6

The Sermon on the Mount

It was last April—the month of flowers. As often he did, he would meditate over the landscape before the people arrived. The landscape was his liturgy. The "lilies of the field," the pristine blue and white anemones dotting the hillside before him, became a subject of his sermon that day. He had walked up the rock-strewn slope to the highest point and sat down. His vantage point yielded a commanding view of the lake and the surrounding countryside.

Below the hills were the springs of Ma-gadan, seven springs of fresh, living water—as life of faith, he taught, should have a source from which it is renewed and replenished. Beyond was the harp-shaped Sea of Galilee, now gentle but often exploding into dark, thunderous tempests, as ever changing in demeanor as were the people around it who learned life and gained sustenance by way of it. Below and on all sides were fields of grain and well-ordered orchards of grapes, apricots, figs, olives, walnuts, and almonds—a land so greatly blessed by the Father.

Just beyond identifiable vision was a surprising spot of red among the rich greens and golds of the orchards and fields and the black of the soil—a meadow of blood-red flowers. These were flowers unique to this area, with multiple buds on each bloom, each resembling falling drops of blood.

They were said to commemorate the blood of martyrs shed in that meadow. The expansive beauty and heroic destiny of this location framed the seriousness of the moment as he saw his disciples and a multitude of followers approaching up the hill. So much blood and sacrifice had been given for this moment in history when the Chosen People would finally be able to achieve the ever-promised and longed-for Kingdom of Heaven. The people came to him, and he began to teach them.

> *Blessed are the poor in spirit,*
> *for theirs is the Kingdom of Heaven.*
>
> *Blessed are those who mourn,*
> *for they will be comforted.*
>
> *Blessed are the meek,*
> *for they will inherit the earth.*

The Sermon on the Mount

*Blessed are those who hunger and thirst for
righteousness, for they will be filled.*

*Blessed are the merciful,
for they will be shown mercy.*

*Blessed are the pure in heart,
for they will see God.*

*Blessed are the peacemakers,
for they will be called sons of God.*

*Blessed are those who are persecuted because of
righteousness, for theirs is the Kingdom of
Heaven.*

*Blessed are you when people insult you, persecute
you and falsely say all kinds of evil against you
because of me.
Rejoice and be glad, because great is your reward
in heaven, for in the same way they persecuted the
prophets who were before you.*[1]

"Blessed are my people who hear these words with ears of
faith and hands of action to serve," said Yeshua, lost in the
mixed emotions it brought back to him, of days of innocence
and hope in his ministry. He searched the faces of the crowd,
as he had done on that day, looking for the bright spots of
living faith that had become a magnet for his words that
morning—perhaps now looking for some source of hope he
might have missed.

He returned his attention to the scene.

*"You are the salt of the earth. But if the salt loses
its saltiness, how can it be made salty again? It is
no longer good for anything, except to be thrown*

– 135 –

Not as I Will, But as You Will   Chapter 6

out and trampled by men.

"You are the light of the world. A city on a hill cannot be hidden. Neither do people light a lamp and put it under a bowl. Instead they put it on its stand, and it gives light to everyone in the house. In the same way, let your light shine before men, that they may see your good deeds and praise your Father in heaven.

"Do not think that I have come to abolish the Law or the Prophets; I have not come to abolish them but to fulfill them. I tell you the truth, until heaven and earth disappear, not the smallest letter, not the least stroke of a pen, will by any means disappear from the Law until everything is accomplished. Anyone who breaks one of the least of these commandments and teaches others to do the same will be called least in the Kingdom of Heaven, but whoever practices and teaches these commands will be called great in the Kingdom of Heaven. For I tell you that unless your righteousness surpasses that of the Pharisees and the teachers of the law, you will certainly not enter the Kingdom of Heaven.[2]

"They will truly be the least in the Kingdom because *this generation will be held responsible,"* Yeshua said, softly.

"You have heard that it was said to the people long ago, 'Do not murder, and anyone who murders will be subject to judgment.' But I tell you that anyone who is angry with his brother will be subject to judgment. Again, anyone who says to his brother, 'Raca,' is answerable to the

– 136 –

The Sermon on the Mount

Sanhedrin. But anyone who says, 'You fool!' will be in danger of the fire of hell.

"Therefore, if you are offering your gift at the altar and there remember that your brother has something against you, leave your gift there in front of the altar.

"First go and be reconciled to your brother; then come and offer your gift. Settle matters quickly with your adversary who is taking you to court. Do it while you are still with him on the way, or he may hand you over to the judge, and the judge may hand you over to the officer, and you may be thrown into prison. I tell you the truth, you will not get out until you have paid the last penny.

"You have heard that it was said, 'Do not commit adultery.' But I tell you that anyone who looks at a woman lustfully has already committed adultery with her in his heart. If your right eye causes you to sin, gouge it out and throw it away. It is better for you to lose one part of your body than for your whole body to be thrown into hell. And if your right hand causes you to sin, cut it off and throw it away. It is better for you to lose one part of your body than for your whole body to go into hell.

"It has been said, 'Anyone who divorces his wife must give her a certificate of divorce.' But I tell you that anyone who divorces his wife, except for marital unfaithfulness, causes her to become an adulteress, and anyone who marries the divorced woman commits adultery.

Not as I Will, But as You Will   Chapter 6

"Again, you have heard that it was said to the people long ago, 'Do not break your oath, but keep the oaths you have made to the Lord.' But I tell you, do not swear at all: either by heaven, for it is God's throne; or by the earth, for it is his footstool; or by Jerusalem, for it is the city of the Great King. And do not swear by your head, for you cannot make even one hair white or black. Simply let your 'Yes' be 'Yes,' and your 'No,' 'No'; anything beyond this comes from the evil one.

"You have heard that it was said, 'Eye for eye, and tooth for tooth.' But I tell you, do not resist an evil person. If someone strikes you on the right cheek, turn to him the other also. And if someone wants to sue you and take your tunic, let him have your cloak as well. If someone forces you to go one mile, go with him two miles. Give to the one who asks you, and do not turn away from the one who wants to borrow from you.

"You have heard that it was said, 'Love your neighbor and hate your enemy.' But I tell you: Love your enemies and pray for those who persecute you, that you may be sons of your Father in heaven. He causes his sun to rise on the evil and the good, and sends rain on the righteous and the unrighteous. If you love those who love you, what reward will you get? Are not even the tax collectors doing that? And if you greet only your brothers, what are you doing more than others? Do not even pagans do that? Be perfect, therefore, as your heavenly Father is perfect.[3]

Yeshua looked away, those last words of his ringing in his

The Sermon on the Mount

memory, "Be perfect, therefore, as your heavenly Father is perfect. The greatest downfall of my people is they don't understand how possible such perfection is," he said.

"Perfection is not possible, we are mere men, they said, never believing in the possibility.

"Beyond my words, I tried to show them that perfection is just true love. All it takes is true brotherhood and sisterhood without consciousness of barriers. Barriers are the problem. Anything between us is all the result of the evil one. The Father never meant for separation to exist between us—separations due to our national origins, beliefs, or social status. As brothers and sisters in a family have no barriers even though their natures and roles can be very different. In a father's eyes, his son the leader of the Sanhedrin and his crippled daughter have equal value, equal love."

The scene before him continued.

> *"Be careful not to do your 'acts of righteousness' before men, to be seen by them. If you do, you will have no reward from your Father in heaven. So when you give to the needy, do not announce it with trumpets, as the hypocrites do in the synagogues and on the streets, to be honored by men. I tell you the truth, they have received their reward in full. But when you give to the needy, do not let your left hand know what your right hand is doing, so that your giving may be in secret.*
>
> *"Then your Father, who sees what is done in secret, will reward you. And when you pray, do not be like the hypocrites, for they love to pray standing in the synagogues and on the street*

Not as I Will, But as You Will

Chapter 6

corners to be seen by men. I tell you the truth, they have received their reward in full. But when you pray, go into your room, close the door and pray to your Father, who is unseen. Then your Father, who sees what is done in secret, will reward you. And when you pray, do not keep on babbling like pagans, for they think they will be heard because of their many words. Do not be like them, for your Father knows what you need before you ask him. This, then, is how you should pray:

"'Our Father in heaven,
hallowed be your name,
your kingdom come,
your will be done
on earth as it is in heaven.
Give us today our daily bread.
Forgive us our debts,
as we also have forgiven our debtors.
And lead us not into temptation,
but deliver us from the evil one.

"For if you forgive men when they sin against you, your heavenly Father will also forgive you. But if you do not forgive men their sins, your Father will not forgive your sins."

Yeshua whispered, his eyes clenched, the words straining through hoarse emotion, "This is my prayer to you, my children, as well, that you remember this prayer, that you remember my quest for the kingdom, when I am gone, and continue in my stead. That the memory of it will not fade, and the yearning for it will not wither. This is my only hope..." His voice faded, lapsing into tearful silence.

– 140 –

The Sermon on the Mount

The scene in Capernaum continued.

"When you fast, do not look somber as the hypocrites do, for they disfigure their faces to show men they are fasting. I tell you the truth, they have received their reward in full. But when you fast, put oil on your head and wash your face, so that it will not be obvious to men that you are fasting, but only to your Father, who is unseen; and your Father, who sees what is done in secret, will reward you.

"Do not store up for yourselves treasures on earth, where moth and rust destroy, and where thieves break in and steal. But store up for yourselves treasures in heaven, where moth and rust do not destroy, and where thieves do not break in and steal. For where your treasure is, there your heart will be also.

"The eye is the lamp of the body. If your eyes are good, your whole body will be full of light. But if your eyes are bad, your whole body will be full of darkness. If then the light within you is darkness, how great is that darkness! No one can serve two masters. Either he will hate the one and love the other, or he will be devoted to the one and despise the other. You cannot serve both God and Money.

"Therefore I tell you, do not worry about your life, what you will eat or drink; or about your body, what you will wear. Is not life more important than food, and the body more important than clothes? Look at the birds of the air; they do not sow or reap or store away in barns, and yet

Not as I Will, But as You Will   Chapter 6

your heavenly Father feeds them. Are you not much more valuable than they? Who of you by worrying can add a single hour to his life? And why do you worry about clothes? See how the lilies of the field grow. They do not labor or spin. Yet I tell you that not even Solomon in all his splendor was dressed like one of these.

"If that is how God clothes the grass of the field, which is here today and tomorrow is thrown into the fire, will he not much more clothe you, O you of little faith? So do not worry, saying, 'What shall we eat?' or 'What shall we drink?' or 'What shall we wear?' For the pagans run after all these things, and your heavenly Father knows that you need them. But seek first his kingdom and his righteousness, and all these things will be given to you as well. Therefore do not worry about tomorrow, for tomorrow will worry about itself. Each day has enough trouble of its own.[4]

"Do not judge, or you too will be judged. For in the same way you judge others, you will be judged, and with the measure you use, it will be measured to you. Why do you look at the speck of sawdust in your brother's eye and pay no attention to the plank in your own eye? How can you say to your brother, 'Let me take the speck out of your eye,' when all the time there is a plank in your own eye? You hypocrite, first take the plank out of your own eye, and then you will see clearly to remove the speck from your brother's eye.

"Do not give dogs what is sacred; do not throw your pearls to pigs. If you do, they may trample

– 142 –

The Sermon on the Mount

them under their feet, and then turn and tear you
to pieces.

"Ask and it will be given to you; seek and you
will find; knock and the door will be opened to
you. For everyone who asks receives; he who seeks
finds; and to him who knocks, the door will be
opened. Which of you, if his son asks for bread,
will give him a stone? Or if he asks for a fish,
will give him a snake? If you, then, though you
are evil, know how to give good gifts to your
children, how much more will your Father in
heaven give good gifts to those who ask him! So in
everything, do to others what you would have them
do to you, for this sums up the Law and the
Prophets.

"Enter through the narrow gate. For wide is the
gate and broad is the road that leads to destruction,
and many enter through it. But small is the gate
and narrow the road that leads to life, and only a
few find it.

"Watch out for false prophets. They come to you in
sheep's clothing, but inwardly they are ferocious
wolves. By their fruit you will recognize them.
Do people pick grapes from thornbushes, or figs
from thistles? Likewise every good tree bears good
fruit, but a bad tree bears bad fruit. A good tree
cannot bear bad fruit, and a bad tree cannot bear
good fruit. Every tree that does not bear good
fruit is cut down and thrown into the fire. Thus,
by their fruit you will recognize them.

"Not everyone who says to me, 'Lord, Lord,' will

> *enter the Kingdom of Heaven, but only he who does the will of my Father who is in heaven. Many will say to me on that day, 'Lord, Lord, did we not prophesy in your name, and in your name drive out demons and perform many miracles?' Then I will tell them plainly, 'I never knew you. Away from me, you evildoers!'*

"They will not know me," Yeshua said, as in a trance, confronted with the unsummoned specter of his people's future. "When an arrow leaves the bow slightly askew from the target, where it ends up is far removed from the original mark. Thus, I fear, my people, my children will end up far away from my desires for them. My intent was not on saving individuals but on the salvation of the world—the regathering of the whole of Israel as the instrument of the Father in preparation for the coming of His Kingdom." [5] This is the most important point for them to understand. But they do not understand.

"What good is a few saved from drowning, when the many are still perishing in the depths. Can the saved be happy when they tarried and let many drown? The saved must help the others to be saved, quickly before, it is too late.

"Gabriel," Yeshua asked, turning abruptly to the angel, "must I die now? What if my life were extended even a short time? If my death be required as ransom for their failure, perhaps it could be just postponed a bit until I can teach my disciples further—prepare them better for what they must do afterward to further the kingdom. This, so the arrow will be more true to the mark."

Gabriel said, gravely, "That you must decide. But you have already cast the seeds for the Kingdom. What more can you

– 144 –

The Sermon on the Mount

do? Your parables help them understand. Simple people need pictures to understand. And perchance they will, when they can think back over the great value you brought to them. But Satan is crouched at the door waiting his due. You decide how he is to be satisfied; one life—though the most precious—now; or the lifeblood of the world, later, if you fail. You have not failed yet; this sacrifice is an offering to forestall that failure."

Taciturn and thoughtful, Yeshua did not answer. Given the choices the angel offered, he knew what decision he would make. Never would he risk others' lives for his. But a part of him was still unconvinced these were the only choices.

The scene changed to the lakeshore where a very large crowd had gathered around Yeshua—so many that they stretched back and up the green hillside before him. Yeshua remembered this great setting for teaching that allowed his voice to carry far up the hillside. He had boarded a boat and sat facing the crowd, speaking of many things in parables that morning.

> "A farmer went out to sow his seed. As he was scattering the seed, some fell along the path, and the birds came and ate it up. Some fell on rocky places, where it did not have much soil. It sprang up quickly, because the soil was shallow. But when the sun came up, the plants were scorched, and they withered because they had no root. Other seed fell among thorns, which grew up and choked the plants. Still other seed fell on good soil, where it produced a crop—a hundred, sixty or thirty times what was sown. He who has ears, let him hear."

– 145 –

Not as I Will, But as You Will

Chapter 6

The disciples came to him and asked, "Why do you speak to the people in parables?"

He replied, "The knowledge of the secrets of the Kingdom of Heaven has been given to you, but not to them. Whoever has will be given more, and he will have an abundance. Whoever does not have, even what he has will be taken from him. This is why I speak to them in parables: Though seeing, they do not see; though hearing, they do not hear or understand. In them is fulfilled the prophecy of Isaiah:

"'You will be ever hearing but never understanding; you will be ever seeing but never perceiving. For this people's heart has become callused; they hardly hear with their ears, and they have closed their eyes. Otherwise they might see with their eyes, hear with their ears, understand with their hearts and turn, and I would heal them.'

"But blessed are your eyes because they see, and your ears because they hear. For I tell you the truth, many prophets and righteous men longed to see what you see but did not see it, and to hear what you hear but did not hear it.

"Listen then to what the parable of the sower means: When anyone hears the message about the kingdom and does not understand it, the evil one comes and snatches away what was sown in his heart. This is the seed sown along the path. The one who received the seed that fell on rocky places is the man who hears the word and at once receives it with joy. But since he has no root, he

– 146 –

The Sermon on the Mount

lasts only a short time. When trouble or persecution comes because of the word, he quickly falls away. The one who received the seed that fell among the thorns is the man who hears the word, but the worries of this life and the deceitfulness of wealth choke it, making it unfruitful. But the one who received the seed that fell on good soil is the man who hears the word and understands it. He produces a crop, yielding a hundred, sixty or thirty times what was sown.

"The Kingdom of Heaven is like a man who sowed good seed in his field. But while everyone was sleeping, his enemy came and sowed weeds among the wheat, and went away. When the wheat sprouted and formed heads, then the weeds also appeared.

"The owner's servants came to him and said, 'Sir, didn't you sow good seed in your field? Where then did the weeds come from?'

"An enemy did this," he replied.

"The servants asked him, 'Do you want us to go and pull them up?'

"'No,' he answered, 'because while you are pulling the weeds, you may root up the wheat with them. Let both grow together until the harvest. At that time I will tell the harvesters: First collect the weeds and tie them in bundles to be burned; then gather the wheat and bring it into my barn.'

"Once again, the Kingdom of Heaven is like a net that was let down into the lake and caught all

– 147 –

Not as I Will, But as You Will   Chapter 6

kinds of fish. When it was full, the fishermen
pulled it up on the shore. Then they sat down and
collected the good fish in baskets, but threw the
bad away. This is how it will be at the end of the
age. The angels will come and separate the wicked
from the righteous and throw them into the fiery
furnace, where there will be weeping and gnashing
of teeth.

"The Kingdom of Heaven is like a mustard
seed, which a man took and planted in his field.
Though it is the smallest of all your seeds, yet
when it grows, it is the largest of garden plants
and becomes a tree, so that the birds of the air
come and perch in its branches.

"The Kingdom of Heaven is like yeast that a
woman took and mixed into a large amount of
flour until it worked all through the dough.[6]

"The Kingdom of Heaven is like treasure hidden
in a field. When a man found it, he hid it again,
and then in his joy went and sold all he had and
bought that field. Again, the Kingdom of Heaven
is like a merchant looking for fine pearls. When he
found one of great value, he went away and sold
everything he had and bought it.

"Have you understood all these things?" he asked.

"Yes," they replied.

He said to them, "Therefore every teacher of the
law who has been instructed about the Kingdom
of Heaven is like the owner of a house who brings
out of his storeroom new treasures as well as old."[7]

– 148 –

The Sermon on the Mount

"Did they understand?" asked Yeshua, turning from the vision to Gabriel. "Did they understand what a precious circumstance they were in? Did they realize how much their fathers toiled and longed for the opportunity they now participate in—the chance to bring in the Kingdom and the Father's reign?"

Though his remark was to Gabriel, Gabriel realized his question was directed more at himself. He had noted, in wonder, how Yeshua was ever mindful of his own responsibility before convicting others of failure.

"This precious being," he thought, "who took upon himself the fearfully daunting task to demolish Satan's nation, to do away with Satan's kingship and fulfill the long-standing dream of the Father, was always looking for any way to be this sacrificial offering for Heaven's providence. From his position, he could have set the entire universe in motion to breathe a deep sigh of despair with him. Instead, he showed only a sense of being apologetic toward Heaven for having been rejected. Without his heart of clinging to his people and their innocence, the Father would have a mind to pass a judgment on the people greater than that of Noah's time. Because of this heart of the forgiving son, the Father will be unable to abandon these flagitious offspring."

Gabriel could only mourn in silence and prayerful apology that those meant to see and attend could not behold this most precious of all jewels, a true son of Heaven.

Not as I Will, But as You Will

Chapter 7

Parables of the Kingdom

Looking desperately for an opportunity to reach Yeshua and quell his pain, Gabriel responded: "There is still hope, my Lord, of your words hitting their mark. Some will hear them as you intended. Maybe it will be generations from today, but people will finally begin to understand, and take up your burden for establishing the Kingdom."

His words seemed lost as, following Yeshua's thoughts, a new vision opened before them of a ridge on the Mount of Olives overlooking the city, where Yeshua was speaking to his disciples.

> *"At that time the kingdom of heaven will be like ten virgins who took their lamps and went out to meet the bridegroom. Five of them were foolish and five were wise. The foolish ones took their*

Not as I Will, But as You Will

Chapter 7

lamps but did not take any oil with them. The wise, however, took oil in jars along with their lamps. The bridegroom was a long time in coming, and they all became drowsy and fell asleep.

"At midnight the cry rang out: 'here's the bridegroom! Come out to meet him!' Then all the virgins woke up and trimmed their lamps. The foolish ones said to the wise, 'Give us some of your oil; our lamps are going out.'

"'No,' they replied, 'there may not be enough for both us and you. Instead, go to those who sell oil and buy some for yourselves.'

"But while they were on their way to buy the oil, the bridegroom arrived. The virgins who were ready went in with him to the wedding banquet. And the door was shut.

"Later the others also came. 'Sir! Sir!' they said. 'Open the door for us!'

"But he replied, 'I tell you the truth, I don't know you.'

"Therefore keep watch, because you do not know the day or the hour." [1]

Yeshua turned, looking back once again to the silent trio under the olive tree. "They will miss the new bridegroom, if I cannot succeed. I feel like I must prepare my people more or they will misstep. They will be responsible for what they know. It is better for them that they never knew me, if my words cannot lead them to the right direction in preparation for that all important moment." He sighed heavily, as the scene continued.

– 152 –

Parables of the Kingdom

"*Again, it will be like a man going on a journey, who called his servants and entrusted his property to them. To one he gave five talents of money, to another two talents, and to another one talent, each according to his ability. Then he went on his journey. The man who had received the five talents went at once and put his money to work and gained five more. So also, the one with the two talents gained two more. But the man who had received the one talent went off, dug a hole in the ground and hid his master's money.*

"*After a long time the master of those servants returned and settled accounts with them. The man who had received the five talents brought the other five. 'Master,' he said, 'you entrusted me with five talents. See, I have gained five more.'*

"*His master replied, 'Well done, good and faithful servant! You have been faithful with a few things; I will put you in charge of many things. Come and share your master's happiness!'*

"*The man with the two talents also came. 'Master,' he said, 'you entrusted me with two talents; see, I have gained two more.'*

"*His master replied, 'Well done, good and faithful servant! You have been faithful with a few things; I will put you in charge of many things. Come and share your master's happiness!'*

"*Then the man who had received the one talent came. 'Master,' he said, 'I knew that you are a hard man, harvesting where you have not sown and gathering where you have not scattered seed.*

— 153 —

Not as I Will, But as You Will   Chapter 7

So I was afraid and went out and hid your talent in the ground. See, here is what belongs to you.'

"His master replied, 'You wicked, lazy servant! So you knew that I harvest where I have not sown and gather where I have not scattered seed? Well then, you should have put my money on deposit with the bankers, so that when I returned I would have received it back with interest.

"'Take the talent from him and give it to the one who has the ten talents. For everyone who has will be given more, and he will have an abundance. Whoever does not have, even what he has will be taken from him. And throw that worthless servant outside, into the darkness, where there will be weeping and gnashing of teeth.'[2]

"When the Son of Man comes in his glory, and all the angels with him, he will sit on his throne in heavenly glory. All the nations will be gathered before him, and he will separate the people one from another as a shepherd separates the sheep from the goats. He will put the sheep on his right and the goats on his left.

"Then the King will say to those on his right, 'Come, you who are blessed by my Father; take your inheritance, the kingdom prepared for you since the creation of the world. For I was hungry and you gave me something to eat, I was thirsty and you gave me something to drink, I was a stranger and you invited me in, I needed clothes and you clothed me, I was sick and you looked after me, I was in prison and you came to

– 154 –

Parables of the Kingdom

visit me.'

"Then the righteous will answer him, 'Lord, when did we see you hungry and feed you, or thirsty and give you something to drink? When did we see you a stranger and invite you in, or needing clothes and clothe you? When did we see you sick or in prison and go to visit you?'

"The King will reply, 'I tell you the truth, whatever you did for one of the least of these brothers of mine, you did for me.'

"Then he will say to those on his left, 'Depart from me, you who are cursed, into the eternal fire prepared for the devil and his angels. For I was hungry and you gave me nothing to eat, I was thirsty and you gave me nothing to drink, I was a stranger and you did not invite me in, I needed clothes and you did not clothe me, I was sick and in prison and you did not look after me.'

"They also will answer, 'Lord, when did we see you hungry or thirsty or a stranger or needing clothes or sick or in prison, and did not help you?'

"He will reply, 'I tell you the truth, whatever you did not do for one of the least of these, you did not do for me.' Then they will go away to eternal punishment, but the righteous to eternal life."[3]

Yeshua said to Gabriel, "That is the problem, as I was not recognized, so those sent to follow in my footsteps may not be recognized. My disciples must judge the heart, the fruits, not the appearance. If they have the right heart, if their hearts resemble my heart, they will recognize the same in others. But

– 155 –

Not as I Will, But as You Will   Chapter 7

they cannot recognize what they do not possess.

"Do my children want to be servants to their Heavenly Father or sons and daughters? A son takes responsibility for his father's needs, and doesn't wait to be told what must be done. I am first of all the elder son, trying to unite the children around the Parent's will. That is what my parables say, how to have the heart of a son to the Father instead of a hired servant. Servants sleep in the back away from the family. The son sleeps in the Father's house."

Gabriel was silent. His position was the servant. He could not advise the sons on how best to be sons. Now another scene appeared before them, Yeshua teaching on a hillside in Judea.

"There was a man who had two sons. The younger one said to his father, 'Father, give me my share of the estate.'

So he divided his property between them.

"Not long after that, the younger son got together all he had, set off for a distant country and there squandered his wealth in wild living. After he had spent everything, there was a severe famine in that whole country, and he began to be in need. So he went and hired himself out to a citizen of that country, who sent him to his fields to feed pigs.

"He longed to fill his stomach with the pods that the pigs were eating, but no one gave him anything. When he came to his senses, he said, 'How many of my father's hired men have food to spare, and here I am starving to death! I will set out and go back to my father and say to him:

– 156 –

Parables of the Kingdom

Father, I have sinned against heaven and against you. I am no longer worthy to be called your son; make me like one of your hired men.'

So he got up and went to his father.

"But while he was still a long way off, his father saw him and was filled with compassion for him; he ran to his son, threw his arms around him and kissed him.

"The son said to him, 'Father, I have sinned against heaven and against you. I am no longer worthy to be called your son.'

"But the father said to his servants, 'Quick! Bring the best robe and put it on him. Put a ring on his finger and sandals on his feet.

"'Bring the fattened calf and kill it. Let's have a feast and celebrate. For this son of mine was dead and is alive again; he was lost and is found.' So they began to celebrate.

"Meanwhile, the older son was in the field. When he came near the house, he heard music and dancing. So he called one of the servants and asked him what was going on. 'Your brother has come,' he replied, 'and your father has killed the fattened calf because he has him back safe and sound.'

"The older brother became angry and refused to go in. So his father went out and pleaded with him. But he answered his father, 'Look! All these years I've been slaving for you and never disobeyed your orders. Yet you never gave me even a young goat so

– 157 –

Not as I Will, But as You Will   Chapter 7

I could celebrate with my friends. But when this son of yours who has squandered your property with prostitutes comes home, you kill the fattened calf for him!'

"'My son,' the father said, 'you are always with me, and everything I have is yours. But we had to celebrate and be glad, because this brother of yours was dead and is alive again; he was lost and is found.'" [4]

Turning away, Yeshua said, "Come home my brothers, *'Turn! Turn from your evil ways! Why will you die, O house of Israel?'"* [5] Yeshua fought the tears in his now-swollen eyes. "How happy this elder brother would be to welcome his younger brothers and sisters in the kingdom, to celebrate their overcoming this world's pain and temptation. Will I get the chance? If the Chosen People do not understand the Father has sent me, then my words fall on deaf ears. If my words could not convince them, my actions—driving out demons, healing the sick—should have been enough to show from whom I came. But they say my powers of healing are from the devil, and so they open the door to the devil to close it on me."

A scene in the Jerusalem temple courtyard opened before them. Yeshua was addressing a man disturbed by a demon, as he expelled the malevolent spirit from the cowering figure.

When the demon left, the man who had been mute spoke, and the crowd was amazed. But some of them said, "By Beelzebub, the prince of demons, he is driving out demons." Others tested him by asking for a sign from heaven.

Yeshua knew their thoughts and said to them:

– 158 –

Parables of the Kingdom

"Any kingdom divided against itself will be ruined, and a house divided against itself will fall. If Satan is divided against himself, how can his kingdom stand? I say this because you claim that I drive out demons by Beelzebub. Now if I drive out demons by Beelzebub, by whom do your followers drive them out? So then, they will be your judges. But if I drive out demons by the finger of God, then the kingdom of God has come to you.

"When a strong man, fully armed, guards his own house, his possessions are safe. But when someone stronger attacks and overpowers him, he takes away the armor in which the man trusted and divides up the spoils. He who is not with me is against me, and he who does not gather with me, scatters. When an evil spirit comes out of a man, it goes through arid places seeking rest and does not find it. Then it says, 'I will return to the house I left.' When it arrives, it finds the house swept clean and put in order. Then it goes and takes seven other spirits more wicked than itself, and they go in and live there. And the final condition of that man is worse than the first."

Yeshua said, "If Satan is driven out, but God does not come in, then Satan will come back twice as strong. They may cast out demons, but they do not bring God in; so, to what purpose is their effort?"

Gabriel replied abruptly, seeking to thrust his words between Yeshua's consciousness and the vision. "My Lord, you are the healer of the lineage of the Father, something they cannot conceive of as yet."

Not as I Will, But as You Will Chapter 7

The scene continued with Yeshua unmindful of Gabriel's appeal. The strength of his will was a formidable wall Gabriel felt incapable to breach.

> *As Yeshua was saying these things, a woman in the crowd called out, "Blessed is the mother who gave you birth and nursed you." He replied, "Blessed rather are those who hear the word of God and obey it."*
>
> *As the crowds increased, he said, "This is a wicked generation. It asks for a miraculous sign, but none will be given it except the sign of Jonah. For as Jonah was a sign to the Ninevites, so also will the Son of Man be to this generation. The Queen of the South will rise at the judgment with the men of this generation and condemn them; for she came from the ends of the earth to listen to Solomon's wisdom, and now one greater than Solomon is here. The men of Nineveh will stand up at the judgment with this generation and condemn it; for they repented at the preaching of Jonah, and now one greater than Jonah is here."*[6]

As the scene faded, Yeshua concluded, "Even those who followed me did so mostly for my miracles and healings, not for my words. Thus, few can believe without seeing."

Parables of the Kingdom

Gabriel responded diffidently, wanting to move beyond this thought sequence but seeing Yeshua captured by it, "Yes, the miracles and healings were merely signs to fulfill the prophesy so that people would know you are who you say." The scene changed to the outskirts of Gennesaret, a fishing village on the lakeshore.

Yeshua started at the memory of this morning, a morning when, besieged by many for healing over the past days, he had been seeking solitude. But word had gone out to all in the surrounding country that he was there. People brought all their sick to him, and some begged him to let the sick just touch the edge of his cloak. All who touched him were healed.[7]

He replied, "Would that they could have known the purpose that I had come for, the things that made for true peace. I spent all my energy in healing the physical bodies, with no time to heal the spirits. Because their spirits were filled with evil, the sicknesses would return, as they resumed a life of sin."

The scene in Gennesaret continued.

> *Some Pharisees and teachers of the law came to him from Jerusalem and asked, "Why do your disciples break the tradition of the elders? They don't wash their hands before they eat!"*
>
> *Yeshua replied, "And why do you break the command of God for the sake of your tradition? For God said, 'Honor your father and mother' and 'Anyone who curses his father or mother must be put to death.' But you say that if a man says to his father or mother, 'Whatever help you might otherwise have received from me is a gift devoted to God,' he is not to 'honor his father' with it.*

– 161 –

Not as I Will, But as You Will   Chapter 7

Thus you nullify the word of God for the sake of your tradition. You hypocrites! Isaiah was right when he prophesied about you, 'These people honor me with their lips, but their hearts are far from me. They worship me in vain; their teachings are but rules taught by men.'" [8]

He called the crowd to him and said, "Listen and understand. What goes into a man's mouth does not make him 'unclean,' but what comes out of his mouth, that is what makes him 'unclean.'"

Then the disciples came to him and asked, "Do you know that the Pharisees were offended when they heard this?"

He replied, "Every plant that my heavenly Father has not planted will be pulled up by the roots. Leave them; they are blind guides. If a blind man leads a blind man, both will fall into a pit."

Peter said, "Explain the parable to us."

"Are you still so dull?" he asked them. "Don't you see that whatever enters the mouth goes into the stomach and then out of the body? But the things that come out of the mouth come from the heart, and these make a man 'unclean.' For out of the heart come evil thoughts, murder, adultery, sexual immorality, theft, false testimony, slander. These are what make a man 'unclean'; but eating with unwashed hands does not make him 'unclean.'" [9]

Yeshua lowered his eyes to shield them from the emotional impact of the series of visions. The contrast to those early

– 162 –

Parables of the Kingdom

days in the beginning of his ministry, which had held so much hope for success, was unbearable. He thought back to those words of the Sermon on the Mount, when his pure instruction to his followers was untainted by responding to negative reproof, uninfluenced by his later observance of their weaknesses. He had spoken to them purely, simply how to be heavenly children, objects of joy to their Heavenly Father, with belief that they could achieve it.

Later on, he thought, he accommodated their prosaic understandings. He taught more and more through parables of the simplicity of the Kingdom, as near to them as true, faithful family relations, with the relationship with their true Father, their heavenly Parent, being the core. This was something that even simple people could understand, he had thought. How he ached for that simple faith in them to be justified by their actions, by their attendance to him as he had attended to them.

To Gabriel, he said, "I spoke those words with the belief I would be with them, to help them find their way to the blessing. But now they will be alone, without my guidance. They are children," he continued sadly, "left alone to fend for themselves among the wild animals—Satan's minions, who will devour them!"

Gabriel's expression was transfixed with concern. He studied Yeshua's face, the pensively drawn tenseness of his body and face, but those eyes still unyieldingly calm. Gabriel shook his head, marveling at the heart that would not let go of responsibility, even though he was utterly blameless. Yeshua had forgotten—if ever he had recognized it—any pain caused by the failures of those around him. All his energy and concern was concentrated in saving them.

– 163 –

Not as I Will, But as You Will   Chapter 7

Yeshua continued, "Like pearls before swine, they failed to understand my words. They looked for tricks, miracles and healings like children transfixed by a magician—which I was then accused of being. Thus, my time, energy and words were wasted. And now this opportunity is doomed to failure, to be buried, unfulfilled; and all the sacrifice of the prophets and their forefathers will be trampled into the mud with it."

Gabriel replied, crystallizing the paradox at the root of Yeshua's suffering. "Your audience was always meant to be the scribes, Pharisees, Sadducees, the educated. The Father and I planned it as such. You should have grown up in Judea where you were born, in close proximity to the Jerusalem temple and the religious community in power. And you would have been raised with your cousin, John. That's why I had your mother visit Elizabeth, John's mother, when they were both with child.

"That was their chance to unite these two families who were sharing a destiny of such heavenly significance. Your home should have been the temple, to have been raised in the temple together with John, with skin-touch opportunity to speak to and influence the educated leadership class. Nazareth was far away from the temple in Jerusalem, from Zechariah and Elizabeth and your cousin John; and opportunity for you while growing up. That's my greatest regret. You have done well under the circumstances."

Yeshua said softly, "True, I could never teach them to understand things of the spirit. They could not understand my parables because they looked at things so concretely. When I spoke of bread, they saw physical bread, yet I meant it as a symbol. How difficult it is to teach this to people without training in things of the spirit. Of course, the Father meant for my audience to be the rabbis and scribes, those

– 164 –

Parables of the Kingdom

learned in the use of symbolic language and the meaning behind. But they could not accept me or my words. It was only the simple people who could respond."

Gabriel waved his hand and again the smooth, glassy, azure blue of the lake appeared, with Yeshua standing on the shore before a crowd. Yeshua recognized it as the day following the meeting where he had produced multiple loaves of bread and fish to feed five thousand from only five loaves and three fish. The people had been amazed at the miracle and had been looking for him ever since.

> When they found him on the other side of the lake, they asked him, "Rabbi, when did you get here?"
>
> He answered, "I tell you the truth, you are looking for me, not because you saw miraculous signs but because you ate the loaves and had your fill. Do not work for food that spoils, but for food that endures to eternal life, which the Son of Man will give you. On him God the Father has placed his seal of approval."
>
> Then they asked him, "What must we do to do the works God requires?"
>
> He answered, "The work of God is this: to believe in the one he has sent."
>
> So they asked him, "What miraculous sign then will you give that we may see it and believe you? What will you do?
>
> "Our forefathers ate the manna in the desert; as it is written: 'He gave them bread from heaven to eat.'"

Not as I Will, But as You Will   Chapter 7

He said to them, "I tell you the truth, it is not Moses who has given you the bread from heaven, but it is my Father who gives you the true bread from heaven. For the bread of God is he who comes down from heaven and gives life to the world."

"Sir," they said, "from now on give us this bread."

Then he declared, "I am the bread of life. He who comes to me will never go hungry, and he who believes in me will never be thirsty. But as I told you, you have seen me and still you do not believe. All that the Father gives me will come to me, and whoever comes to me I will never drive away. For I have come down from heaven not to do my will but to do the will of him who sent me.

"And this is the will of him who sent me, that I shall lose none of all that he has given me, but raise them up at the last day. For my Father's will is that everyone who looks to the Son and believes in him shall have eternal life, and I will raise him up at the last day."

At this the Jews began to grumble about him because he said, "I am the bread that came down from heaven."

They said, "Is this not... the son of Joseph, whose father and mother we know? How can he now say, 'I came down from heaven?'"

"Stop grumbling among yourselves," he answered. "No one can come to me unless the Father who sent me draws him, and I will raise him up at

– 166 –

Parables of the Kingdom

the last day. It is written in the Prophets: 'They will all be taught by God.' Everyone who listens to the Father and learns from him comes to me. No one has seen the Father except the one who is from God; only he has seen the Father. I tell you the truth, he who believes has everlasting life.

"I am the bread of life. Your forefathers ate the manna in the desert, yet they died. But here is the bread that comes down from heaven, which a man may eat and not die. I am the living bread that came down from heaven. If anyone eats of this bread, he will live forever. This bread is my flesh, which I will give for the life of the world."

Then the Jews began to argue sharply among themselves, "How can this man give us his flesh to eat?"

He said to them, "I tell you the truth, unless you eat the flesh of the Son of Man and drink his blood, you have no life in you. Whoever eats my flesh and drinks my blood has eternal life, and I will raise him up at the last day. For my flesh is real food and my blood is real drink. Whoever eats my flesh and drinks my blood remains in me, and I in him.

"Just as the living Father sent me and I live because of the Father, so the one who feeds on me will live because of me. This is the bread that came down from heaven. Your forefathers ate manna and died, but he who feeds on this bread will live forever."

Yeshua said, "The flesh and blood I brought should have

– 167 –

Not as I Will, But as You Will — Chapter 7

been the cleansing of their lineage by grafting on to mine—the restoration of the lineage of Adam lost through the fall. But with that opportunity lost, bread and wine become a symbol of another path to salvation—more circuitous, more tortuous and finally more tenuous for them to understand. Like the manna and quail given their ancestors in the wilderness, it provides temporary relief and sustenance until the promised land, the kingdom, can be reached. They must never see it as the promise fulfilled in itself and be satisfied. Sadly, we have a long way to go before we can rest in the kingdom."

The scene changed to the synagogue in Capernaum following Yeshua's speech, as he met with his disciples.[9]

> On hearing it, many of his disciples said, "This is a hard teaching. Who can accept it?"
>
> Aware that his disciples were grumbling about this, he said to them, "Does this offend you? What if you see the Son of Man ascend to where he was before! The Spirit gives life; the flesh counts for nothing. The words I have spoken to you are spirit and they are life. Yet there are some of you who do not believe." For he had known from the beginning which of them did not believe and who would betray him. He went on to say, "This is why I told you that no one can come to me unless the Father has enabled him."
>
> From this time many of his disciples turned back and no longer followed him. "You do not want to leave too, do you?" he asked the Twelve.[10]

Yeshua said, "The same temptation that brought down their fathers may bring them down. It corrupted the priesthood to be like whitewashed tombs so that they sought praise

Parables of the Kingdom

for outward appearances but were deaf to the heart of the words of the prophets to the responsibility to attend in action those words. The same judgments I spoke against the scribes and Pharisees, they will find themselves tempted to do.

"This generation will be held responsible for it all," [11] said Yeshua, his eyes lowered and clenched, his body shuddering. "They don't understand how Satan works to trick them into thinking they are following the right path. Narrow is that path, and so easily you can diverge from it, if you do not have a heart of attendance to the Father before your own desires. Can the children follow with that heart? I fear the answer!

"And my children will be like children who quarrel when their parents are not around to help them value one another. They will tear asunder my body, the house of God, from within. They will dispute small points of difference, neglecting the real responsibility they share, as brothers and sisters, and as the foundation of the Kingdom on Heaven on Earth," Yeshua said. "I will no longer be with them to help them find their way, to teach them to love one another as I love them, as the Father loves them.

"The Chosen People, with steadfastness trained into them through four thousand years of direct chastisement and nurturing by the Father, were the rock upon which the Kingdom of Heaven could rest. Without it, the kingdom will rest upon sand, shifting as human concerns are put before Heaven's. And, Heaven demands more of us now under the new covenant brought with my ministry.

"Laws of Heaven will now demand right action as well as obedience to the law. Leadership, blessed by Heaven, will be from those who serve rather than those with power and authority. Blessings will come to the poor but rich in spirit,

– 169 –

Not as I Will, But as You Will   Chapter 7

rather than to those endowed with earthly riches.

"James, my younger brother, you know these things; you know the things that make for peace. You the peacemaker, you are my hope now for a bridge to our people. Why were you not here this evening? You know the truth but are too much led by opinion around you. Heaven needs you now. Come to me, James, and answer Heaven's call before it is too late.

"Without the Chosen People, how will the wider world come to know their true Father and true family. They live as orphans, abandoned to the whim of apostasy, diverse gods, strange beliefs and violent confrontations. Where is the hope for them if my children, who should know my voice through the tradition of their prophets and thus should know I came from the Father in Heaven, cannot love me and love one another and be together as a family?

"If I leave, they will be alone against the forces of evil arrayed against them. How gleeful Satan is to divide the Father's family against itself! This is the source of his power over them, turning one against the other. Gabriel, what will happen if I leave them *now?*"

Gabriel replied, impassioned with regard for this inestimably precious being before him, "When the leadership rejected you, the people could not follow you; they were blocked. Sadly, for the sin of a few all must suffer, just as by the victory of a few all could have received salvation. That is the blessing or the curse of being the Chosen People. The few powerful have condemned the nation."

Yeshua bowed his head sorrowfully, "Once I was asked by the Pharisees when the Kingdom of God would come. I told them, *"The Kingdom of God does not come with your careful observation, nor will people say, 'Here it is,' or 'there it is,'*

– 170 –

because the kingdom of God is in your midst."[12] The Kingdom is present in me, and when I am gone, it will be gone for a very long time and they will mourn its loss. I suffer for that day when it will return."

He sighed, long and painfully, murmuring, "Perhaps *this* is my failure; I quit emphasizing the goal of building the kingdom, when I had to speak about the change of plans—that I might have to die. My grief, which will never fully be assuaged, is that my mission's ending says the Father may have lost faith in me. Could that be true?"

Gabriel looked at the crumpled figure, and moved to encircle him with his arms. "My Lord," he whispered, "Fear not, the Father loves you more than the sum of heaven and earth combined; you are His only truly begotten son. The son is as the Father. The Father Himself takes the responsibility for this missed opportunity."

Not as I Will, But as You Will

Chapter 8

Keys to the Kingdom

In the darkening pale of the waning moonlight a thick mist was descending. The mist, mingled with tears and sweat, glistened on Yeshua's face. A heavy silence surrounded them as Gabriel waited and watched compassionately Yeshua's intense struggle—a struggle against powers and principalities not visible to the eye, but stronger than death is to life. The future of all in heaven and earth hung in the balance, weighed by the coming action of this lone tortured figure.

After many moments Yeshua finally spoke. "The kingdom had been in jeopardy for some time, I knew. It was hard for the disciples to accept the change of mission from establishing the kingdom to my having to die. I understand their struggle. For two years, we had been totally focused on the message, repent and unite with us to build the Kingdom of Heaven. Now all of a sudden, they faced not only the

Not as I Will, But as You Will   Chapter 8

prospect of the kingdom being delayed, but also I, their leader, having to die. I struggled to find the way to explain such a drastic change of plans—my having to sacrifice my life as atonement for the failure of the people to accept me.

"The Father has purposed it and His will must be accomplished. The Kingdom will be established with those He prepared or with someone else, if they fail. In the past the failure of the Chosen People could be restored because it was only His servants, the prophets, who were rejected. But this time it is His son whom they are rejecting. They must understand the great calamity this brings upon them. To illustrate it, I taught them a parable."

A scene from the past day opened before them, the temple courts where Yeshua had often come to teach and engage people in dialogue. Yeshua was addressing the chief priests and temple elders who had demanded to know by what right he spoke. They interrupted him as he was teaching a gathering of holiday pilgrims drawn to him after his prophecy-laden entry into the city that morning riding an ass's colt. Those gathered had the look of intense curiosity mixed with apprehension. "Could this be the anointed one?" was the unceasingly murmured question in the air.

Yeshua rose out of his seated, informal pose and replied, partly in answer to the query of these interlopers standing behind his small gathering but hardly looking at them as his attention was fixed on the gathering with riveted eyes, drawing out those sparks of living faith in the crowd with purposeful intensity.

> *"Hear another parable. There was a householder*
> *who planted a vineyard, and set a hedge around*
> *it, and dug a winepress in it, and built a tower,*

– 174 –

Keys to the Kingdom

*and let it out to tenants, and went into another
country. When the season of fruit drew near, he
sent his servants to the tenants to get the fruit;
and the tenants took his servants and beat one,
killed another, and stoned another. Again he sent
other servants, more than the first; and they did
the same to them.*

*"Afterwards he sent his son to them, saying, 'They
will respect my son.' But when the tenants saw
the son, they said to themselves, 'This is the heir;
come, let us kill him and have his inheritance.'
And they took him and cast him out of the
vineyard, and killed him. When therefore the
owner of the vineyard comes, what will he do to
these tenants?*

*"They said, 'He will put those wretches to a
miserable death, and let out the vineyard to other
tenants who will give him the fruits in their
season.'"*

*Yeshua said to them, "Have you never read in
the scriptures; 'The very stone which the builders
rejected has become the head of the corner; this
was the Lord's doing, and it is marvelous in our
eyes?' Therefore I tell you, the kingdom of God
will be taken away from you and given to a
nation producing the fruits of it."* [1]

Yeshua repeated, his voice seemed far away lost in memory of that time, *"Then the owner of the vineyard said, 'What
shall I do? I will send my son, whom I love; perhaps they will
respect him.'* [2] It was the son's responsibility to reason with
them. Could he have done more?"

– 175 –

Not as I Will, But as You Will   Chapter 8

As if to shake off the despair this momentary thought brought him, Yeshua roused himself and said, "The temple leadership demands to know by what right I speak as God's representative. 'Why are your words better than ours?' they ask. 'You speak from the same Torah but you are not even trained as one of us. Why should we follow you?' they ask—but not with sincere desire to know. They see only from their perspective—what they will lose—not from the Father's perspective of what the Chosen People and the world can gain through me. Who is the son? We are all children of the Father. But, the true son, fundamentally, is the one who has the interests of the father in mind.

"The Law was given to our people for the sake of the world. We are to be the light of the world, the bridge from darkness to light through the Law—and through the Law we are led to discover the Father's love that is even greater than the law; that ultimately, the law becomes a vassal to it. How am I different from them? I know this greater destiny for our people and am prepared to lead them there. If they were leading us there, I would not have to. They would keep our light under a bushel, keep our treasure to themselves and put a fence around it. This is why I am necessary: to throw open the doors to our treasure and lead the world in to share it. But these leaders! Not only do they refuse to serve the kingdom, but they block others from serving as well!

"In my parable the workers in the vineyard reject the son, as those same leaders are now poised to do with me. The parable is coming to pass. How much greater now will be the judgment and punishment upon our people! Whose blood can amend for so great a failure, where all of them should be tortured and killed for their failure? The devil owns them now, for they have proved by their actions that they are of his

Keys to the Kingdom

blood and not the Father's. Only the true son of the Father, petitioning and making amends for them in his own blood, like the blood of Isaac, the most faithful son, can recompense for their failure.

"This was to be the most important step in all of God's historical providence, receiving the Anointed One for mankind, as predicted. The Father is tortured with the prospect that the mission of His long-suffering, long-tended root of the Kingdom is failing; tortured with the prospect of losing His earthly lineage meant to descend from me. The first Adam failed as parents of humanity. I, the last Adam, was meant to succeed and forge a new beginning. It is my damnable position to choose which torture the Father will face, losing me and His lineage or the complete destruction of his Chosen People, root and branch.

"The Father could save my life, if I choose so. But then, without my blood being shed, the Chosen People will have to face up to their fate fully, with no requital. By my death, at least a part of the root and a tiny shoot of the providence to be nurtured and developed can be saved. It was this inexplicable choice that the Father was facing, which I had to explain to my disciples. I was afraid to tell them all this, for their faith is tender as a child's; they would have become defeated. I just tried to have them believe in me and that the victory could still be accomplished even without me."

Gabriel was silent. He was watchful and intuitive to Yeshua's quest, seeing that in spite of the anguish this reliving brought to him, he was trying to find meaning and hope in his past actions.

A new vision then opened before them.

Yeshua recognized the scene of the deep grotto of a rocky

– 177 –

Not as I Will, But as You Will   Chapter 8

spring—the fountainhead of the Jordan River—nestled among rich red-colored cliffs where the water trickled in many paths from the snow-capped Mount Hermon rising majestically in the background. It was late summer and this cool respite, fragrant with the scent of laurel, had been a place where he had stopped en route to Caesarea Philippi to discuss seriously with his disciples about the future.

> *Yeshua asked them, "Who do people say I am?"*
>
> *They replied, "Some say John the Baptist; others say Elijah; and still others, one of the prophets."*
>
> *"But what about you?" he asked. "Who do you say I am?"*
>
> *Peter answered, "You are the Christ."*
>
> *Yeshua warned them not to tell anyone about him.*
>
> *He then began to teach them that the Son of Man must suffer many things and be rejected by the elders, chief priests and teachers of the law, and that he must be killed and after three days rise again. He spoke plainly about this, and Peter took him aside and began to rebuke him.*
>
> *But when he turned and looked at his disciples, he rebuked Peter. "Get behind me, Satan!" he said. "You do not have in mind the things of God, but the things of men."* [3]

Reflecting on that time, Yeshua said, "It had not been a new idea to the disciples, that I might have to die if the foundation for success were not firmly established. But, somehow, they never really took seriously the possibility. The disciples' response told me they were far away from me in heart. Rather

– 178 –

Keys to the Kingdom

than repenting for their own part in the failure of the providence, they could only think of how this change would affect them.

"I told them, '*If anyone would come after me, he must deny himself and take up his cross and follow me. For whoever wants to save his life will lose it, but whoever loses his life for me and for the gospel will save it.*'[4]

"My cross—my challenge—was building the Kingdom of Heaven. This was the cross, the symbolism of the cross, and that was what I meant. My cross, the Kingdom of Heaven, still needs to be accomplished, with or without me. Now it will have to be without me.

"It is this I am trying to prepare them for, but they can't see beyond my death. For them, without me the Kingdom is impossible. Perhaps this is the fault of my miracles. They believed too much in what seemed to be my magical powers. I told them, '*I tell you the truth, anyone who has faith in me will do what I have been doing. He will do even greater things than these.*'[5] If they have the attitude to lose their life for the Father's will, then they can do anything—the Father can do anything through them, as He has through me."

Yeshua rose, pacing thoughtfully, and continued, "Repentance for our failures is the base through which we can begin again and the Father can empower us thusly. I chose the Day of Atonement (*Yom Kippur*) to speak to them about it further as we returned to the vicinity of Mount Herman. In the same way that this day means to make amends or to reconcile—becoming 'at one'—with God through afflicting ourselves in fasting, my sacrifice would be the affliction to reconcile those united in heart with me to the Father, despite the overall failure of the Chosen People.

Not as I Will, But as You Will   Chapter 8

"What I needed to make them understand was that atonement would be only the beginning, making possible a new beginning. Through this time of holy convocation, they must reorient their hearts from the path that led them to sin and failure. Out of that must come rebirth and renewal of the commitment for the Kingdom. If this happens, then the sacrifice of my life would be worthwhile. I needed also a way to give them hope to continue. For this I went back to Mount Herman with them."

The scene reappeared, the same backdrop of the grotto and spring, the fountainhead of the Jordan. This spring, the root of the spinal column of the land of Israel, the Jordan River, seemed to bubble up out of nowhere from its source Mount Herman—looming majestically, like God's mountain surveying His vineyard, Israel, lying before it in its shadow. The mists of morning hung over the grotto, in lacy ephemeral shards, almost sparkling in the dim growing light. Yeshua took Peter, James and John up the steep mountainside to an overhanging cliff midway up the mountain.

> *There he was transfigured before them. His face shone like the sun, and his clothes became as white as the light. Just then there appeared before them Moses and Elijah, talking with him.*
>
> *Peter said to him, "Lord, it is good for us to be here. If you wish, I will put up three shelters— one for you, one for Moses and one for Elijah."*
>
> *While he was still speaking, a bright cloud enveloped them, and a voice from the cloud said, "This is my Son, whom I love; with him I am well pleased. Listen to him!"*
>
> *When the disciples heard this, they fell face down*

– 180 –

Keys to the Kingdom

to the ground, terrified. But he came and touched
them. "Get up," he said. "Don't be afraid." When
they looked up, they saw no one except him.

As they were coming down the mountain, he
instructed them, "Don't tell anyone what you have
seen, until the Son of Man has been raised from
the dead."

The disciples asked him, "Why then do the teachers
of the law say that Elijah must come first?"

He replied, "To be sure, Elijah comes and will
restore all things. But I tell you, Elijah has
already come, and they did not recognize him, but
have done to him everything they wished. In the
same way the Son of Man is going to suffer at
their hands."[6]

Yeshua said, "Then the disciples understood that I was
talking to them about John the Baptist. John, the promised
Elijah, died without fulfilling his mission, and now I too must
die. During the autumn and winter I continued to try to reach
the people, looking for faith that might change that fate. I
reached out to all, looking for such faith and commitment.
Maybe, like the people of Ninevah, my people could still
change. *When God saw what they did and how they turned*
from their evil ways, he had compassion and did not bring upon
them the destruction he had threatened.[7]

"But my hope was short-lived. Even my own brothers have
proved callous and ignorant of my purpose and mission, at
one point pushing me to appear at the temple when I had
been warned against it. The priests were looking for me,
probably to arrest me. They challenged me to demonstrate my
position to the people through more miracles. They said, *"You*

Not as I Will, But as You Will

Chapter 8

ought to go to Judea, so that your disciples may see the miracles you do. No one who wants to become a public figure acts in secret. Since you are doing these things, show yourself to the world." [8] But their motivation was wrong, as they themselves did not believe in me, all but my brother James. I still have hope for James. It is only a matter of time before he comes to me. His conscience is already beginning to tell him the others are wrong. If only I had more time!

"But that season I did appear at the Temple, to worshipers there for the holy day feasts."

A scene of the temple courtyard opened before them. A milieu of people loitered noisily in the common ground. Many of them were in colorful exotic dress, reflecting the distant parts of the Diaspora they were from.

"The Temple authorities were looking for you to arrest you," said Gabriel, finally breaking his silence. "People were stunned when you still showed up to teach. This brashness stayed the hand of the authorities and allowed you to continue teaching."

Yeshua and Gabriel returned their attention to the scene at hand. The festive atmosphere of the feast was one with rich and poor dwelling away from home together, side by side, in small tents or tabernacles, reliving the ancestral heritage of the wilderness course. As Yeshua entered the courtyard, people made way for him, whispering about him, aware of the controversy surrounding him and voicing divided opinions among themselves. In the background passed the solemn procession of priests, carrying willow branches to pass seven times around the burnt offering of the altar symbolizing the falling of the walls of Jericho. The ritual of the moment was rich in everybody's thoughts. It was the last day of the feast as

– 182 –

Keys to the Kingdom

the chief priest was preparing to pour the holy water drawn from the Pool of Siloam on the altar.

Yeshua then addressed a small gathering, speaking loudly above the din, adding his own special emphasis to the occasion:

> *"If anyone is thirsty, let him come to me and drink. Whoever believes in me, as the Scripture has said, streams of living water will flow from within him."*

> *On hearing his words, some of the people said, "Surely this man is the Prophet."*

> *Others said, "He is the Christ."*

> *Still others asked, "How can the Christ come from Galilee? Does not the Scripture say that the Christ will come from David's family and from Bethlehem, the town where David lived?"*

Murmurings rose to a crescendo from the crowd showing their divided reactions: some were in support and others condemned him. Some even moved to seize him, but others stayed their hand so as no one interfered with him speaking.

> *"Finally the temple guards went back to the chief priests and the Pharisees, who asked them, "Why didn't you bring him in?"*

> *"No one ever spoke the way this man does," the guards declared.*

> *"You mean he has deceived you also?" the Pharisees retorted. "Has any of the rulers or of the Pharisees believed in him? No! But this mob that knows nothing of the law——there is a curse*

– 183 –

Not as I Will, But as You Will

Chapter 8

on them."

Nicodemus, who had gone to Yeshua earlier and who was one of their own number, asked, "Does our law condemn anyone without first hearing him to find out what he is doing?"

They replied, "Are you from Galilee, too? Look into it, and you will find that a prophet does not come out of Galilee."[9]

Yeshua looked sadly at the sight of Nicodemus. Glancing at Gabriel, he said, "He was the only one of the leadership of the Temple or of the Jewish ruling council who sincerely tried to understand me."

The temple scene changed to an earlier time. It was nightfall and Yeshua was alone.

Nicodemus approached him, the open, genuine expression on his face immediately apparent to Yeshua, saying, *"Rabbi, we know you are a teacher who has come from God. For no one could perform the miraculous signs you are doing if God were not with him."*

Yeshua remembered his initial impression of Nicodemus, noticing that the barriers seemed to be lifted with this priest, an unusual situation for one of the Jewish leadership. He had decided to challenge him deeper, more intimately then he normally would do. He declared,

"I tell you the truth, no one can see the kingdom of God unless he is born again."

"How can a man be born when he is old?" Nicodemus asked. "Surely he cannot enter a second time into his mother's womb to be born!"

– 184 –

Keys to the Kingdom

Yeshua answered, "I tell you the truth, no one can enter the kingdom of God unless he is born of water and the Spirit. Flesh gives birth to flesh, but the Spirit gives birth to spirit. You should not be surprised at my saying, 'You must be born again.' The wind blows wherever it pleases. You hear its sound, but you cannot tell where it comes from or where it is going. So it is with everyone born of the Spirit."

"How can this be?" Nicodemus asked.

"You are Israel's teacher," said Yeshua, "and do you not understand these things? I tell you the truth, we speak of what we know, and we testify to what we have seen, but still you people do not accept our testimony. I have spoken to you of earthly things and you do not believe; how then will you believe if I speak of heavenly things?" [10]

Turning away from the scene, looking at the clouds darkening to pale the moon now centered over the Temple mount, Yeshua said, "Nicodemus saved my life during the Feast of Tabernacles, but, alas, he was too concerned about his position and his comfortable orthodoxy to go beyond that moment and follow me."

A new vision appeared of the Temple foreground.

The Scribes and the Pharisees, trying to trap him, had brought a woman caught in adultery. They made her stand before the group Yeshua was teaching and they said to Yeshua,

"Teacher, this woman was caught in the act of adultery. In the Law Moses commanded us to stone such women. Now what do you say?" They

– 185 –

Not as I Will, But as You Will   Chapter 8

*were using this question as a trap, in order to
have a basis for accusing him.*

When they kept on questioning him, Yeshua finally
answered them, saying, *"If any one of you is without sin, let
him be the first to throw a stone at her."*

Those who heard began to go away one at a time, the older
ones first, until only Yeshua was left, with the woman still
standing there. He asked her, *"Woman, where are they? Has no
one condemned you?"*

"No one, sir," she said.

*"Then neither do I condemn you," he declared.
"Go now and leave your life of sin."* [11]

Addressing Gabriel, Yeshua said, "Nicodemus and this
adulterous woman had so much in common! One thought he
was above reproach and the other thought she was hopelessly
lost—but actually both were equal in sin before the Father.
Their sin was not what they did but more what they failed to
do, as with the rest of the people of Israel. Their self-absorp-
tion blocked them from using their lives in a way to glorify
the Father. But from the moment that they had to release this
woman, the Temple leadership, having been soundly embar-
rassed, was determined to stop me."

He returned his attention again to the temple scene.

When Yeshua finally spoke to the people, he said, responding to the atmosphere of the lights around the temple,

*"I am the light of the world. Whoever follows me
will never walk in darkness, but will have the
light of life."*

The Pharisees challenged him, "Here you are,

– 186 –

Keys to the Kingdom

appearing as your own witness; your testimony is not valid."

Yeshua answered, "Even if I testify on my own behalf, my testimony is valid, for I know where I came from and where I am going. But you have no idea where I come from or where I am going. You judge by human standards; I pass judgment on no one. But if I do judge, my decisions are right, because I am not alone. I stand with the Father, who sent me. In your own Law it is written that the testimony of two men is valid. I am one who testifies for myself; my other witness is the Father, who sent me."

Then they asked him, "Where is your father?"

"You do not know me or my Father," Yeshua replied. "If you knew me, you would know my Father also. I am going away, and you will look for me, and you will die in your sin. Where I go, you cannot come."

This made them ask among themselves, "Will he kill himself? Is that why he says, 'Where I go, you cannot come'?"

But he continued, "You are from below; I am from above. You are of this world; I am not of this world. I told you that you would die in your sins; if you do not believe that I am the one I claim to be, you will indeed die in your sins."

"Who are you?" they asked.

"Just what I have been claiming all along," Yeshua replied. "I have much to say in judgment of you.

– 187 –

Not as I Will, But as You Will   Chapter 8

But he who sent me is reliable, and what I have heard from him I tell the world."

But nobody seemed to understand that he was telling them about his and their Father, *Abba Elihenu* (Our Father God).

So Yeshua said, "When you have lifted up the Son of Man, then you will know that I am the one I claim to be and that I do nothing on my own but speak just what the Father has taught me. The one who sent me is with me; he has not left me alone, for I always do what pleases him."

As he spoke, many in the crowd of worshippers nodded their heads, their faces showing their faith in him.[10]

Yeshua continued, "If you hold to my teaching, you are really my disciples. Then you will know the truth, and the truth will set you free."

One answered him, challengingly, "We are Abraham's descendants and have never been slaves of anyone. How can you say that we shall be set free?"

Yeshua replied, "I tell you the truth, everyone who sins is a slave to sin. Now a slave has no permanent place in the family, but a son belongs to it forever. So if the Son sets you free, you will be free indeed. I know you are Abraham's descendants. Yet you are ready to kill me, because you have no room for my word. I am telling you what I have seen in the Father's presence, and you do what you have heard from your father."

"Abraham is our father," they responded.

– 188 –

Keys to the Kingdom

"If you were Abraham's children," said Yeshua, "then you would do the things Abraham did. As it is, you are determined to kill me, a man who has told you the truth that I heard from God. Abraham did not do such things. You are doing the things your own father does."

"We are not illegitimate children," they protested. "The only Father we have is God himself."

Yeshua said to them, "If God were your Father, you would love me, for I came from God and now am here. I have not come on my own; but he sent me. Why is my language not clear to you? Because you are unable to hear what I say. You belong to your father, the devil, and you want to carry out your father's desire. He was a murderer from the beginning, not holding to the truth, for there is no truth in him. When he lies, he speaks his native language, for he is a liar and the father of lies. Yet because I tell the truth, you do not believe me! Can any of you prove me guilty of sin? If I am telling the truth, why don't you believe me? He who belongs to God hears what God says. The reason you do not hear is that you do not belong to God."

Some, listening to this drew back, thoughtfully, but one of the more vocal ones answered him, "Aren't we right in saying that you are a Samaritan and demon-possessed?"

"I am not possessed by a demon," said Yeshua, "but I honor my Father and you dishonor me. I am not seeking glory for myself; but there is one

– 189 –

Not as I Will, But as You Will   Chapter 8

who seeks it, and he is the judge. I tell you the truth, if anyone keeps my word, he will never see death."

At this they exclaimed, "Now we know that you are demon-possessed! Abraham died and so did the prophets, yet you say that if anyone keeps your word, he will never taste death. Are you greater than our father Abraham? He died, and so did the prophets. Who do you think you are?"

Yeshua replied, "If I glorify myself, my glory means nothing. My Father, whom you claim as your God, is the one who glorifies me. Though you do not know him, I know him. If I said I did not, I would be a liar like you, but I do know him and keep his word. Your father Abraham rejoiced at the thought of seeing my day; he saw it and was glad."

"You are not yet fifty years old," the pious ones said to him, "and you have seen Abraham!"

"I tell you the truth," Yeshua answered, "before Abraham was born, I am!" [12]

At this, the more angry ones went to seek stones with which to stone him, but Yeshua quickly left the temple grounds.

Yeshua turned his head away again, protesting, "I have to speak the truth, whether they want to hear it or not! Above all I must speak the truth. Would that some had ears to hear it the way it is meant. I mourn most for those who listened and almost heard, but didn't have the strength to act and follow. I saw it in their eyes that they would have liked to hear more,

– 190 –

Keys to the Kingdom

but the pressure of the angry ones made them pull back."

Gabriel replied, "They are still listening and watching. You have not lost them, they have just not found themselves yet. Whatever path you must go, it will glorify the Father and inspire them. Secretly they admire you for saying such things that no one else would have the courage to say."

The scene changed again. Before them now was the Temple's Solomon's Porch. Yeshua recognized it as around the same time as the previous scene, this past December, during the Festival of the Lights and the Feast of Dedication. Yeshua had entered the Porch, a favorite teaching spot, with a crowd in tow behind him. He had stood by the edge of the porch built into the eastern wall of the Temple, enjoying for a moment the sights and sounds, before he spoke.

The Porch overlooked the Kidron Valley, with the musical tinkle of falling water from the creek, newly replenished by rains, meandering through the valley below, and the gentle rock-strewn slopes of the Mount of Olives rising beyond. The Festival of Lights was, perhaps, Yeshua's favorite of the Temple holidays. It celebrated the miracle of the lights, generations earlier, when with fuel for one day, the lights magically kept burning for eight, as the Temple was rededicated.

It also celebrated the courage of the Maccabees—Maccabee means "the hammer"—in refusing to surrender their faith even unto death. The Maccabees were five brothers who led the Jewish army to defeat the armies of the Seleucid Greek king, Antiochus Epiphanes, against fantastically impossible odds and reestablished the kingdom of Judah. His speech to his followers during that time was often about lights: about being lights themselves unto the world to dispel fear and ignorance as a candle scatters the darkness.

– 191 –

Not as I Will, But as You Will

Chapter 8

The various people, mainly pious Jews, gathered around him, saying, "How long will you keep us in suspense? If you are the Christ, tell us plainly."

Yeshua answered, "I did tell you, but you do not believe. The miracles I do in my Father's name speak for me, but you do not believe because you are not my sheep. My sheep listen to my voice; I know them, and they follow me. I give them eternal life, and they shall never perish; no one can snatch them out of my hand. My Father, who has given them to me, is greater than all; no one can snatch them out of my Father's hand. I and the Father are one."

The pious ones had picked up stones to throw at him, but Yeshua said to them, "I have shown you many great miracles from the Father. For which of these do you stone me?"

"We are not stoning you for any of these," replied the pious ones, "but for blasphemy, because you, a mere man, claim to be God."

Yeshua answered them, "Is it not written in your Law, 'I have said you are gods?'[13] If he called them 'gods,' to whom the word of God came—and the Scripture cannot be broken—what about the one whom the Father set apart as his very own and sent into the world? Why then do you accuse me of blasphemy because I said, 'I am God's Son?' Do not believe me unless I do what my Father does. But if I do it, even though you do not believe me, believe the miracles that you may

– 192 –

Keys to the Kingdom

*know and understand that the Father is in me,
and I in the Father." Again they tried to seize him,
but he escaped their grasp.*[14]

Gabriel then quietly said, "As you say, your sheep know your voice and will not forget. Take heart from that."

Yeshua shook his head in puzzlement. "But those who seemed to respond to me the most were often gentiles, the ones we called 'God-fearers,'" replied Yeshua, his voice betraying both surprise and anguish. "What could that mean? I found myself struggling with the mandate of having to deal only with the Chosen People, when the harvest among these God-fearing gentiles seemed at times more promising."

Following Yeshua's thoughts, a scene opened that he recognized as the ancient well, known as Jacob's Well, on the heavily traveled road through the Samarian hills where he often walked when returning to Galilee from Jerusalem. He and his disciples had stopped there midday to rest from their journey. They had gone into the town nearby for food while he rested by the well.

A Samaritan woman came to draw water. Yeshua said to her, 'Will you give me a drink?'

The Samaritan woman said to him, 'You are a Judean[15] *and I am a Samaritan woman. How can you ask me for a drink?*

Yeshua answered her, "If you knew the gift of God and who it is that asks you for a drink, you would have asked him and he would have given you living water."

"Sir," the woman said, "you have nothing to draw with and the well is deep. Where can you get this

– 193 –

Not as I Will, But as You Will Chapter 8

living water? Are you greater than our father Jacob, who gave us the well and drank from it himself, as did also his sons and his flocks and herds?"

Yeshua answered her, "Everyone who drinks this water will be thirsty again, but whoever drinks the water I give him will never thirst. Indeed the water I give him will become in him a spring of water welling up to eternal life."

The woman said to him, "Sir, give me this water so that I won't get thirsty and have to keep coming here to draw water."

He told her, go, call your husband and come back.

"I have no husband," she replied.

Yeshua said to her, "You are right when you say

Keys to the Kingdom

you have no husband. The fact is you have had five husbands, and the man you now have is not your husband. What you have just said is quite true."

"Sir," the woman said, "I can see that you are a prophet. Our fathers worshiped on this mountain, but you Judeans claim that the place where we must worship is in Jerusalem."

Yeshua declared, "Believe me, woman, a time is coming when you will worship the Father neither on this mountain nor in Jerusalem. You Samaritans worship what you do not know; we worship what we do know, for salvation is from the Jews. Yet a time is coming and has now come when the true worshippers will worship the Father in spirit and truth, for they are the kind of worshippers the Father seeks. God is spirit and his worshippers must worship in spirit and in truth."

The woman said, "I know that Mashiah is coming. When he comes, he will explain everything to us."

Then Yeshua declared, "I who speak to you am he."

Just then his disciples returned and were surprised to find him talking with a woman. But no one asked: what do you want? or why are you talking with her?

Then, leaving the water jar, the woman went back to the town to tell the people about the prophet she met at the well, one who had told her everything

– 195 –

Not as I Will, But as You Will

Chapter 8

she ever did.

His disciples urged him, "Rabbi, eat something."

He replied, "I have food to eat that you know nothing about."

The disciples looked perplexed at one another. "Could someone have brought him food?" they murmured.

"My food," said Yeshua, "is to do the will of him who sent me and to finish his work. Do you not say, four months more and then the harvest? I tell you, open your eyes and look at the fields. They are ripe for harvest, even now he harvests the crop for eternal life so that the sower and the reaper may be glad together. Thus the saying, 'one sows and another reaps' is true. I sent you to reap what you have not worked for. Others have done the hard work, and you have reaped the benefits of their labor." [16]

Yeshua said to Gabriel, "The words I spoke to this woman were the words I longed to speak to my people. My people demanded healings and miracles. What I wanted to give them were words of eternal life, about the heavenly kingdom of love that would be so much more satisfying than the things of this world they were so easily appeased with. She listened and she believed and returned to us with many of her townsfolk. Many of them accepted me and I stayed for days there to minister. I would have stayed with them, rather than go on to further rejection in Judea and Galilee, if it were my choice. But I know that the seeds of the Kingdom of Heaven have been generated in this land. When you have seeds, you can plant them anywhere; but without seeds you have no place to

– 196 –

begin. Now I must spawn this regeneration. Is my blood the fertilizer for this new seed?"

Gabriel hesitated, his expression betrayed an uncertainty heretofore uncharacteristic—he would rather not answer this question. Finally he replied, "It is not for me to say. So much will be lost with the failure of the sons of Nehemiah and Ezra, but the gentiles' time will come, perhaps sooner than expected. All I can say is that whatever your sacrifice, it will not be lost. Your sheep will wear coats of many colors."

They fell silent, contemplating the meaning of these last words to each. To Gabriel, it was a challenge to bring to fruition; to Yeshua, it was a final dictum of his position and responsibility.

Not as I Will, But as You Will

Chapter 9

Three Days, Cleansing and Controversy

Yeshua pressed the back of his hand against his eyes, a dam to the outbreak of despair he would not permit himself to acknowledge, saying, "the seeds of the kingdom need food to grow. But my voice will no longer speak to them. The thought keeps coming back to me that there is so much more to teach them. The thought I cannot stifle is that there is now no more time to teach them the things I want to teach them. What I have left them is so small.

"'The son of man came to seek and save what was lost.'[1] What was lost by our first parents Adam and Eve—their fall from the Father—was an intangible sense of their position, not easily identified, much less reclaimed. This was the purpose of my coming; my responsibility, to give the fallen generations of mankind back that position they lost as children of the father. It's not something regained by certain actions or beliefs. It is an attitude that was lost before it was ever gained by the first parents. This is the attitude of a mature filial child, taking responsibility for what the parent—the Heavenly Father—is concerned with, recognizing how much this parent has loved and sacrificed for you." He paused. "And of course, the preparation..." Then he roused himself again, to exclaim:

"How important was the mission of Elijah, John's mission, to prepare the people with this attitude? The prophet Malachi spoke of Elijah's mission at this time when he said, *'He will turn the hearts of the fathers to their children and the hearts of the children to their fathers or else I will come and strike the land with a curse.'* [2] The family united, centered upon their original Heavenly Father, is the lasting seed of the Kingdom of Heaven! What a wonderful vision for the future of humankind!" Blood spotted his mouth from his chewed lips.

"The forefathers had the mind and vision of the kingdom; the children have the body and opportunity to bring it to pass. Together, the mind and body united, the vision can become reality. Like a bow and arrow, the bow is the parents, pointing the children in the proper direction; the children are the arrow; leaving the parents to speed toward the mark. The parents will never touch the mark; but through the children, they will experience it. This way, the Father's goal of the Kingdom was to be kept alive down through the generations. "He pushed his dampened, long hair back. The emotion was overcoming him, and he didn't want it to. He continued musing.

"And as the generations following Moses in the wilderness embraced the Tabernacle as the embodiment of their anointed one, so today's generation should also treasure the Temple as the glorified ideal of him. Today my people think that the

Three Days, Cleansing and Controversy

Law is the point of worship, where it is meant to witness to the man who is the epitome of that Law. They confuse their needs; the messiah is not a judge, he is a parent. This is the message that has been lost."

Yeshua stood up suddenly, wearily, and threw up his arms, as if throwing off the emptiness left by the death of a great hope. He moaned loudly, "Adonai, Adonai! What a great plan you had! Eyes have not seen nor ears heard what Your heart has prepared for those who can respond to Your love! But now, how do we avoid the curse?" Yeshua fell silent again, his head bowed, pacing erratically. Finally, falling again to his knees on the grassy mound now soaked with his tears, he spoke with a muted, subdued passion, picking up where he had left off.

At the same time, he became mindful once again of Gabriel's lingering, earnest presence. He could not define the nature of the way Gabriel looked at him, except it was the look, as always, of extreme attentiveness. He perceived that Gabriel's interest was more than just providing a sympathetic ear. To what ends, he knew not; but he felt it was important that these words be said—words he had as yet been unable to speak to another human being—words that, until now, he could share only with the Father. He turned, as if addressing the words to Gabriel, even though he did not look at him. He began quietly, as if building his case in his mind.

"If the children feel the love and gratitude of loving parents, the children can never do anything to hurt them or separate from them. Isn't that an exemplar of universal, unconditional love? To some extent, even fallen families behave this way. Adam and Eve, the first parents, should have perceived that their loving parent invested His whole energy and zeal to create the beautiful garden of creation for His children, giv-

– 201 –

Not as I Will, But as You Will   Chapter 9

ing everything for them and longing for their grateful response. If they had had such an attitude of mature love, those first parents could never have fallen, they never would have separated from the Father." He paused; the next words became more urgent.

"If human children can have such a feeling toward their physical parents here on earth, shouldn't this at least have been expected of humankind toward their original Heavenly Parent who gave absolutely, unconditionally everything to His children of the earth, seeking only responsive love and gratitude in return? I am the first-begotten son of that original nature, which makes me become the mediator to bring the other siblings back, teaching them the attitude they need to have to resolve the pain and resentment of the parents, reestablishing those children's position in the family." He realized he was reaching the heart of his great argument. It had to be right!

"Yet how to help them identify that responsible attitude? This was what I was trying to transmit through all my teachings. It's not actions but an attitude, a willingness to do or be anything, putting the Father's desire, your neighbor's needs— your siblings—above your own in all circumstances. I could not say these actions would lead to the Kingdom of Heaven, because actions are not enough. First—first—I sought to teach the *attitude* of faithful children! That is the cornerstone of perfect faith and love! I knew that, Gabriel! I knew it better than anyone because I was the first-begotten son of the Father, and I shared His heart! I was the one He was counting on!" He paused again.

"I was teaching this new attitude of heart by symbol and parable, the difference between a servant's attitude and a loving child's attitude, but the people could not transcend their literal old way of thinking. The tragedy is that I never really

– 202 –

Three Days, Cleansing and Controversy

reached the point to teach right actions. For all my excellent intentions, I failed them. And now, I will not be here to be the example of life of faith for them to follow."

Gabriel responded quietly, "I am only a servant, so I can never give the children more than a loyal servant's heart. This we, the ministering spirits, have sought to do throughout the ages. But now is your time, the son who is with the Father to teach this attitude to the prodigal and scattered children who have grown up as orphans. They must love the Father with a different quality of love then we possess."

Yeshua concurred sorrowfully. "Yes, that was the plan. With such love they will be spurred to take responsive action, to take ownership of the task of expanding the Father's Kingdom—the Father's kingship and reign of heart over the Earth. That will be the Kingdom of Heaven on the Earth, when all the children are united with one another as brothers and sisters of the Heavenly Parent. Alas, I fear, what I have left behind is not enough for such love to be transmitted—for the Kingdom to be established without me!" Yeshua slowly rose from the ground. He now faced the listening Gabriel.

"The Chosen People still think that it is through miraculous actions that the Father will manifest Himself, like the manna falling from heaven to their fathers in the wilderness, to feed them. But such signs are for those whose hearts cannot be touched with love, inspired to action and protection, as a family should be able to do among themselves. I told them, 'The bread of God is he who comes down from heaven and gives life to the world.' [3] I am that bread. But they could not understand what I meant." Gabriel nodded and said nothing. It was Yeshua's job to speak of this great mission.

"By eating me, drinking my blood, figuratively—becoming

me in thought, word and deed—they would regain the heart of the child to the Heavenly Father that would bring them into eternal loving relationship with Him—eternal life. Of course, my words were not enough, I knew. I must transmit a spiritual element to them as well as words, to elevate their spirits to higher understandings—a change of blood lineage that will change them from the lineage of the Adversary to that of the Father."

He tried to frame the next thought in the most neutral way that he could, for without his bidding it, the thought of Miriam fleetingly crossed his mind. Miriam! Slowly he began, "For this my bride, as Holy Spirit, and I, would be the parents for their rebirth. The only person I could even begin to share this content with was the Pharisee Nicodemus. But, alas, he was not ready to receive it. How can they understand heavenly things when they cannot yet understand earthly things? I knew that, of course. So all I asked was for them to just believe in me until they could understand. It wasn't enough." He lowered his head.

Gabriel spoke. "Do not chastise yourself so, Yeshua! You have done all that is possible to do. If they are not ready to receive or to believe, then, sadly, they must taste the orphaned life even more, in order to appreciate what it was you offered them."

Yeshua paused at that thought, then said, "I don't believe that they, the simple people of faith, have rejected me. I spoke of this to you before. I have never given up that hope throughout the months since John's death. It is that hope that grasps at my heart now, to not let those down who could believe even now. When I entered Jerusalem this last time, I was struck by the reality of my death fast approaching, and how far from my goal of establishing the restored tribes I was.

– 204 –

Three Days, Cleansing and Controversy

"Coming over the crest of the Mount of Olives from Bethpage, I was overwhelmed with the beauty of the panorama of the city. The Temple walls and columns, radiant with the setting sun, project a glow that seemed like another light source itself—the radiance of the blessings of God wrought by the sacrifice of holy men of ages past. How can I let this be lost, destroyed, if there is anything possible I can do to save it?" He gestured with his right arm and hand.

"This is the same mount that the Prophet Zechariah identified as the place that the feet of the Lord would first touch the earth, as judgment was brought to Jerusalem. I was overwhelmed with the sense of the tragic love affair that had existed between the Father and this city and its people—His pain at its betrayal, and fear of what will now have to become of it." [4]

As if bid by silent spirits, a vision opened before Yeshua of his arrival at the Temple mount. As Yeshua described it, he saw himself collapsing to the earth weeping in prayer, with the vista before him of the holy city Jerusalem. Tears gushed from his eyes as Yeshua, hearing his words spoken that day in prayer, was struck again with the unbearably sad presence of that moment.

> *"If you, even you, had only known on this day what would bring you peace—but now it is hidden from your eyes. The days will come upon you when your enemies will build an embankment against you and encircle you and hem you in on every side. They will dash you to the ground, you and the children within your walls. They will not leave one stone on another, because you did not recognize the time of God's coming to you."* [5]

Not as I Will, But as You Will   Chapter 9

Yeshua shuddered. "It has been my desperation, from that moment, to use what time I have left in the best way possible. But I am overwhelmed by my smallness for the immensity of the task. Why couldn't I have been more charismatic—like John? Maybe that was what was needed to break through to the people. What more could I have done?" he said in a grieved hush, the tears soaking his clothes like rain.

Breathing deeply to regain his composure, he continued in the same hushed tone, "Since arriving in Jerusalem, It has been my all-consuming goal to capture the heart of the simple faithful, through teaching and example; to inspire the disciples to stand up and move beyond the failed leadership and take responsibility for the Kingdom's establishment in Israel. Even if I am not here to guide them, they can take that responsibility upon themselves. Too much is at stake—the Father's entire historical preparation of over four thousand years—for our nation to fail."

Gabriel nodded, saying compassionately, "The memories of these days will live in people's hearts; it will not be lost. All Jerusalem knew about you from these past three days. If you are to die, the one thing that cannot be expunged is the people's memory of you. Memories will live in them of moments like your cleansing the Temple of those who were buying and selling offerings; and challenging the religious leadership in front of the Passover crowds."

As he spoke, the vision opened up, this time of Yeshua in the Temple. Before him were the tables of the moneychangers and the benches of those selling doves and grain to the Temple visitors for offerings.

Yeshua had charged into the bustling fray of merchants and Temple visitors carrying their purchases of offerings,

– 206 –

Three Days, Cleansing and Controversy

overturning the tables of the merchants. All had retreated before this wild-eyed apparition, reminiscent of a latter-day Elijah on the mountain, challenging the prophets of Baal.

> *"Is it not written," said Yeshua, "'My house will be called a house of prayer for all nations,'[6] but you have made it 'a den of robbers.'"[7,8]*

Gabriel continued, "The chief priests and the teachers of the Law heard this and began looking for a way to kill you, for they feared you, because the whole crowd was drawn to you, amazed at your teaching."

His tone still hushed and emotionally charged, Yeshua said, "Yes, I knew this time, the priests would have to act. I had to expose them once and for all as the hypocrites they have become, empty of godliness in their actions, filled to the brim with self-motivated appetites. This was especially important for the sake of the disciples, to inflame their passion for right-eousness. They are too passive to deal with the times of tribu-lations to come if I have to die."

"Your public ministry in the Temple bespoke eloquently that heart," said Gabriel, gesturing to a vision of two days ear-lier, Yeshua at the Temple, confronted by the chief priests, scribes and elders as he was walking in the Temple courts.

> *"By what authority are you doing these things?" the spokesman asked. "And who gave you authority to do this?"*
>
> *Yeshua replied calmly, smiling, "I will ask you one question. Answer me, and I will tell you by what authority I am doing these things. John's baptism—was it from heaven, or from men? Tell me, if you want my answer!"*

– 207 –

Not as I Will, But as You Will   Chapter 9

The group backed away and in whispers discussed among themselves. One saying, "If we say, 'from heaven,' he will ask, 'then why didn't you believe him?' But if we say, 'From men'..." Yes, interrupted another, if we say from men, we are in trouble. The people loved John, for everyone held that John really was a prophet. They returned to Yeshua and answered, "We don't know."

Yeshua said, "Neither will I tell you by what authority I am doing these things."[9]

A murmur then arose, and the priests looked around to see a crowd had gathered, listening to their exchange. Yeshua continued speaking loudly so the crowd could hear.

"What do you think? There was a man who had two sons. He went to the first and said, 'Son, go and work today in the vineyard.' 'I will not,' he answered, but later he changed his mind and went.

"Then the father went to the other son and said the same thing. He answered, 'I will, sir,' but he did not go.

"Which of the two did what his father wanted?"

"The first," they answered.

Yeshua said to them, "I tell you the truth, the tax collectors and the prostitutes are entering the kingdom of God ahead of you. For John came to you to show you the way of righteousness, and you did not believe him, but the tax collectors and the prostitutes did. And even after you saw this, you did not repent and believe him."[10]

– 208 –

Three Days, Cleansing and Controversy

A few stories later, noting their discomfort with the message, Yeshua said, "Listen to another parable." He spoke another parable aimed at the priests and Pharisees, saying:

*The kingdom of heaven is like a king who
prepared a wedding banquet for his son. He
sent his servants to those who had been invited to
the banquet to tell them to come, but they refused
to come. Then he sent some more servants and
said, "tell those who have been invited that I have
prepared my dinner: My oxen and fattened cattle
have been butchered, and everything is ready.
Come to the wedding banquet."*

*But they paid no attention and went off——one to
his field, another to his business. The rest seized
his servants, mistreated them and killed them. The
king was enraged. He sent his army and destroyed
those murderers and burned their city.*

*Then he said to his servants, "The wedding
banquet is ready, but those I invited did not
deserve to come. Go to the street corners and
invite to the banquet anyone you find."*

*So the servants went out into the streets and
gathered all the people they could find both good
and bad, and the wedding hall was filled with
guests. But when the king came in to see the
guests, he noticed a man there who was not
wearing wedding clothes.*

*"Friend," he asked, "how did you get in here
without wedding clothes?" The man was speechless.
Then the king told the attendants, "Tie him hand
and foot, and throw him outside, into the*

– 209 –

Not as I Will, But as You Will

Chapter 9

darkness, where there will be weeping and gnashing of teeth." For many are invited, but few are chosen.[11]

When the priests and the temple leadership heard Yeshua's parables, their expressions said it all: they knew he was talking about them. They looked around in fear and confusion at the rapt attention of the crowd as Yeshua continued speaking. Grasping the damning inference delivered them by Yeshua's parables, they whispered among themselves as they were leaving of plans to trap him in his own words.

As Yeshua continued to speak, some of their disciples returned to him along with the men Yeshua had recognized as being from Herod's government.

"Teacher," one spokesman said, "we know you are a man of integrity and that you teach the way of God in accordance with the truth. You aren't swayed by men, because you pay no attention to who they are. Tell us then, what is your opinion? Is it right to pay taxes to Caesar or not?"

Yeshua, knowing their evil intent, said, "You hypocrites, why are you trying to trap me? Show me the coin used for paying the tax." They brought him a denarius.

He asked them, "Whose portrait is this? And whose inscription?"

"Caesar's," they replied.

Then he said to them, "Give to Caesar what is Caesar's, and to God what is God's."[12]

Another Pharisee whom Yeshua knew as expert in the Law,

– 210 –

Three Days, Cleansing and Controversy

tested him with this question: "Teacher, which is the greatest commandment in the Law?" Yeshua replied:

> "'Love the Lord your God with all your heart and with all your soul and with all your mind.' This is the first and greatest commandment. And the second is like it: 'Love your neighbor as yourself.' All the Law and the Prophets hang on these two commandments."

> While the Pharisees were there, Yeshua asked them, "What do you think about the Christ?[13] Whose son is he?"

> "The son of David," they replied.

> He said to them, "How is it then that David, speaking by the Spirit, calls him 'Lord'? For he says, 'The Lord said to my lord 'Sit at my right hand until I put your enemies under your feet.' If then David calls him 'Lord,' how can he be his son?"[14, 15]

The priests and Pharisees were confounded. They asked no more questions.

Turning from them to the crowds and to his disciples, Yeshua said:

> "The teachers of the law and the Pharisees sit in Moses' seat. So you must obey them and do everything they tell you. But do not do what they do, for they do not practice what they preach. They tie up heavy loads and put them on men's shoulders, but they themselves are not willing to lift a finger to move them.

Not as I Will, But as You Will

Chapter 9

"Everything they do is done for men to see: They make their phylacteries wide and the tassels on their garments long; they love the place of honor at banquets and the most important seats in the synagogues; they love to be greeted in the marketplaces and to have men call them 'Rabbi.' But you are not to be called 'Rabbi,' for you have only one Master and you are all brothers.

"And do not call anyone on earth 'father,' for you have one Father, and he is in heaven. Nor are you to be called 'teacher,' for you have one Teacher, the Christ. The greatest among you will be your servant. For whoever exalts himself will be humbled, and whoever humbles himself will be exalted.

"Woe to you, teachers of the law and Pharisees, you hypocrites! You shut the kingdom of heaven in men's faces. You yourselves do not enter, nor will you let those enter who are trying to.

"Woe to you, teachers of the law and Pharisees, you hypocrites! You travel over land and sea to win a single convert, and when he becomes one, you make him twice as much a son of hell as you are.

"Woe to you, teachers of the law and Pharisees, you hypocrites! You devour widows' houses and for a show make lengthy prayers. Therefore you will be punished more severely.

"Woe to you, blind guides! You say, 'If anyone swears by the temple, it means nothing; but if anyone swears by the gold of the temple, he is

– 212 –

Three Days, Cleansing and Controversy

bound by his oath.' You blind fools! Which is greater: the gold, or the temple that makes the gold sacred? You also say, 'If anyone swears by the altar, it means nothing; but if anyone swears by the gift on it, he is bound by his oath.' You blind men! Which is greater: the gift, or the altar that makes the gift sacred? Therefore, he who swears by the altar swears by it and by everything on it. And he who swears by the temple swears by it and by the one who dwells in it. And he who swears by heaven swears by God's throne and by the one who sits on it.

"Woe to you, teachers of the law and Pharisees, you hypocrites! You give a tenth of your spices— mint, dill and cumin. But you have neglected the more important matters of the law—justice, mercy and faithfulness. You should have practiced the latter, without neglecting the former. You blind guides! You strain out a gnat but swallow a camel.

"Woe to you, teachers of the law and Pharisees, you hypocrites! You clean the outside of the cup and dish, but inside they are full of greed and self-indulgence. Blind Pharisees! First clean the inside of the cup and dish, and then the outside also will be clean.

"Woe to you, teachers of the law and Pharisees, you hypocrites! You are like whitewashed tombs, which look beautiful on the outside but on the inside are full of dead men's bones and everything unclean. In the same way, on the outside you appear to people as righteous but on the inside you

– 213 –

Not as I Will, But as You Will
Chapter 9

are full of hypocrisy and wickedness.

"Woe to you, teachers of the law and Pharisees, you hypocrites! You build tombs for the prophets and decorate the graves of the righteous. And you say, 'If we had lived in the days of our forefathers, we would not have taken part with them in shedding the blood of the prophets.' So you testify against yourselves that you are the descendants of those who murdered the prophets. Fill up, then, the measure of the sin of your forefathers!

"You snakes! You brood of vipers! How will you escape being condemned to hell? Therefore I am sending you prophets and wise men and teachers. Some of them you will kill and crucify; others you will flog in your synagogues and pursue from town to town. And so upon you will come all the righteous blood that has been shed on earth, from the blood of righteous Abel to the blood of Zechariah son of Berekiah, whom you murdered between the temple and the altar. I tell you the truth; all this will come upon this generation.

"O Jerusalem, Jerusalem, you who kill the prophets and stone those sent to you, how often I have longed to gather your children together, as a hen gathers her chicks under her wings, but you were not willing. Look, your house is left to you desolate. For I tell you, you will not see me again until you say, 'Blessed is he who comes in the name of the Lord.'" [16]

"After we left the temple," Yeshua said, reflectively, gazing

– 214 –

Three Days, Cleansing and Controversy

fixedly at the gathering at the temple, "my disciples called my attention to the buildings—to the buildings!" He threw up his arms exasperatedly. "As if they had any significance in the coming trials that were about to descend! I wondered if they had heard anything I had just said. In their obtuse comments, I knew that they really didn't understand what had just transpired between the priests and I. That right now these men plotted my death. They understood nothing of what this dialogue that I had just had with the temple leadership portended for the future—mine, theirs, the nation of Israel, and the world.

"'Do you see all these things?' I asked. 'I tell you the truth, not one stone here will be left on another; every one will be thrown down.' Their blank expressions told me that indeed they did not understand nor believe that this was possible."

Gabriel said, "They may only understand through experience of trial. You cannot protect or cushion them from their fate." He waved his hand to manifest the scene of the gathering that Yeshua had with the disciples on the hillside of the Mount of Olives, after they left the temple.

"Teacher," one of the disciples asked, "When will these things that you speak of, the end of days, happen?" Yeshua responded:

> "When you hear of wars and revolutions, do not be frightened. These things must happen first, but the end will not come right away." Then he said to them: "Nation will rise against nation, and kingdom against kingdom. There will be great earthquakes, famines and pestilences in various places, and fearful events and great signs from heaven.

– 215 –

Not as I Will, But as You Will   Chapter 9

"But before all this, they will lay hands on you and persecute you. They will deliver you to synagogues and prisons, and you will be brought before kings and governors, and all on account of my name. This will result in your being witnesses to them.

"But make up your mind not to worry beforehand how you will defend yourselves. For I will give you words and wisdom that none of your adversaries will be able to resist or contradict. You will be betrayed even by parents, brothers, relatives and friends, and they will put some of you to death. All men will hate you because of me. But not a hair of your head will perish. By standing firm you will gain life.[17]

"When you see Jerusalem being surrounded by armies, you will know that its desolation is near. Then let those who are in Judea flee to the mountains, let those in the city get out, and let those in the country not enter the city. For this is the time of punishment in fulfillment of all that has been written.

"How dreadful it will be in those days for pregnant women and nursing mothers! There will be great distress in the land and wrath against this people. They will fall by the sword and will be taken as prisoners to all the nations. Jerusalem will be trampled on by the Gentiles until the times of the Gentiles are fulfilled.

"There will be signs in the sun, moon and stars. On the earth, nations will be in anguish and

– 216 –

Three Days, Cleansing and Controversy

perplexity at the roaring and tossing of the sea.
Men will faint from terror, apprehensive of what
is coming on the world, for the heavenly bodies
will be shaken. At that time they will see the Son
of Man coming in a cloud with power and great
glory. When these things begin to take place, stand
up and lift up your heads, because your redemption
is drawing near."

He told them this parable: "Look at the fig tree
and all the trees. When they sprout leaves, you can
see for yourselves and know that summer is near.
Even so, when you see these things happening, you
know that the kingdom of God is near." [18]

Ignoring the shocked expression on the faces of many of
the gathering, he continued his prophecy of the coming end
times.

"I tell you the truth; this generation will certainly
not pass away until all these things have happened.
Heaven and earth will pass away, but my words
will never pass away. Be careful, or your
hearts will be weighed down with dissipation,
drunkenness and the anxieties of life, and that
day will close on you unexpectedly like a trap.
For it will come upon all those who live on the
face of the whole earth. Be always on the watch,
and pray that you may be able to escape all that
is about to happen, and that you may be able to
stand before the Son of Man." [19]

Yeshua turned back to Gabriel, his voice rushed and
urgent. "They just don't understand what is going to happen
to them now, because of their action! The Father cannot let

– 217 –

Not as I Will, But as You Will   Chapter 9

the temple or the nation stand! They will have defiled His law, detested and persecuted His prophets, and destroyed His one true son, the restored Adam from which a new lineage was to have been born to Him! This providence that culminated in me was to be the hope of the world!

"My offspring, my family line, descended by blood from King David, was to be a new kingly line directly connected to the Father, to which all of the rest of mankind could have engrafted and received a new blood lineage. This would be a lineage pure and undefiled by the Original Sin of the fall of man. For this assault on the Kingdom of God, the Chosen People will be decimated for who knows how long—maybe hundreds, maybe thousands of years! The world will suffer much war and destruction for its rejection today of the Prince of Peace, until conditions can come again such as we have today for the end times, for the final fulfillment of the Father's Kingdom. That will be the price to the people of my death. Why can't they see that?"

"Because they can't," said Gabriel as he gazed at Yeshua, his body trembling, overcome with emotion. Yeshua's pain was visible in the streaks on his face and clothing of blood mixed with sweat and tears. He was weeping convulsively, uncontrollably. Barely audible, the emotion stifling his voice, he whispered, "The simple innocent people will bear such a terrible fate for generations from this point on, for the sins of the few, and I can do nothing!"

Gabriel waited. He could do nothing but let the wave of pain wash over Yeshua, wait for the surge of emotion to recede—Yeshua's final realization that his hope was demolished, that he could somehow prepare these innocents to go through that tribulation with faith and perseverance to be blessed in the end. He was indeed the Father's true son, whose

– 218 –

Three Days, Cleansing and Controversy

tortuous agony was the Father's pain manifest for the lost and suffering children, Gabriel reflected.

Yeshua whispered, "Satan knows the Chosen People have failed. And as with Job, asks for their punishment. The Father's *Mizpah* (justice) is absolute, but he seeks a route for *Chesed* (forgiveness or mercy). He can only give forgiveness if there is intercession by one undefiled by the sin, supplicating to take the punishment in their stead."

Gabriel was taken aback. Suddenly seeing Yeshua's fate before him, he found himself strangely unable to embrace that which until now he had been advancing. "But, Yeshua," he exclaimed, "Wait! Didn't our God Almighty also ask that of Abraham, the founder of the nation? And wasn't Isaac also willing to do as our God asked? And didn't our God ultimately refuse that sacrifice because our God wanted no one to sacrifice their children to Him, as did those who burned their sons in the fires of Gehenna to bloodthirsty idols? Contrition, asking for forgiveness, perhaps, in the end, that is the only sacrifice demanded!"

Yeshua looked intently at Gabriel. "But if I am the true son of the true Father God, my Father is in me, and I am in Him, then isn't it my choice to make this sacrifice should it be necessary? Wouldn't a loving Father die for His son? And wouldn't a loving son also die for a loving Father?"

Gabriel shook his head, the dichotomy of his true desire for Yeshua's welfare now coming to the forefront. "Of course it is not that the Father requires this of you after He has forbidden it to His very own people! Satan is expecting some sacrifice to stay his hand. I only bring this up to suggest that perhaps, as at the time of Isaac, there can be found some 'lamb in the bush' to replace your sacrificing your life."

Not as I Will, But as You Will   Chapter 9

Yeshua replied quietly, "Gabriel, it is my choice. I choose to be the lamb. If my suffering now saves suffering in the times to come, wouldn't it be better so? Too many would have to die to be such a lamb, and who knows if it would be enough to hold back the bloodthirsty hand of Satan? Unfortunately, Satan has a freedom to act due to man's failure. The Father can't interfere there."

Gabriel said grimly, "Truly, Isaiah the prophet was describing you when he said:

> *"He was despised and rejected by men, a man of*
> *sorrows, and familiar with suffering. Like one*
> *from whom men hide their faces he was despised,*
> *and we esteemed him not. Surely he took up*
> *our infirmities and carried our sorrows, yet*
> *we considered him stricken by God, smitten by*
> *him, and afflicted. But he was pierced for our*
> *transgressions, he was crushed for our iniquities;*
> *the punishment that brought us peace was upon*
> *him, and by his wounds we are healed."* [20]

Yeshua nodded, deep in contemplation. A look of serenity had begun to take hold, the serenity of a victory over pain. "My sacrifice is nothing when I think of the alternative. I too will see my day of victory, when I will drink again of the fruit of the vine on that day in the kingdom of God.[21] My agony is that it will be later rather than sooner—much, much later with so much suffering in the intervening time. As I must undergo a course of sacrifice and suffering, so must my followers. How long will that last, how much suffering will it take? Alas, *that* is the question!"

His thought of the week before, his arrival in Jerusalem, when he had set out to see, as if for one last time, all that had

– 220 –

Three Days, Cleansing and Controversy

touched his life to this point. He knew the temple priests were looking for him, since forty days earlier when the authorities had put out a bulletin for his capture. He stayed with friends who he knew would protect him in Ephraim.[22] And then before setting out for Jerusalem, in a last preparation for the end, he went to visit Miriam.

Not as I Will, But as You Will

Chapter 10

Miriam, the Last Visit

"Miriam, Miriam," he breathed the words through deep sighs. Another thought intrusively compelled itself into his mind, almost beyond his will to stifle. It was a private thought that he was loath to speak out loud, even though he knew Gabriel could perceive his thoughts. This moment with Miriam was too private to share. Gabriel honored this personal memory and stayed in the background.

He had ventured out alone early that morning. He allowed himself this one time to visit Miriam, because he had a message to deliver to her. The path took him over the mount and down to the little hamlet on the road to Jericho where Miriam lived as part of the outer Essene community. For years now, Miriam was almost always in his thoughts, but never would he allow words concerning her to pass his lips. She was in his heart even though he could never see her and touch her. In his

Not as I Will, But as You Will

Chapter 10

mind, she was to be protected from humiliation and abandonment in the event of his death. Therefore his determination had been that until his future success was secure, he would not allow himself to see her. She must be free to make a new life with someone else, if he could not live to be her husband.

But until now, always in the forefront of his mind had been the indomitable hope that he was protecting her for the day when he could make her his wife. The two would become one, and then no man could ever separate them. And as God had promised his forefather David, they would see their children, grandchildren, and descendants number forever. King David had looked to this future descendant as the hope for the salvation of his people, spawning an eternal kingdom. The Heavenly Father's words to David came to mind.

> *"When your days are over and you rest with your fathers, I will raise up your offspring to succeed you, who will come from your own body, and I will establish his kingdom. He is the one who will build a house for my name, and I will establish the throne of his kingdom forever. I will be his father, and he will be my son. When he does wrong, I will punish him with the rod of men, with floggings inflicted by men. But my love will never be taken away from him, as I took it away from Saul, whom I removed from before you.*
> *Your house and your kingdom will endure forever before me; your throne will be established forever."* [1]

Yeshua thought of that bittersweet journey of several hours in the soft dewy morning ten days ago. Once again— maybe for the last time—he had savored the spectacular panoramic view: the horizon and the glowing dawn that met over the Judean wilderness as he walked down the incline of

– 224 –

Miriam, the Last Visit

the Roman-made road that traversed the rocky hills for the day's journey from Ephraim to Jericho. The landscape was like a metaphor for a religious life: the intense red of the cliffs reflecting the dawn's light was like the color of blood, the hills alive with color, in contrast to the bleak and colorlessness of the desert plains stretching beyond them—life and death in comparison.

At first observation one was struck by the emptiness, the barrenness and the lack of color, seeing just the shades of brown in the gentle rises and dips in the landscape. Deep wadis slashed through the landscape on either side of the road as he descended toward Jericho. Color was only visible in the most surprising places when it was searched out, or unexpectedly and delightfully come across, such as the pink and white spring clusters of wildflowers, sparingly scattered among the sparse grasses of the rocky plateaus. This was the wilderness landscape that had been so much a part of his religious experience and discovery of himself and his mission with the Father.

Passing through the old city of Jericho, Yeshua saw the hill beside the road under which was buried the fort that Joshua brought down through prayer. At the southern edge of the city was the spring that was noxious and undrinkable but restored to fresh water by the prophet Elisha when he sprinkled salt on it. South of the hills out of which the spring emerged and a garden in the desert suddenly appeared was the transcending view of the barren wilderness of Judah.

In Yeshua's mind, a cavalcade of the history of the past two thousand years that took place along this narrow strip of land ran. From young Joshua and Caleb's crossing the river with the remnant of the refugees Moses brought from Egypt; to the judges establishing the first rule of law and court system in the history of humankind; to the kings' rule, which expanded the tiny strip of land into the greatest world power of its era by the time of King Solomon. Already the Chosen People had impacted the history of the human race substantially, though this was nothing compared to what they were being prepared to do. But it was a destiny that was now in grave doubt, Yeshua's troubled thoughts had begun to conclude.

The Essene village was located slightly off the main thoroughfare of the busy crossroads center of Jericho, just beyond the main part of the city, on the way to Bethabara. This was an anonymous trip. He did not look to meet anybody he knew except Miriam. The next morning, familiar as he was with the typical morning schedules of young maidens, he went to the community well, knowing that at some time during the morning she would probably come here. In the early morning women already congregated, veiled and unveiled, chatting, laughing, drawing the water for the day and returning with their large urns full. Nobody seemed to take note of the nondescript-looking stranger resting in the shade from his journey. Many strangers did likewise here, as this was one of the few sources of water in close proximity to the Dead Sea valley ahead.

Following his thoughts, the scene appeared before Yeshua. Miriam came to the well and immediately noticed Yeshua sitting apart from the well, alone. She was dressed as he remembered, with the same blue headdress and veil. As before, it was only her deep, open, sensitive eyes that set her apart from the other young women at the well. Their eyes met, and Miriam acknowledged his gaze. Her own glance was a mixture of joy and alarm, unsure if this most unusual meeting spelled good or bad news.

Once again her thoughts became perceptible to Yeshua.

– 226 –

Miriam, the Last Visit

She had not seen Yeshua for many months, since before John had died. A few times she had tried visiting Yeshua when he was teaching in the area, but he would not acknowledge her. She had come to realize their relationship must remain strictly between them, until he was ready to move it further into the public. So those visits ceased. She knew it was his way of protecting her, and she accepted it, even though she longed to meet him: to touch, to talk, to revive that connection from those last moments they had shared.

He arose and retreated to a secluded grassy slope hidden from view of the well. Within a brief space of time Miriam joined him there. She cautiously lowered her veil, looking around to make sure they were alone and not followed.

Yeshua's eyes were steady, open, too honest and guileless to hold any response back. Both were held by the moment between them now, unable to move forward or retreat. They were captive to the emotion—the unconscious interplay of the intense sensual communication happening between them. In the space of that moment of silent expectation between them, Yeshua meditated on the underlying cause and process happening between them. It was the same emotions that had brought together man and woman as husband and wife since the dawn of history, overcoming seeming incompatible natures.

It was the kind of kinetic spark that God had built into human bodies to bond them together initially. That priming ember tapped the latent energy of the love relationship, of which the Father's energy could be a part and multiply in relationship to their shared investment. This, until at a later point, when the longer term bonding took place based on mutual respect and gratitude—gratitude for what they had received from one another as the challenges of life were faced

Not as I Will, But as You Will

Chapter 10

as husband and wife and parents, which was the foundation of mature eternal marital love. "What God has put together, let no man separate." What a beautiful plan the Father had for us! he thought. Would that it could happen to me, he had mused so often these past few years. But that steady inexorable drumbeat of desire in recent days had become a tightly controlled, patiently borne torture.

Miriam blurted out, "I longed to talk to you, to see you even for a moment."

"I know," he responded, almost on top of her words in the same hushed, explosively emotional tone as hers.

His stance, his legs grew weak, as he realized the implications of this shared emotion—a meeting more intimate than any physical touch, an action he had explicitly avoided. He lowered himself to sit on the grass, and she followed. But he motioned for her to stay at a distance.

Miriam then exclaimed, "I'm so worried about you. Your life is in danger. Don't you know the temple authorities are searching you out? They want to kill you; you are too dangerous to their authority."

Yeshua nodded, but with an unconcerned shrug.

Miriam continued, "I was going to search you out and speak to you, no matter what it would mean for me. You know I have waited for you, and will wait as long as you want. But I can't stay home any longer. I must help you."

Yeshua shook his head strongly and held his palm up to her to stop her. "You cannot join me. Where I am going, you cannot go; you cannot be with me. I told you that my life might have to be sacrificed for this mission. Such has now come to pass."

– 228 –

Miriam, the Last Visit

Miriam interrupted, rising slightly, "Rabboni, you can't. Your life is too precious—"

Yeshua cut off her words, and said sharply, "No! You must listen! There is no choice!" He settled back on the grass and motioned for her to do the same. "I am first a warrior for the Kingdom of God, bringing about the Father's reign over His children and this world. Understand that this is a spiritual war between God the Father and Satan for the souls of the world. The children give Satan power over them because they listen to his temptations. The human race is like a child tempted by a seducer who means them harm but offers them sweet things that they like if they will follow him away. They listen to his temptations and leave their home and their loving parent, the Heavenly Father, to follow him. I must bring them back; that is the task I was born for."

Miriam paused, her eyes glazed with tears; she fell back, limply and listened.

Yeshua continued, "This is a spiritual war between God and Satan for the souls of the children. The battle has now come to a head. Satan says to the Father, 'See they have chosen me, they do not belong to you. They even have rejected your son.' I came on behalf of the Father to reclaim those children, my siblings. But what will the Father do if I am rejected, as well?"

Miriam shook her head, a confused, troubled expression on her face.

Struggling to give her clarity, Yeshua fell back on his stories, saying, "listen to a parable:

> *"There was a landowner who planted a vineyard.*
> *He put a wall around it, dug a winepress in it*

Not as I Will, But as You Will   Chapter 10

> *and built a watchtower. Then he rented the vineyard to some farmers and went away on a journey. When the harvest time approached, he sent his servants to the tenants to collect his fruit. The tenants seized his servants; they beat one, killed another, and stoned a third. Then he sent other servants to them, more than the first time, and the tenants treated them the same way.*
>
> *"Last of all, he sent his son to them. 'They will respect my son,' he said. But when the tenants saw the son, they said to each other, 'This is the heir. Come, let's kill him and take his inheritance.' So they took him and threw him out of the vineyard and killed him."* [2]

"The vineyard is the world, the landowner is God," said Yeshua, "the tenants are the Chosen People, I am the son. What should God do to those tenants? Shouldn't he kill them? That is what Satan wants! That will give him glee, to see the Father having to abandon His children, completely, to their deserved fate. My rejection by our people means Satan can have a right to them, and the Father can say nothing."

Miriam sighed, shaking her head, "But you are only one person, Rabboni, what can you do against the world—why you?"

Yeshua looked at her gently, easing her confusion with his calmness, "There is no one else who understands the Father. I am the only son who sees His pain, so I must be the one to resolve it," he said, searching her eyes for an ember of understanding. Sensing it in her searching eyes, yet composed and not overcome with emotion, he continued. It was at this moment he realized more than ever how strong, how prepared

– 230 –

Miriam, the Last Visit

she was for this role that sadly now would never materialize, as Eve restored.

In that instant he mourned most for her loss—the world's loss of her. How much the world needed the Holy Spirit, the feminine aspect of God in the flesh, to nurture, guide, forgive and comfort as only the feminine nature can! He spoke to her more deeply than he had ever spoken to any other human being, paying tribute to the greatness he perceived in her that must now remain latent.

> *"Our Heavenly Father is at the pinnacle of suffering, and has been throughout human history, with none of his children understanding it. The fall of God's children, Adam and Eve, is the focal point of His difficulty. Their separation from God was a very pitiful and tearful situation. God is the Father of mankind and Adam and Eve are His first children, the ancestors of fallen mankind. When these children fell, the consequences had a direct impact on the Father and caused Him incredible suffering. Because the fall was a physical act, the Father lost His connection with the physical world, and in addition, He endured the suffering of the loss of his children that he had loved before they were created, and planned for so carefully over eons of struggle and preparation.*

> *"The fall of man brought three consequences: God lost His children and He lost His temple, because man was to be the dwelling place of God. Furthermore, God lost the only home in which His love could be manifested; Adam and Eve were not only to be the children of God but to be the recipients of His love. With the fall of man God*

– 231 –

Not as I Will, But as You Will   Chapter 10

*lost everything He had hoped for in the love of
His own children, the love between husband and
wife, and the love between parent and child that
He would have experienced through His children
had they not fallen away from Him."* [3]

"I came... my mission is to restore that bond between the
Father and his lost children, because I am the first born to
understand what was lost both for the children and the
Father."

Miriam looked at Yeshua, perplexed, not understanding,
but seeking to understand for his sake, for the sake of her
desire to fuse in heart with him. "But, Rabboni, if you die,
how can you help anyone?"

Yeshua said, "Yes, that is the problem, the children cannot
understand even earthly things, so I have been unable to teach
them heavenly things. And now, by the pain they will cause
the Father—rejecting me, his seed, his lineage for the
future—the Father will have lost everything, if I cannot find
a way to bridge the gulf between them. My death must
become a bridge to that gulf between the Father and the children or all will be lost forever between the Father and His
children; lost to Satan who can claim them as rightfully his
then."

Yeshua, realizing his words were beyond her understanding, said patiently, "Believe in me, who I am. That you must
do now to do the will of the Father. *'The work of God is this:
to believe in the one he has sent.'* [4] I am completely outside the
sin of the Chosen People. If I who was most wronged by
these same people can seek forgiveness for them, and take
their punishment upon my body in place of them, then Satan
has no base to claim them. I will be an intercessor—a ransom,

– 232 –

Miriam, the Last Visit

if you will—for those who unite with me. Then some can be saved from the fate the Chosen People as a whole will face. If everyone could unite with me, then none would have to suffer. That was my goal.

"Now because of my sacrifice, at the very least, the Chosen People will be thrown out of the vineyard—not killed—but banished, exiled; and others, maybe gentiles, the other nations, the *goyyim*, will become the caretakers. Those caretakers will be the ones who can unite with me; to believe in me, whom He has sent.

"I take a chance to explain these things to you now. I feel the Father has given you special eyes to see, ears to hear, and a heart to understand my words. My regret is that I raised hopes in you to be dashed now, after all this time of your faithful sacrifice, waiting for me."

He continued, with an ever-so-slight pause, to recover his failing breath, choked with emotion. "But, I will soon die. As a warrior, I am a eunuch for the sake of the Kingdom of Heaven. Warriors should be young men without families, so they don't leave behind a family without support. So I must never marry. I can leave no family dependent upon me, to starve and be mistreated. When the battle, the war is won, the warrior can settle down. I have yearned for that day to come, but the battle rages on even more heatedly.

"These are the last days. Either the Father's long-suffering providence will be vindicated by faith, and his Kingdom for all the children, the *goyyim* included, will be established; or this opportunity will be lost and Satan's rule will greatly be extended. If this is so, then so much suffering will be inflicted on the world before another opportunity will come! Because of the faithlessness of the Chosen People, it appears

– 233 –

that chance for the Kingdom has now been lost. But, by my actions, I can bring about a realm of protection—of life—for those who unite with me, until that new opportunity returns."

Yeshua continued, his tone lowered, reflecting tenderness, "How many times I thought about you and wished to see you in the crowd—longed to see you. How glad, in one sense, I would have been!" He recovered his composure and continued, "I am a man; I want what you want, but it is impossible. Because of that, I need you to be strong, so we can both do the right thing. Help me to do what I must do, for the Father's Kingdom."

Miriam whispered, slowly, deliberately, "Then I will be a eunuch for the Kingdom of Heaven as well. I want no children but yours. I want to help you."

Yeshua rose to his feet, with palms up, "No, that's not the way," he whispered emphatically. "Help me by finding happiness with another. Live the life I could have had; have my chil-

dren for me, with another. Then I will be at peace. That is how you help me."

Miriam nodded, her eyes moist with sadness but also with acceptance. Her look and composure said she would accept this ultimate request, knowing that it was from God.

As Yeshua reluctantly, forcedly, moved to go, he said, his words leaden with emotion, "When I see you now I know that my physical life is not my greatest sacrifice."

She lowered her head, emotion overwhelming her. She didn't watch as Yeshua left—perhaps holding those last words of his in her heart as the final memory of him.

Leaving, Yeshua's body trembled as the magnitude of this sacrifice he was embracing flashed through his mind. A forced gasping response of understanding was wrung from him, in pity for her expressed devotion to him. She had been prepared for something he and the Father had hoped for, that the historical providence demanded—the True Mother's position. She had been faithful to that promise; which he now, uncontrollably, had to abandon. How great was her faith and devotion; how much he would grieve the loss. He felt like he had died at that moment—as did their future together.

Yeshua wiped the tearful scene away, as his consciousness returned to the Garden. Mesmerized by the intensity of that memory, he reflected on it. His words to her had been a form of surrender to the moment. Something that he had to give them both, even if it would be the last. He was forced to speak to the desire they shared and place it in perspective to the reality. That she would live a normal, natural life, but that his life would be ending soon. Her future would be wrapped up in building a family. His would be focused beyond death to the recapturing of the lost providence of the Father—

damage control to save a shattered remnant of the four thousand year providence of the nation of Israel, the prepared cornerstone of God's purposed Kingdom, before all was lost.

His hope for a destiny of promise was drowned in salvaging the past, for the sake of some time in the future when building could again begin—maybe not for a long, long time to come. For the sake of all he held dear about her, he wanted her nowhere near this impending destiny of his. She was meant for life and love, to bring glory to the Father in the fulfillment of both with whoever the Father had prepared for her to take his place.

That there was such a person was not even a question to him, it was something he intuitively knew. Her future was light, bright. His was with a detour through the deep valley of death to emerge as a much greater and higher light with a vaster radiance and responsibility. His connection to her now could no longer be as potential husband but as spiritual parent alone.

Gabriel knelt closer to Yeshua and said, "I know it is the most difficult thing you do. More difficult than giving your life is denying the Father His lineage. Would that there was another way. What could have been will now never be, the sinless begotten son of the Father having a lineage to carry on from generation to generation, to multiply his goodness like the stars in heaven, such as was the promise to your forefather David. It is, indeed, a sad day for the Father and for the world."

"Yes," said Yeshua, quietly. "I died there at Jericho first; along with my hope for the future. There is no greater death than the death of our lineage—it is something that is greater than love, greater than life. Because without it, there is no future."

– 236 –

Gabriel continued, "But by you the seeds for the kingdom have been sown. Whether sooner or later, the Kingdom of God will come because of your sacrifice."

Yeshua nodded. "Yes, this is my only hope."

Not as I Will, But as You Will

Chapter 11

The Last Supper

Yeshua saw that the moon had moved substantially across the sky; a blanket of shadow cast by the moonlight lay between him and the olive trees. The hour was advancing. He rose again and for the third time went to where the disciples were reclining, finding them still sleeping. He made no effort this time to rouse them but sighed deeply, a sound so desolate it seemed to still the breeze rustling the olive tree branches, as if nature participated in this travail with him. Finally, he returned to his vigil.

When he spoke, his voice was calm and objective; his eyes held a serenity that can only come from absolute domination of one's body and emotions—the closest kin to the desensitization from having endured extreme torture. "If I leave, what will happen to them? They did not understand when I told them I had to die. We were establishing the Kingdom. How

– 239 –

Not as I Will, But as You Will   Chapter 11

could I die before that was accomplished? How could they believe in someone coming to the throne of David to bring about God's kingly rule but who is killed before the Kingdom comes? It only made them lose faith in me to a degree that they won't admit, but I see it in their eyes. How can their savior be so weak as to be destroyed? When will I take possession of the Kingdom if I am dead, is their thinking?

"It was a change of the providence, from what they understood. And I know their hearts; I know their pain, because it was mine as well. I am sacrificing my position by my actions. Of course there must be a kingly rule on the earth, with a lineage to carry on. That is how complete resurrection will take place, both in body and in spirit; for the children of Adam to become the children of the Father, as they were meant to be from the beginning. Thus, my position will have to be completed by someone else, who will be able to do what I am unable to do because I must sacrifice my life now. Therefore, the Lord must come again. This is so difficult for them to understand. As difficult as it is for me, I fear, it is harder for them.

"It means that they, like I, will probably not see the kingdom in their lifetime. All their effort and sacrifice will seem to them for naught. I can bear it, because I know the Father's pain at my loss is so much greater than mine that I can't suffer only for myself. The Father has waited for thousands of years for this one moment, when His son could be born. The four thousand year preparation of the Chosen People and the coming of His son were the vast and precisely wrought heavenly conflagration that would bring forth the Kingdom of Heaven and the destruction of the satanic world.

"The Father's original intent was that starting from me, his first born sinless Adam, the lineage of the Kingdom would

The Last Supper

begin. From there it would multiply as the stars, and the rest of fallen mankind would be grafted on to that lineage and be a part of the Kingdom manifest on the earth as in Heaven. My sacrifice is nothing, compared to the Father's. It is the Father who is inconsolable and must be comforted, which is my position. Who will liberate his sorrow and give him what he has been denied all these generation since Adam, a family to truly understand Him, to be His body, His temple of flesh rather than a temple of stone?

"But my children, my brothers, can't understand this. They only see their own pain, as children will. They only see their own efforts made null, their hopes and dreams dashed. Will they give up? Then any hope for the future victory will be lost. They must have the strength and faith to carry on without me, to begin the foundation for the completion of our great commission. I fear they don't have that. I am tortured to do this thing. It appears as if I am abandoning all who believed in the Father, the children, and me and who vested all their hopes in me succeeding. If I leave now, I am forsaking all that—yet if I live, all will be lost as well."

"Forgive me, Lord," Gabriel whispered, "your pain will not be lost. Remember the meal you just shared with the twelve. They understood little, it is true, but the time will come when the words will resonate in their hearts."

A vision opened of the scene that evening in the upstairs room of one of Yeshua's followers. The space had been given over to him and the Twelve to have their evening meal together, a Passover meal. For Yeshua the greater meaning and solemnity of coming events overwhelmed the normal Passover traditions of the meal:

He got up from the meal, took off his outer

– 241 –

Not as I Will, But as You Will — Chapter 11

clothing, and wrapped a towel around his waist. After that, he poured water into a basin and began to wash his disciples' feet, drying them with the towel that was wrapped around him.

He came to Simon Peter, who said to him, "Lord, are you going to wash my feet?"

Yeshua replied, "You do not realize now what I am doing, but later you will understand."

"No," said Peter, "you shall never wash my feet."

Yeshua answered, "Unless I wash you, you have no part with me."

"Then, Lord," Simon Peter replied, "not just my feet but my hands and my head as well!"

The Last Supper

Yeshua answered, "A person who has had a bath needs only to wash his feet; his whole body is clean. And you are clean, though not every one of you." For he knew who was going to betray him, and that was why he said not every one was clean. When he had finished washing their feet, he put on his clothes and returned to his place. "Do you understand what I have done for you?" he asked them. "You call me 'Teacher' and 'Lord,' and rightly so, for that is what I am. Now that I, your Lord and Teacher, have washed your feet, you also should wash one another's feet. I have set you an example that you should do as I have done for you. I tell you the truth, no servant is greater than his master, nor is a messenger greater than the one who sent him. Now that you know these things, you will be blessed if you do them.

"I am not referring to all of you; I know those I have chosen. But this is to fulfill the scripture: 'He who shares my bread has lifted up his heel against me.' I am telling you now before it happens, so that when it does happen you will believe that I am He. I tell you the truth, whoever accepts anyone I send accepts me; and whoever accepts me accepts the one who sent me."

After he had said this, Yeshua was troubled in spirit and testified, "I tell you the truth, one of you is going to betray me." His disciples stared at one another, at a loss to know which of them he meant. One of them, the disciple whom Yeshua loved, was reclining next to him.

Simon Peter motioned to this disciple and said,

Not as I Will, But as You Will

Chapter II

"Ask him which one he means."

Leaning back against Yeshua, he asked him, "Lord, who is it?"

Yeshua answered, "It is the one to whom I will give this piece of bread when I have dipped it in the dish." Then, dipping the piece of bread, he gave it to Judas Iscariot, son of Simon. As soon as Judas took the bread, Satan entered into him.

"What you are about to do, do quickly," Yeshua told him, but no one at the meal understood why Yeshua said this to him. Since Judas had charge of the money, some thought Yeshua was telling him to buy what was needed for the Feast, or to give something to the poor. As soon as Judas had taken the bread, he went out. And it was night.

When he was gone, Yeshua said, "Now is the Son of Man glorified and God is glorified in him. If God is glorified in him, God will glorify the Son in himself, and will glorify him at once. My children, I will be with you only a little longer. You will look for me, and just as I told the Jews, so I tell you now: Where I am going, you cannot come.

"A new command I give you: Love one another. As I have loved you, so you must love one another. By this all men will know that you are my disciples, if you love one another."

Simon Peter asked him, "Lord, where are you going?"

Yeshua replied, "Where I am going, you cannot

– 244 –

The Last Supper

follow now, but you will follow later."

Peter asked, "Lord, why can't I follow you now? I will lay down my life for you."

Then Yeshua answered, "Will you really lay down your life for me? I tell you the truth, before the rooster crows, you will disown me three times!" [1]

Yeshua prayed, "Father, forgive them. They don't know what they do. It is out of the ignorance and fear of the moment that they act. They will regret their actions." The vision continued.

"Do not let your hearts be troubled. Trust in God; trust also in me. In my Father's house are many rooms; if it were not so, I would have told you. I am going there to prepare a place for you. And if I go and prepare a place for you, I will come back and take you to be with me that you also may be where I am. You know the way to the place where I am going."

Thomas said to him, "Lord, we don't know where you are going, so how can we know the way?"

Yeshua answered, "I am the way and the truth and the life. No one comes to the Father except through me. If you really knew me, you would know my Father as well. From now on, you do know him and have seen him."

Philip said, "Lord, show us the Father and that will be enough for us."

Yeshua answered: "Don't you know me, Philip, even after I have been among you such a long

– 245 –

Not as I Will, But as You Will   Chapter 11

*time? Anyone who has seen me has seen the
Father. How can you say, 'Show us the Father'?
Don't you believe that I am in the Father, and
that the Father is in me? The words I say to you
are not just my own. Rather, it is the Father,
living in me, who is doing his work. Believe me
when I say that I am in the Father and the Father
is in me; or at least believe on the evidence of the
miracles themselves.*

*"I tell you the truth; anyone who has faith in me
will do what I have been doing. He will do even
greater things than these, because I am going to
the Father. And I will do whatever you ask in
my name, so that the Son may bring glory to the
Father. You may ask me for anything in my name,
and I will do it."*

Yeshua whispered, "*Abba,* I offer a prayer for my people,
that they believe in themselves, as I have believed in them.
That they will do more than I, and that the Heavenly
Kingdom can come quickly." The vision continued.

*"If you love me, you will obey what I command.
And I will ask the Father, and he will give you
another Counselor to be with you forever—the
Spirit of truth. The world cannot accept him,
because it neither sees him nor knows him. But
you know him, for he lives with you and will be
in you. I will not leave you as orphans; I will
come to you. Before long, the world will not see
me anymore, but you will see me. Because I live,
you also will live. On that day you will realize
that I am in my Father, and you are in me, and I
am in you. Whoever has my commands and obeys*

– 246 –

The Last Supper

*them, he is the one who loves me. He who loves
me will be loved by my Father, and I too will love
him and show myself to him."*

Yeshua whispered, "love one another as I have loved you."
The vision continued.

*Then Judas (brother of James, not Judas Iscariot)
said, "But, Lord, why do you intend to show
yourself to us and not to the world?"*

*Yeshua replied, "If anyone loves me, he will
obey my teaching. My Father will love him, and
we will come to him and make our home with
him. He who does not love me will not obey
my teaching. These words you hear are not my
own; they belong to the Father who sent me. All
this I have spoken while still with you. But the
Counselor, the Holy Spirit, whom the Father will
send in my name, will teach you all things and
will remind you of everything I have said to you.*

*"Peace I leave with you; my peace I give you. I
do not give to you as the world gives. Do not let
your hearts be troubled and do not be afraid. You
heard me say, 'I am going away and I am coming
back to you.' If you loved me, you would be glad
that I am going to the Father, for the Father is
greater than I. I have told you now before it
happens, so that when it does happen you will
believe. I will not speak with you much longer, for
the prince of this world is coming. He has no hold
on me, but the world must learn that I love the
Father and that I do exactly what my Father has
commanded me. Come now; let us leave."[2]*

– 247 –

Not as I Will, But as You Will

Chapter II

Yeshua prayed sobbing, *"Abba, Abba,* I know your heart breaks to ask this of me, and it is because of this that I hesitate now. How can I know that Your desire can still be fulfilled? I care not for myself, but only that Your purpose for creation is fulfilled, that Your loneliness for Your children to wrap in Your arms, finally is fulfilled. It is You that will now suffer, not I. How can I solve that? My life, my sacrifice is nothing—phantoms and shadows—next to Your coming suffering and lonely vigil for the next chance to bring the Kingdom. And You will see every child in the world suffer apart from You, orphaned and abandoned to Satan's whims and tortures, unable to do anything about their sufferings.

"Father, if it is not possible for this cup to be taken away unless I drink it, let Your will be done. If there a way I can still succeed with my mission, show me now before it is too late." His tears were like water on the ground and so intense was the anguish that blood mixed with the sweat and tears falling on the grass beneath him.

Gabriel touched Yeshua gently on the shoulder and said, "The Father knows your heart and loves you all the more for it, but destiny has already been set in motion."

The vision continued.

> *"I am the true vine, and my Father is the gardener.*
> *He cuts off every branch in me that bears no*
> *fruit, while every branch that does bear fruit*
> *he prunes so that it will be even more fruitful.*
> *You are already clean because of the word I have*
> *spoken to you. Remain in me, and I will remain*
> *in you. No branch can bear fruit by itself; it*
> *must remain in the vine. Neither can you bear*
> *fruit unless you remain in me.*

– 248 –

The Last Supper

"I am the vine; you are the branches. If a man remains in me and I in him, he will bear much fruit; apart from me you can do nothing. If anyone does not remain in me, he is like a branch that is thrown away and withers; such branches are picked up, thrown into the fire and burned. If you remain in me and my words remain in you, ask whatever you wish, and it will be given you. This is to my Father's glory, that you bear much fruit, showing yourselves to be my disciples. As the Father has loved me, so have I loved you. Now remain in my love.

"If you obey my commands, you will remain in my love, just as I have obeyed my Father's commands and remain in his love. I have told you this so that my joy may be in you and that your joy may be complete. My command is this: Love each other as I have loved you. Greater love has no one than this: that he lay down his life for his friends.

"You are my friends if you do what I command. I no longer call you servants, because a servant does not know his master's business. Instead, I have called you friends, for everything that I learned from my Father I have made known to you. You did not choose me, but I chose you and appointed you to go and bear fruit—fruit that will last. Then the Father will give you whatever you ask in my name. This is my command: Love each other.

"If the world hates you, keep in mind that it hated me first. If you belonged to the world, it

Not as I Will, But as You Will

Chapter II

would love you as its own. As it is, you do not belong to the world, but I have chosen you out of the world. That is why the world hates you. Remember the words I spoke to you: 'No servant is greater than his master.' If they persecuted me, they will persecute you also. If they obeyed my teaching, they will obey yours also.

"They will treat you this way because of my name, for they do not know the One who sent me. If I had not come and spoken to them, they would not be guilty of sin. Now, however, they have no excuse for their sin. He who hates me hates my Father as well. If I had not done among them what no one else did, they would not be guilty of sin. But now they have seen these miracles, and yet they have hated both me and my Father. But this is to fulfill what is written in their Law: 'They hated me without reason.'

"When the Counselor comes, whom I will send to you from the Father, the Spirit of truth who goes out from the Father, he will testify about me. And you also must testify, for you have been with me from the beginning.[3]

"All this I have told you so that you will not go astray. They will put you out of the synagogue; in fact, a time is coming when anyone who kills you will think he is offering a service to God. They will do such things because they have not known the Father or me. I have told you this, so that when the time comes you will remember that I warned you. I did not tell you this at first because I was with you.

The Last Supper

"Now I am going to him who sent me, yet none of you asks me, 'where are you going?' Because I have said these things, you are filled with grief. But I tell you the truth: It is for your good that I am going away. Unless I go away, the Counselor will not come to you; but if I go, I will send him to you. When he comes, he will convict the world of guilt in regard to sin and righteousness and judgment: in regard to sin, because men do not believe in me; in regard to righteousness, because I am going to the Father, where you can see me no longer; and in regard to judgment, because the prince of this world now stands condemned.

"I have much more to say to you, more than you can now bear. But when he, the Spirit of truth, comes, he will guide you into all truth. He will not speak on his own; he will speak only what he hears, and he will tell you what is yet to come. He will bring glory to me by taking from what is mine and making it known to you. All that belongs to the Father is mine. That is why I said the Spirit will take from what is mine and make it known to you.

"In a little while you will see me no more, and then after a little while you will see me."

Some of his disciples said to one another, "What does he mean by saying, 'In a little while you will see me no more, and then after a little while you will see me,' and 'Because I am going to the Father?'

They kept asking, "What does he mean by 'a little

Not as I Will, But as You Will   Chapter II

while?' We don't understand what he is saying."

Yeshua saw that they wanted to ask him about this, so he said to them, "Are you asking one another what I meant when I said, 'In a little while you will see me no more, and then after a little while you will see me?' I tell you the truth; you will weep and mourn while the world rejoices. You will grieve, but your grief will turn to joy. A woman giving birth to a child has pain because her time has come; but when her baby is born she forgets the anguish because of her joy that a child is born into the world. So with you: Now is your time of grief, but I will see you again and you will rejoice, and no one will take away your joy.

"In that day you will no longer ask me anything. I tell you the truth; my Father will give you whatever you ask in my name. Until now you have not asked for anything in my name. Ask and you will receive, and your joy will be complete. Though I have been speaking figuratively, a time is coming when I will no longer use this kind of language but will tell you plainly about my Father. In that day you will ask in my name. I am not saying that I will ask the Father on your behalf. No, the Father himself loves you because you have loved me and have believed that I came from God. I came from the Father and entered the world; now I am leaving the world and going back to the Father."

Then Yeshua's disciples said, "Now you are speaking clearly and without figures of speech.

– 252 –

The Last Supper

Now we can see that you know all things and that you do not even need to have anyone ask you questions. This makes us believe that you came from God."

"You believe at last!" Yeshua answered. "But a time is coming, and has come, when you will be scattered, each to his own home. You will leave me all alone. Yet I am not alone, for my Father is with me. "I have told you these things, so that in me you may have peace. In this world you will have trouble. But take heart! I have overcome the world." [4]

After Yeshua said this, he looked toward heaven and prayed: "Father, the time has come. Glorify your Son, that your Son may glorify you. For you granted him authority over all people that he might give eternal life to all those you have given him. Now this is eternal life: that they may know you, the only true God, and [the] Christ, whom you have sent. I have brought you glory on earth by completing the work you gave me to do. And now, Father, glorify me in your presence with the glory I had with you before the world began.

"I have revealed you to those whom you gave me out of the world. They were yours; you gave them to me and they have obeyed your word. Now they know that everything you have given me comes from you. For I gave them the words you gave me and they accepted them. They knew with certainty that I came from you, and they believed that you sent me. I pray for them. I am not praying for the world, but for those you have given me, for they

– 253 –

Not as I Will, But as You Will

Chapter 11

are yours. All I have is yours, and all you have is mine. And glory has come to me through them.

"I will remain in the world no longer, but they are still in the world, and I am coming to you. Holy Father, protect them by the power of your name—the name you gave me—so that they may be one as we are one. While I was with them, I protected them and kept them safe by that name you gave me. None has been lost except the one doomed to destruction so that Scripture would be fulfilled. 'I am coming to you now, but I say these things while I am still in the world, so that they may have the full measure of my joy within them. I have given them your word and the world has hated them, for they are not of the world any more than I am of the world.'

"My prayer is not that you take them out of the world but that you protect them from the evil one. They are not of the world, even as I am not of it. Sanctify them by the truth; our word is truth. As you sent me into the world, I have sent them into the world. For them I sanctify myself, that they too may be truly sanctified.

"My prayer is not for them alone. I pray also for those who will believe in me through their message, that all of them may be one, Father, just as you are in me and I am in you. May they also be in us so that the world may believe that you have sent me. I have given them the glory that you gave me, that they may be one as we are one: I in them and you in me. May they be brought to complete unity to let the world know that you sent me and

– 254 –

The Last Supper

have loved them even as you have loved me.

"Father, I want those you have given me to be with me where I am, and to see my glory, the glory you have given me because you loved me before the creation of the world. Righteous Father, though the world does not know you, I know you, and they know that you have sent me. I have made you known to them, and will continue to make you known in order that the love you have for me may be in them and that I myself may be in them." [5]

As the scene faded, Yeshua's gaze turned to Gabriel. He said, his voice now composed and calm, "It is finished." He rose and stood before Gabriel. The softness of his voice was threaded with a steely tone as he continued, "My mind is set. The travails of the birth of peace will now begin. I die for the Kingdom to come, on earth as it is in Heaven. Thank you for your comfort and counsel." He bowed his head, partly in reverence, but also hiding his eyes, which betrayed his extreme exhaustion.

Gabriel looked at the slender figure before him—too slender, as if never having had enough to eat. Although he knew food was both a necessity and a desire, Yeshua had long since mastered his body over such a desire, denying it for the sake of higher concerns. His exhaustion—some of which had been apparent even when he came to the garden—said silently that he had probably slept recently as little as he ate. His robe, threadbare and travel-worn, looked as if it were all he had worn for several years. Long, dark creeping stains from sweat and tears crisscrossed it; some darker streaks were recognizable as blood shed from the intense mental and spiritual travail he had just endured. But to Gabriel, there was never

– 255 –

Not as I Will, But as You Will — Chapter 11

a more kingly bearing then he witnessed at that moment, transcendent over all the fragility of Yeshua's physically tormented body.

Gabriel, the captivating celestial eyes sparkling with tears, bowed very low, touching Yeshua's hands in a deep gesture of fealty and respect. "It is my honor, Lord, that the Father extended this opportunity to me to serve His glorious son in such an ennobling way. Truly I, your servant, am the better for it."

Chapter 12

The End of the Road

Yeshua's head was bowed, the tears spent; only the sorrow remained. He knelt again in prayer, with quiet, strong words.

"Father, not my will, but *Your* will be done. I was willing that my life would be lived on the dark side of the mountain striving for the crest. With the only hope of at least dying within the touch of the sun's rays streaming from the summit and the hope of this future ideal illuminated for the children to come." He paused.

"Yet I know, it is worse for your providence that I would die in obscurity, my message lost—a seed on rocky ground with no hope to take root. For Your sake and for the sake of the future Kingdom of God, my death must not be buried in long-suffering darkness and anonymity. Better that I suffer defeat in a blazing pyre-light of public remembrance!

Not as I Will, But as You Will

Chapter 12

"But how can I leave with the fate of your Kingdom so uncertain? What will happen to your Will, if I leave? Before I drink this bitter cup, what hope do I have that this message will not be lost?

"How can I communicate to my future followers to understand the meaning of my sacrifice? I died as a sacrifice for the iniquity and failure of men. My death can only be vindicated if they take up my cross and follow me—my cross not of dying but of building the Kingdom of Heaven. I am paying the price for their iniquity. Now they must follow through on my mission that I would have accomplished if I had not had to amend for their failure, in preparation for the return of the anointed one.

"To future generations I ask this. My brethren, my children, do not think that you are waiting for the Father; the Father is waiting for you.

> "Watch out that no one deceives you. For many will come in my name, claiming, 'I am the Christ,' and will deceive many. You will hear of wars and rumors of wars, but see to it that you are not alarmed. Such things must happen, but the end is still to come. Nation will rise against nation, and kingdom against kingdom. There will be famines and earthquakes in various places. All these are the beginning of birth pains.
>
> "Then you will be handed over to be persecuted and put to death, and you will be hated by all nations because of me. At that time many will turn away from the faith and will betray and hate each other, and many false prophets will appear and deceive many people. Because of the

– 258 –

The End of the Road

increase of wickedness, the love of most will grow cold, but he who stands firm to the end will be saved. And this gospel of the kingdom will be preached in the whole world as a testimony to all nations, and then the end will come.[1]

"I sincerely wish that you would reflect deeply upon the circumstances when I, the messiah of this age, was crucified. I hope they pray about my life and about God's view on human salvation. Think about the fact that Mary, my mother, had to give birth to the son of God in a manger. How much she grieved over this! Could this have been God's will? Think about the circumstances that I could not be married even though I was thirty-three. Think of how my disciples and I often went hungry. My life was filled with grievances.

"My future followers may surmise that everything that happened to me was God's will. However, think whether there was any responsibility on the part of human beings. I came as the messiah and the son of man. As the begotten son of God I did my very best to fulfill my messianic mission, but I could not fully accomplish my dreams and desires. Had my will been entirely accomplished, there would be no need for the messiah to return. Pray with fasting to know the truth of my life, and I will come to you and reveal it."[2]

Gabriel touched Yeshua's shoulders and spoke softly. "The Father sent me with a special message. 'Tell My son:

'My most beloved, our time has not yet come. Will the Sabbath—a day of rest for Me when I find my lost children and build a family of peace—ever come on this earth? Because of your sacrifice now, I still have hope. Because the seed of the kingdom is lost, I have to put things back together in Heaven before it can be finished on earth. Therefore, I

– 259 –

Not as I Will, But as You Will   Chapter 12

cannot avoid having you go the way of death.

'By going this way, you can work freely through the hearts of men on earth. By those coming after you uniting in love with you and attending you as the bridegroom—loving you more than anyone else—they can escape hell and come into Paradise above the angels. The day will come when all people and all things welcome springtime and sing songs of the Sabbath for the first time in a world of peace, and the Kingdom of Heaven will be opened on earth.

'So, you and I together will take responsibility for this loss, so that a new opportunity in the future can be bought. My son, do not worry, I will take over your mission. I will raise up your children, followers of the Way, to prepare a bride for the coming of the new bridegroom and their marriage supper in the Heavenly Kingdom on Earth—the chance denied you. At such time, your way will be completed and you and I will finally be victorious.'"

Yeshua took in the words reverently, with bowed head. He said to Gabriel, "I've tried never to pray to the Father from weakness for my own needs, because the Father's pain is so much greater than mine. His word is the last word. I submit my body to whatever fate lies ahead. His will be done," he said quietly, resolutely.

The expression of Gabriel's eyes had the luminous adamant simplicity of a last rites pledge before a dying man, as he replied, "As your mission is laid down here in Gethsemane in sorrow and tears, this I will do for you. I was with you at the beginning of your ministry and at the end. And I will keep it going when you leave. *I will make the day of your birth the greatest holiday celebrated by the world.*

"It will give the Festival of Lights new and greater mean-

– 260 –

The End of the Road

ing, celebrating the light of truth and illumination that you brought to this darkened world—the hope that drives away the dark—transforming it forever. It will be a day when the world is reminded that the King of Kings came to build the Heavenly Kingdom so the world could live in peace. He had to die because the world was not yet ready for him." Gabriel's excitement built as his voice began to rise.

"Every year when the world celebrates this day, they will remember this promise. Through this day, hidden seeds will be sown, ready to be generated in the future when the time is ripe—a time when the completion of the Kingdom of Heaven will be accomplished. They will feel a bit of that Kingdom of Heaven in the goodwill they feel that day toward their fellow man. They will be reminded that someday the whole year will be as that one day is, Peace on Earth; Good Will Toward Men. This I pledge before you; I will accomplish this, my Lord.

"And by your victory through death today, you will be res-urrected as the victor and ruler over heaven—if not yet earth. That victory will remain for the next time, when someone can come on the shoulders of this victory you have gained and complete it for you."

"Thank you, my brother," Yeshua said, tremendously moved by Gabriel's declaration. "I believe you. You give me peace. I ask the Father for one thing only; that I may freely travel between this world and the next to anyone who may sin-cerely seek to know me and to receive my message."

"That would be wonderful!" Gabriel exclaimed softly. Yeshua went on.

"Think of it, Gabriel! Whether kings or outcasts, I will come to those who seek me in their heart at the extremity of

– 261 –

Not as I Will, But as You Will   Chapter 12

their will and endurance. Anytime they seek to rise above this world and live for my ideal, I wish to be there! If given the chance, I pledge to always be there, to strengthen them and guide them to continue to seek the Kingdom and its righteousness."

Gabriel thought about this. Would such a thing be possible or even to be desired? He commented, "The prophets could not do this, nor anyone in the past. No one has been able to freely go beyond the veil of death to reach the living. Even the angels can do this only if sent by the Father. But you are the Lord of both worlds, if not yet able to take your position in this one. For you it can be as you ask. This will be the realm of resurrection paid for by your sacrifice that any can seek by believing in you. Your sheep can find a home there with their shepherd."

Yeshua then said, "My friend, there is one other matter you can help me with, and that is my brother James. He has long suffered in my shadow, caring for our family that I as the eldest had to sacrifice to pursue my mission. Now I must ask him to take on another burden that I must lay aside. This is my message to him;

"'Son of Man, no less one than I, put aside old contentions. The prophets wait for your resolve, for greater things must you do than I. This is the hour of decision drawn for our people, whether they live or die; whether the Kingdom comes or is postponed and they suffer the consequences. Do not let our people fail! You are righteous and just and know my heart better than any! Do not let my death be in vain!'"

Gabriel bowed his head. "It will be done!" he said, his voice gentle but impassioned.

A peace now descended upon Yeshua's face. Things

The End of the Road

endured and to be endured receded into some outer fog-like pain that still exists but has no power any longer to hurt. His words as he spoke were calm. "Then I will take the cup. Amen! Amen! Amen! *'I will not drink again of the fruit of the vine until that day when I drink it anew in the kingdom of God.'"* [3]

Yeshua rose and walked back to the shadowy knoll where the three slept still.

> *"Look, the hour is near, and the Son of Man is betrayed into the hands of sinners. Rise, let us go! Here comes my betrayer!"* [4]
>
> *While he was still speaking, Judas, one of the Twelve, arrived. With him was a large crowd armed with swords and clubs, sent from the chief priests and the elders of the people. Now the betrayer had arranged a signal with them: 'The one I kiss is the man; arrest him.' Going at once to Jesus, Judas said, 'Greetings, Rabbi!' and kissed him."* [5]

"Judas, are you betraying the Son of Man with a kiss?" [6] said Yeshua with sorrow, as his captors approached.

The scene was eerily lit with the flaming torches of the soldiers and the servants of the elders, as the soldiers took Yeshua by the arms and started to lead him out of the garden. The crowd moved noisily, as the disciples quickly roused themselves and followed after. What a strange, sad scene, thought Gabriel, as he began, finally, to mourn the fate of his master, saying to himself silently, "After the Kingdom of Heaven has come and when all other pain has passed away, one anguish will still remain, the anguish between Father and son of the lost potential that they held for one another which

– 263 –

can never through eternity be realized, the eternal lineage of that son."

Perhaps catching the poignancy of this thought, Yeshua looked back into the garden. Noticing Gabriel was still there, he whispered, "Farewell, my true friend, we will meet again very soon."

The crowd of soldiers, elders, servants, and the babbling curious vanished among the gnarled trees, their flickering torchlights growing dimmer in the distance. Finally, the garden was silent, as still as the star-lit night. Oh, death! Be not proud!

And Gabriel slowly left the garden.

Afterword

Gabriel's Legacy

I Heard the Bells on Christmas Day

(Traditional Christmas carol adapted from the poem, *"Christmas Bells"* by Henry Wadsworth Longfellow.)

I heard the bells on Christmas Day
Their old familiar carols play
And wild and sweet the words repeat
Of peace on earth good will to men!

I thought how as the day had come
The belfries of all Christendom
Had rolled along the unbroken song
Of peace on earth good will to men!

And in despair I bowed my head
There is no peace on earth I said
For hate is strong and mocks the song
Of Peace on earth good will to men!

I heard a voice within me say
Do not despair, this holy day
On Christmas morn, New Hope is born
For peace on earth, good will to men!

– 265 –

Not as I Will, But as You Will

Chapter 1

1 Luke 13:34
2 Mark 3:4
3 Mark 2:27
4 Mark 2:22
5 John 16:29-31
6 Matthew 26:36-42
7 Matthew 24:2
8 Jeremiah 13:12-14
9 Isaiah 20:1-6
10 Ezekiel 4:1-8
11 "A Marginal Jew: Volume 3" by John P. Meier, Page 153
12 Matthew 26:39
13 John 14:12
14 Daniel 7:13
15 Luke 22:43
16 Matthew 6:33
17 Zechariah 9:10
18 Isaiah 9:6, 7
19 Isaiah 11.9,10
20 Malachi 4:2-6
21 Matthew 11:12
22 Luke 1:25
23 Luke 1:11-20
24 Luke 1:32, 33
25 Luke 1:28-38
26 Luke 1:34-35
27 Luke 2:48-51
28 Isaiah 56, 57
29 Matthew 13:54-58
30 John 15:5

Chapter 2

1 John 2:3, 4
2 I Samuel 13:13
3 Revelation 3:16

4 Malachi 4
5 Matthew 19:4-6
6 "The Unknown Life of Jesus Christ from Buddhist Records," Nicholas Natovich, Page 204-207
7 Malachi 2:15
8 "The Unknown Life of Jesus Christ from Buddhist Records," Nicholas Natovich, Page 184
9 Isaiah 11
10 "The Unknown Life of Jesus Christ from Buddhist Records," Nicholas Natovich, Page 185,
11 Ezekiel 33:11
12 Psalms of Solomon
13 Assumption of Moses
14 Psalms of Solomon
15 Mishnah, Pesahim 10.5
16 II Samuel 7:4-16
17 Psalm 2:7-10
18 Luke 1:68-79
19 Matthew 3:9
20 Mishnah, Berakhot 2:2
21 Deuteronomy 6:4,5
22 Isaiah 5:1, 2
23 Ezekiel 16
24 Ezekiel 23
25 Malachi 2:2
26 Isaiah 61:9-11
27 Psalm 133
28 Matthew 6:33
29 Genesis 28:14
30 Isaiah 52:7-10
31 "The Unknown Life of Jesus Christ from Buddhist Records," Nicholas Natovich, Page 188
32 "The Unknown Life of Jesus Christ from Buddhist Records," Nicholas Natovich, Page 190

Notes

33 "The Unknown Life of Jesus Christ from Buddhist Records," Nicholas Natovich, Page 191
34 Isaiah 40:29-31
35 Matthew 9:17
36 Luke 17:20-22
37 Romans 1:20
38 Jeremiah 31:31-34

Chapter 3

1 Matthew 23:24
2 Deuteronomy 9: 1-3
3 "The Signs of the Messiah," 4Q521, Dead Sea Scrolls (Michael O. Wise, translation)
4 Isaiah 61:1
5 Isaiah 40: 3
6 Isaiah 40:1
7 John 1:29-34
8 Matthew 3:13-16
9 John 1:35
10 John 1:19-23
11 John 1:24-27
12 Luke 3:16, 17
13 John 3:26-33
14 Matthew 22:37
15 Malachi 3:1
16 Matthew 11:2-15
17 Matthew 11:16-30
18 Mark 14:37, 38
19 Jeremiah 18:7

Chapter 4

1 John 5:20
2 Exodus 32:9-14
3 Deuteronomy 8:3
4 Deuteronomy 6:16

5 Deuteronomy 6:13
6 Deuteronomy 8:24
7 Matthew 4:1-11
8 Revelation 12:9
9 Genesis 3:14
10 "Exposition of The Divine Principle," Page 61
11 Daniel 9:21
12 Matthew 11:12
13 Mark 10:37
14 Matthew 4:13-16
15 Isaiah 9:1-6

Chapter 5

1 Matthew 4:18-22
2 Luke 12:49
3 Luke 12:48
4 2 Chronicles 7:13, 14
5 Matthew 21:43
6 Matthew 19:28
7 Ezekiel 43:7
8 Zechariah 8:23
9 Isaiah 11:9
10 Isaiah 53:3
11 Hebrews
12 Isaiah 11:10-12
13 Micah 2:12
14 Ezekiel 44:3
15 Ezekiel 43:7
16 Jeremiah 18:7-10
17 Jeremiah 26:2, 3
18 Ezekiel 18:23
19 Ezekiel 33:11
20 Matthew 10:24
21 Matthew 5-42
22 Mark 8: 34-38
23 Mark 14: 37, 38
24 Luke 11: 51

Not as I Will, But as You Will

Chapter 6

1 Matthew 5:1-12
2 Matthew 5:13-20
3 Matthew 5:21-48
4 Matthew 6
5 Matthew 7:1-23
6 "A Marginal Jew: Volume 3," by John P. Meier, Page 229
7 Matthew 13:4-52

Chapter 7

1 Matthew 25:1-13
2 Matthew 25:14-46
3 Luke 15:1-32
4 Ezekiel 33:11
5 Luke 11: 14-32
6 Matthew 14:34-36
7 Isaiah 29:13
8 Matthew 15:1-20
9 John 6: 25-59
10 John 6: 60-71
11 Luke 11:51
12 Luke 17:20, 21

Chapter 8

1 Matthew 21:33-43
2 Luke 20:13
3 Mark 8:27-33
4 Mark 8:34-37
5 John 14:12
6 Matthew 17:1-13
7 Jonah 3:10
8 John 7:3-5
9 John 7:37-52
10 John 3:1-12
11 John 8:2-11

12 John 8: 12-59
13 Psalm 82:6
14 John 10: 23-39
15 The Hebrew is Yehud, meaning man or person of God; derived from Judea, the southern part of the kingdom that survived after the fall of the northern part, Israel. Judeans was the more likely term; however it is possible that Yeshua would have used Yehudim where the translation reads "Jews." Samaritans were also part of the ancestral Hebrew people. Yehud would have been more likely to have been used in that period between the first and second temple than Benai Y'srael, children of God, or even which is translated as Israelite, up to the time of the first temple. Another, later, usage is Am Y'srael, People of Israel.
16 John 4:7-41

Chapter 9

1 Luke 19:10
2 Malachi 4:5
3 John 6:33
4 Zechariah 14:4
5 Luke 10:41-44
6 Isaiah 56:7
7 Jeremiah 7:11
8 Mark 11:17
9 Mark 11:28-33
10 Matthew 21:28-32
11 Matthew 22:1-14
12 Matthew 22:16-21
13 Actually, Mashiah in Hebrew, which means anointed or the anointed one; in Greek, Christus.

Notes

14 Psalm 110, 111
15 Matthew 22:35-46
16 Matthew 23
17 Luke 21:1-19
18 Luke 21:20-32
19 Luke 21:32-36
20 Isaiah 53:3
21 Mark 15:25
22 John 11:54

Chapter 10

1 Samuel 7:12-16
2 Matthew 21:33-39
3 Adapted from speech, "The
   Pinnacle of Suffering," by Rev.
   Sun Myung Moon, 1976
4 John 6:29

Chapter 11

1 John 13:4-38
2 John 14
3 John 15
4 John 16
5 John 17

Chapter 12

1 Matthew 24:4-14
2 "A Cloud of Witnesses: God is
   the Parent of Humanity," Book
   5, Pages 15, 16
3 Mark 14:25
4 Matthew 26:45, 46
5 Matthew 26:47-49
6 Luke 22: 48

Acknowledgements

My gratitude is boundless to those whose great and small efforts helped bring this book to fruition:

Rev. Paulina K. Dennis,
for your insight into the deep heart of the Jewish people and Yeshua's love for them.

Minister (Pandit) Amar Nath Gi Gupta,
Dr. Akbar Ahmed,
for your inspired understanding of the expansive heart of Yeshua that sought to embrace all peoples of faith.

Msgr. John P Meier,
for your research of the "Marginal Jew" which gave us a picture of Yeshua that more—if not all—could agree upon.

Rev. Kevin McCarthy,
my Unificationist mentor.

Rhonda Williams
for your truly inspired art.

Svemir Brkic,   Jerry Ciemny,
Clark Eberly,   Dorothy Kolomeisky,
Bert Leavitt,   Vicki Phelps,
Edwin Pierson,
for your generous technical expertise and editing skills.

Rev. Sun Myung Moon,
You led me into the Garden of Gethsemane to meet Jesus, rather than standing on the outside, looking in.

Biography

Kathleen Goto is a pastor's wife and mother to twenty-year-old triplet boys and a fifteen-year-old daughter. At the time of the birth of her boys she was a features writer for "The News World," a daily newspaper in New York City. She put aside her writing career to dedicate herself to her family and faith.

Born in Colorado Springs, Colorado, in a Unity of Christianity background, she attended college in Denver, Colorado. She continued this religious view by embracing Unificationism of the Rev. Sun Myung Moon, which she has been a missionary for and advocate of for 30 years. She resides in the Washington, D.C., area of Northern Virginia with her husband, Hiroshi—from Hiroshima, Japan—and their family.

In the intervening years of raising her family she has become a Unification lay-minister specializing in interfaith dialogue and outreach. It is through the combination of her own Unificationist viewpoint, unique to the general Christian view of the mission of Jesus, and her experience with Hindu and Islamic scholars, she discovered the surprisingly possessive and endearing view of Jesus that other faiths have. From this she formulated this unique fictional narrative of Jesus.